P9-CEC-593

Praise for
When the Truth Unravels

"The four girls at the center of *When The Truth Unravels* are prickly, complicated, and headstrong—and I adored all of them. RuthAnne Snow's debut takes a quintessential high school experience—prom—and fills it with detours and secrets that make it impossible to put down. Across two timelines and multiple POVs, Snow paints an authentic, sensitive picture of depression and shows us how friendship is a delicate but resilient thing. I wish I could hand this to every teen girl trying her best and fearing she isn't enough. (She is.)"

—Rachel Lynn Solomon, author of
You'll Miss Me When I'm Gone

"*When the Truth Unravels* is a captivating, fast-moving exploration of the complexities of female friendship, and a brutally realistic yet sensitive depiction of depression and its intertwining consequences. On a night that's supposed to be about partying and having a good time, tension builds and buzzes just below the surface as each character wrestles with unspoken revelations. Snow handles the story's heavy themes with impressive skill and gentle insight and nails the pressures, uncertainties, and politics of high school."

—Jill Baguchinsky, author of *Mammoth*

"This is the YA friendship book you've been waiting for. Part mystery, part romance, and all authentic, Snow delivers a page-turner that masterfully handles some of the most sensitive topics teens deal with today."

—Natasha Sinel, author of *The Fix* and *Soulstruck*

"Snow masterfully navigates the complexities of female friendships in this powerful and engrossing debut. Intricate storytelling, nuanced protagonists, and a profound examination of adolescence and healing, this novel will claw at your heart and leave you breathless. Flawless, stunning, and unputdownable."

—Whitney Taylor, author of *Definitions of Indefinable Things*

when
the truth
unravels

when
the truth
unravels

ruthanne snow

Sky Pony Press
New York

Copyright © 2019 by RuthAnne Snow

All rights reserved. No part of this book may be reproduced in any manner without the express written consent of the publisher, except in the case of brief excerpts in critical reviews and articles. All inquiries should be addressed to Sky Pony Press, 307 West 36th Street, 11th Floor, New York, NY 10018.

Sky Pony Press books may be purchased in bulk at special discounts for sales promotion, corporate gifts, fund-raising, or educational purposes. Special editions can also be created to specifications. For details, contact the Special Sales Department, Sky Pony Press 307 West 36th Street, 11th Floor, New York, NY 10018 or info@skyhorsepublishing.com.

This is a work of fiction. Names, characters, places, and incidents are either the product of the author's imagination or used fictitiously.

Sky Pony® is a registered trademark of Skyhorse Publishing, Inc®, a Delaware corporation.

Visit our website at skyponypress.com

10 9 8 7 6 5 4 3 2 1

Library of Congress Cataloging-in-Publication Data available on file

Print ISBN: 978-1-5107-3357-2
eBook ISBN 978-1-5107-3358-9

Cover design by Kate Gartner

Printed in the United States of America

For Kristen.
I wish every girl in the world could have a friend as funny and ferocious as you. I am so glad that I did.

when
the truth
unravels

1

Jenna Sinclair
April 18, 10:00 AM

I love Elin Angstrom to death, but it pisses me off that she tried to kill herself.

I stared at the diary on my desk.

I should have been recording my run time and hitting the shower, but the words were a magnet, holding my gaze and refusing to let go. An indictment of my friendship.

No one would ever read my journal—my parents would have trusted me with the nuclear launch codes—but I knew the words were there, and I couldn't stand the sight of them. I snatched a pen out of my desk drawer and drew straight lines through them until they were illegible.

My cell phone buzzed on my desk and I jumped. ELIN CALLING. I put a smile on my face before saying hello—I read once that people on the other end of the line can tell, subconsciously, whether you smiled when they called. "Heeey, what's up?"

"Don't get mad," Elin said.

Not a great way to start a conversation, E. "When do I get mad?"

"You're always mad," she said, a note of amusement in her tone.

"I am not." I scribbled over the next lines, *Most girls go their separate ways in middle school, join new groups, all the stuff Judy Blume is made of. But not me and Elin. We've never even had a real fight.* I winced as my pen tore the thick, creamy paper.

"Whatever. Promise?"

"I promise," I said as I smoothed the ripped paper back into place.

"I kind of . . . need your help covering with my parents."

I paused as her words sank into my brain, the tip of my pen still resting on the page. "What do you mean? They know you're going to prom, right?"

"Well . . ."

"Elin! You said that your doctor recommended it."

"He did! They're just being . . . resistant. So I sort of told them that we were having a girls' night, skipping the dance and having a sleepover. You, me, Ket, Rosie."

I rubbed my left temple. Lying to parents, even other people's parents, practically caused me to break out in hives. But if her doctor said Elin should go to prom, he was probably right. He'd gone to school for that sort of thing.

Expurgate, I wrote carefully next to the blacked out text in my journal. *To edit by omitting or modifying parts considered indelicate.* The SATs had been last fall, but practicing the words had become a habit—it made me feel like all that memorization wouldn't go to waste, and that someday I'd use words like *plenitude* in conversation.

"Where is this girls' night supposed to be?" I said, not bothering with the smile now.

"At Ket's." It was left unsaid that, these days, my house was out of the question.

I frowned. "Rosie's would be better." That wouldn't even require lying to actual parents, since Rosie's parents only considered themselves such in the most technical sense of the word.

"My parents won't let me spend the night at Rosie's anymore. Besides, we'd have to tell Rosie that was the plan if we wanted to use her as an alibi, and she's this close to bailing already."

"Sounds like you've already got this figured out. Why tell me at all?" If resentment bled into my tone, she ignored it. The Elin-Jenna friendship survived on polite smiles and half-truths these days, and I had no idea when the détente was going to end.

Out in the hallway, Lily whimpered and nosed my door open. I beckoned her inside. She padded up next to me, tags on her collar jingling softly, and rested her head on my knee. I felt a pang of guilt as I looked into her soft, brown eyes. I should have taken her with me on my run, but at nearly ten years old, I wasn't sure she could do five miles at my pace.

"I need you to pick me up. And then sell the story to my parents."

I shut my eyes, willing myself to calm down. Was Elin out of line? I couldn't even tell. Elin had been right when she accused me of always being mad, though how she noticed when she kept missing everything else, I had no idea. For weeks, I've felt like I was at the edge of exploding—a formerly dormant rage volcano about to erupt.

Last night, I'd been in the gym with half of prom committee and my boyfriend Miles until 2 a.m., hanging draperies and stringing lights and filling balloons with helium. It was exactly the sort of project I normally loved—and it was my very last high school dance.

I thought I'd feel nostalgic as I curled balloon ribbons with scissors, giggling at silly jokes that were only funny because we were exhausted. If everything had followed the pattern, I would have arrived home and practically floated up the stairs to my room, high on the excitement of planning the dance and the rush of kissing Miles goodnight.

Instead, I'd come home shaking with fury because the deejay hadn't arrived to do the sound check even though we'd paid him for it and our so-called faculty advisor hadn't answered any of my texts. I'd stomped up to my room, whipped out my journal, and written something truly shitty before falling into a fitful sleep.

Adults were always talking about teenagers being angsty and angry. Before, I'd rolled my eyes at how clichéd that was, but now I *was* that teenager and I had no idea how it had happened.

"What am I supposed to say?" I asked, bitterness tingeing my tone. "That my boyfriend is *totally cool* with me spending prom night at a sleepover?"

"Exactly! If that's *your* story, then they'll totally believe me. You're Jenna."

Lily leaped up on my bed, walking in a circle until she found a sufficiently snuggly spot. I made it every morning, crisp corners and decorative pillows beneath the map of China I'd hung over the headboard. A tiny silver star marked the Hubei Province. My dad went there every summer to work in a humanitarian hospital. This year, he was taking me so I could help and practice my Mandarin.

My older siblings, Blake and Holly, asked to go to Cabo for their graduation presents.

I saw Elin's point.

I wedged the phone between my shoulder and ear and pulled my hair out of its sweaty ponytail. I wished Elin hadn't pulled this, but she had to be at prom. The surprise I'd been planning would be a total waste otherwise—which is why, at her request, I had already convinced my boyfriend and our friends that a no-date senior prom was *totally* the way to go. "Okay. Sure."

"Awesome. So, come over here to get me around 4:30, right? Chat with the parents, and then we'll go over to Rosie's to get ready."

I almost bit the words back out of spite, but if I was going to be an accomplice to Elin's plan, I wanted to make sure it was a *good* plan. "How are you getting your dress out of the house?"

"I'm wrapping it into my sleeping bag."

I climbed up beside Lily and lay my head on my pillow. The shower could wait. "You thought of everything. Reminds me of me."

Elin laughed and a weight lifted off my shoulders. Not too long ago, I had thought I'd never hear Elin laugh again. I stroked Lily's silky ears, smiling to myself. This was going to be fine. Elin's doctor was right—Elin's parents were being overprotective. They'd gone completely batshit on my parents for telling the school officials what had happened and hadn't spoken to them since. But what did they expect to happen? Did they think we could all just pretend Elin had gone on vacation in the middle of the semester?

"Can I ask for one more favor?" Elin asked.

My headache throbbed and Lily nudged my hand with her nose, redirecting my hand to the patch of white fur between her eyes. Her eyes closed sleepily as I rubbed her favorite spot, and I fought the urge to yawn. "You might as well."

"And you promise not to . . . judge, or repeat, or anything along those lines?"

"Sure."

Elin paused. "I need you to make sure that Hannah is busy with prom-planning stuff. Especially right before the dance."

I smiled, relieved that she wasn't asking for something bigger. "Is that all? Of course."

Elin laughed again. "See you in a few hours," she said.

"See you," I replied, snuggling my face into Lily's side and shoving my phone under my pillow.

2

Ket West-Beauchamp
April 18, 4:00 PM

Not for the first time, I wished we could just tell Teddy about Elin's Incident.

Partly because, as one of her oldest friends, he deserved to know. Partly—and selfishly—because it would make it a lot easier for me to force him to reconcile with Rosie.

Seriously, wasn't a friend's suicide attempt a much bigger deal than a friend's rejection of your Declaration of True Love?

"How long are you planning to be pissed off at Rosie?" I asked as I followed Teddy into his kitchen. "For reals, I need a ballpark figure."

Teddy laughed, opening the fridge. "Do you want anything? I'm making nachos."

"I'm good." I sat down at the dining room table. "So are you going to answer me? You can't be mad forever, and by forever, I mean until graduation. "

Teddy shut the door with his foot, holding packages of shredded cheese, salsa, and sour cream in his arms. "I'm not going to be mad forever."

I drummed my fingertips on the polished walnut table. "Where are your grandparents?"

"They went to Napa for the weekend." He dumped tortilla chips onto a cookie sheet.

Teddy Lawrence had lived with his grandparents for practically ever, but you would never guess by snooping through their house. If he hadn't been standing in front of me, there would be no evidence of his existence. My house might have been filled with mismatched furniture and too much cat fur, but there wasn't a single spot where I didn't fit.

When my parents called me into our living room to tell me what had happened, I assumed they had seen the tattoo on my hip, the one I had been hoping to keep a secret until college, if not forever. Mama Leanne had her Hard But Necessary Truth face on. Mom Kim was teary eyed. It was their typical reaction to any conflict.

"Sit down, Ket," Mama Leanne said, and I took my place on the Ottoman of Shame.

Something was coming—they never brought me in for a Talk unless I'd done something wrong, so I assumed the lecture was inevitable. Even still, I kept my face impassive, a blank canvas of Whatever and Plausible Deniability. Never give an inch, that's my motto.

And then Mama Leanne did something that she, as the Enforcer of my mothers, never did.

She sat on the edge of the ottoman, next to me, and put her arm around me. Mom Kim remained on the Couch of Judgment, but she covered her face with her hands and burst into tears.

And Mama Leanne told me what Elin had done.

"Ket? Earth to Ket?"

I glanced over to the kitchen where Teddy was putting his nachos into the broiler. My stomach growled, and I knew

I'd probably steal a few despite my determination to fit into my skin-tight dress without a hint of pudge. "Timeline on the Rosie forgiveness?" I asked, flashing my most dazzling smile.

Teddy scowled, plunking down in the chair across from mine. "It's not that easy."

I gazed at him through my lashes. "Oh Teddy, I know it's rough. I mean, she accepted your friendship *for all these years*. Didn't she know that girls are just Sex Dispensing Machines? Put in the Quarters of Kindness, and out pops handies and over-the-jeans action."

Teddy laughed. He nudged my foot with his. "Enough, Ket, okay?"

I smiled and nudged him back. "Okay. But don't be surprised when I start in next week."

He slumped down in his chair, resting his chin in one hand. He was still smiling, but it was a little sad. "I know you're just giving me a hard time, but you know it wasn't like that, right?"

My smile faded. "Of course. I was just trying to get you to laugh."

The truth was, Teddy Lawrence was about as far from those self-proclaimed Nice Guys —you know, the ones who call you a bitch when you won't hook up with a Nice Guy like them?—as you could get. Teddy was pretty much the pinnacle of high school boy. Maybe a bit on the short side, but Rosie was short too, so what did that matter? Elin and I had been as surprised as he had when Rosie turned him down.

The buzzer dinged and we both hopped up. I beat Teddy into the kitchen. "The thing is ... look, you know I think

Rosie is nuts," I said, handing him an oven mitt. "But miscommunication is not a reason to throw away one of your oldest friends."

Teddy pulled the nachos out of the oven, using his bare fingers to pick at bubbling cheese and chips. I winced when he flinched. "It's not just a miscommunication." He set the tray on the stovetop and opened a container of pico, dumping the entire contents over the chips. I fidgeted, wondering if he was going to continue.

"I really thought that she felt the same way," he said finally, pulling a chip from the mass and watching the melty cheese stretch, thin, and snap. "It's embarrassing. That I was so wrong."

Something prickled at my eyes, behind my nose. I reached around Teddy to grab a chip before I did something dumb, like getting weepy. "I know, Teddy. But no one is going to make you feel embarrassed, and definitely not Ro."

Teddy leaned against the sink, holding one hand under his chin to catch dripping grease. "I know she won't *try* to make me feel embarrassed. I just will," he said finally. He grabbed a paper towel to wipe his hands, stalling. I bit the insides of my cheeks, willing myself to not fill the silence.

Finally he turned around to face me, but his eyes were on the floor. "It's just that . . . Rosie was kind of my perfect match, you know? And I'm over it, really, but if Rosie didn't want me, there's no way any other girl would."

"That's stupid," I said. "Besides, we miss you! Rosie especially, but all of us miss you."

"What do you mean, you miss me? I'm still here."

"Yeah, but you don't eat lunch with us anymore," I said. It sounded petty even to me. I stole a few more nachos.

My explanation was pathetic, but Teddy pretending he was still around was worse. He hadn't hung out with our group in almost two months. He still spoke to me, Jenna, and Elin, still played video games with Jenna's boyfriend Miles, but all individually. It was like we'd been drifting apart all spring.

With college around the corner, the thought of graduating with our group already splintered made a band of panic tighten around my heart until I could barely breathe.

My phone buzzed, a reminder text from Jenna to make sure I was on my way.

Ket West-Beauchamp: Perpetually Late.

Jenna Sinclair: Obscenely Annoying.

I sighed as I stood, gathering my dress from where I'd tossed it.

"So what are you guys doing for prom?" Teddy asked as he walked me to the front door.

I rolled my eyes and groaned. Theatrical Ket is always a crowd pleaser. "Oh Teddy, it's going to be such a shit show. Jen decided that she wanted the four of us to just prom-it together. I wish you were coming. Like, couldn't you just throw on a suit real quick?"

Teddy grinned as I stepped out onto the patio. "Tempting . . . but no."

I smiled, wrapping my arms around myself at the chill, the plastic encasing my dress crinkling as I crushed it to my side. Teddy and Rosie had spent every dance of our high school experience hanging out in the band room, eating Cheetos like the dorks they were. If Teddy were to go to prom, it would literally be his very first one. "Well, I figured it was worth it to check," I said, skipping down the steps.

"Hey, Ket?" I heard Teddy say.

I turned. He was leaning against the doorjamb, a faint smile on his face. "I will get over it by graduation."

I smiled in return. "Now, was that so hard?"

Teddy rolled his eyes, but I caught a flash of a bigger smile before he shut the door.

I walked across the Lawrence lawn and ducked through the gap in the lilac bushes that separated Teddy's yard from Rosie's.

Somewhere between Teddy's and Rosie's, the satisfied smile on my face faded away. With no one watching, it was harder to keep the sting away.

One could say many things about Keturah West-Beauchamp. Indian. Slutty. So-so grades. Rainbow flag-wavin' parents.

But the best and truest thing you could say about me was that I was a good friend. I kept secrets, I plotted, and I forced reconciliations.

Even when the reconciliation was between my oldest friend and the guy I'd been in love with since I was ten.

3

Rosie Winchester
April 18, 4:15 PM

The last thing I wanted to do was put on the prom dress hanging on my closet door. But if I didn't get up and change soon, my stepdad Will was going to pop into my room and try to talk about my feelings. And neither one of us was great at talking about feelings.

After, Ket saw an email our school sent her parents, warning them that these things can happen in clusters. Copycats. Girls rushing to follow the next pill-popping-wrist-slicing trend. Very *Virgin Suicides*. I'm sure my parents got a similar email, but per usual, Will is the only one who seems to be taking it seriously.

The doorbell rang. It was probably Jenna, who arrived early to everything. I shut my eyes and put my headphones on, filling my ears with AC/DC. Will would answer the door.

Less than half a song later, the door to my bedroom burst open. "Heeey!" Ket cried, a prom dress of her own slung over one arm.

I propped myself up on my elbows, pulling off my headphones. "You didn't flirt with my stepdad, did you?"

Ket smirked. "Wouldn't you like to know?"

I refused to take the bait.

Ket asked me once if it was weird to have a stepdad who is young and kind of hot. It isn't. Hot or not, I'm pretty sure Will changed my diapers and he was definitely the one who took me to get tampons when I started my period.

She tossed her dress on my desk and hopped onto my bed. "What's wrong with you, Eeyore?"

I frowned. "Nothing."

"Are you going to be a mopey bitch all night?"

"No," I said, rolling off my bed.

Ket raised her eyebrows but didn't argue. "Let's see your dress."

I pulled the plastic sheeting off the hanger. Ket gasped. I suppressed a smile. I might not have been stoked about prom (understatement), but I was pretty into my dress, a floor-length emerald gown with a plunging back that I had purchased with my mom's credit card.

"Holy balls, Ro, this is incredible! How much was it?"

I shrugged. "$400. My mom paid."

Ket whistled. "I thought she was being stingy?"

My smile faded. I tossed the dress back on my bed. "She's only stingy when she thinks my dad should be paying." (Sort of true. She was going to freak when she saw it on her statement. Still, that would not keep her from screaming at my dad, *"I bought Rosie's prom dress!"*)

Ket snorted. "Sounds about right. Here, check out mine."

I oohed and ahhhed over Ket's dress, a sequined rose gold mini with cap sleeves and a plunging neckline. It suited her. Then again, everything suited her. She shaved half of her head freshman year and still managed to look hot. Whereas I had never expanded from the uniform of jeans, tees, and thick-rimmed glasses that I'd been rocking since I was twelve. Most people probably thought I was a tomboy, but really, I loved fashion. I was just too chicken to try anything myself.

I felt a twinge of doubt as I glanced at the dress. I must have been accidentally high when I picked it out. I did not have what it took to pull it off. (Well, except the surfboard chest. That, I had in spades.)

Ket ran off to my mom's bathroom to arrange the makeup she'd brought while we waited for Jenna and Elin to arrive.

I walked over to my bedroom window and peeked behind the curtain. My view looked down into Teddy's window. But Teddy's curtains were drawn, like they had been for two months.

I never planned to go to prom. The thing is, though, when one of your oldest friends *who also tried to kill herself* wants to go to prom . . . well.

There's nothing you can say to get out of that gig.

"Are you coming or what?" Ket called from down the hall. I checked Teddy's window one more time, hoping he would magically appear—but of course he didn't.

I loved Jenna, Ket, and Elin, but there had always been something special about my friendship with Teddy. He lived with his grandparents because his parents were even more dysfunctional than mine—a drug-addicted mom, a dad who had started a new family without him. We both wanted to travel the world, me writing stories and him playing guitar. When I couldn't sleep, I could call him and we would whisper conversations until dawn.

Guys used to tease Teddy about being gay, probably because his name was "Teddy" and he hung out with four girls all the time. He didn't do himself any favors when he started painting his fingernails black and wearing eyeliner.

But the summer before junior year, he shot up a few inches and his grandparents put him in CrossFit. Suddenly he was too muscled to be bullied. Just left alone.

Teddy and I always made excellent co-loners.

My bed squeaked as Ket flopped down. I turned to see her staring up at me, chin propped up on her hands. "Ro? Seriously, what's the deal?"

I shrugged, falling onto my back beside Ket. "Nothing."

"Teddy?"

I shrugged. Ket screwed up her face, her lips puckering prettily. All of Ket's faces were pretty, even her sad and sympathetic ones. But I wasn't in the mood to talk.

The doorbell chimed again. "Ro!" Will called from downstairs. "You gonna get that, kid?"

"Could you?" I yelled, not getting up from my bed. "I'm changing!"

Jenna and Elin pounded up the stairs bearing bags of snacks. We filed into my mom's bathroom. (Technically Will's too, but he took up so little space that it was easy to forget.)

Jenna put her iPod in the dock. Elin set out bags of sour vegan gummy bears, Hot Tamales, canisters of Pringles, and a four-pack of sugar-free Red Bull. I grabbed a drink.

"You know, I thought a girls-night prom was stupid at first, but the concept has grown on me, Jen," Ket said as she plugged in her flat iron and hot rollers. Those were probably for me—Ket's hair was already shiny and stick-straight.

Jenna raised her eyebrow. "Glad I could accommodate you." She was sitting on the edge of the bathtub, brushing through her wavy red hair, a grim look on her face—which was particularly weird, since Jenna had been bouncing off the walls with glee before Homecoming.

This prom group date thing was Jenna's idea. As soon as Elin came back to school, the watercolor version of her former self, Jenna pulled us aside and said, "I've been thinking about prom. I think the four of us should go together. No dates."

It was hard to argue—only Jenna had a boyfriend and Ket hadn't accepted an invitation yet. Jenna insisted it would be good for Elin, and Elin did seem to love the idea. But what I really wanted to do was order takeout and read *A Storm of Swords*. I suspected that Jenna had insisted on driving just so I wouldn't be able to pretend to get sick and go home.

Ket waved a hand impatiently, popping the tab on a Red Bull. "I just mean, who gives up the chance for some prom night romance? Not that Rosie would have had a date. No offense, Ro."

I shrugged.

"But seriously, Jen, I don't know how you can pass on the opportunity to dance the night away with Miles. I mean, *rawr*. If you and I weren't friends . . ."

"Where are you going with this, Ket?" Jenna asked, her mouth thin.

"Nothing, I'm just glad you had this idea. Mama Leanne was *not* pleased with my calc midterm and I thought she was going to lay down the law, but then I was like, *'I don't even have a date. I'm going with my girlfriends, the most wholesome prom night you could imagine.'*"

Jenna reached for a handful of Hot Tamales, her expression softening. "If you're having trouble, why don't you just ask for help?" she asked. "I'd tutor you."

Ket grinned, testing a shimmery eyeshadow on the back of her hand. "Thanks, but I value our friendship too much to subject you to teaching me math."

Jenna rolled her eyes. I felt a serious Jenna lecture coming on, so I cleared my throat. "Help me do my makeup?" I asked Ket.

Elin grabbed Ket's hand, tugging her out of the bathroom. "Help me get into my dress first."

"Change last, you might get makeup on your dress," Jenna said, but Elin and Ket were already out the door.

4

BEFORE
Elin Angstrom
August 25, 7:15 AM

Elin was only wearing jeans and a bra when she heard Rosie honk. She didn't have to glance out her window to know it was Rosie—the Isuzu's horn had a dying cow sound that Elin couldn't have mistaken anywhere.

Pick a shirt. Just pick a shirt.

Piles of clothes lay on her bed. And even though she knew she should hurry, Elin just stared at the options, unsure.

The navy plaid button up?

The sheer coral blouse over a cami?

The violet tunic with white embroidery?

Every first day before this one, Elin had arrived at school baked as golden brown as a Barbie, her blonde hair falling in a wavy waterfall down her back, wearing an outfit she'd selected a week in advance. This year, after spending most of the summer indoors, her complexion was winter-white, freckles MIA, and her damp hair was drying into frizzy cowlicks.

She should have woken up earlier. If she'd just climbed out of bed the first time her alarm sounded, sunshine streaming through her window, she wouldn't have this problem. But she had felt queasy and crampy and hit the snooze button until her mother had finally knocked on her door.

A shower had done nothing to relieve the dull ache settling into her hips. She'd pulled on her new jeans, a designer pair her sister Cat had gotten for her birthday. She hadn't gotten them hemmed, so she had to roll them up. She had considered shirts but found that too overwhelming. She had wandered into her bathroom, dusted bronzer on her cheekbones with a shaking hand, feeling like she was moving in slow-motion. She tried to remember where she put her class schedule.

And now she was standing in her room, unable to escape the shirt decision, with her friends waiting outside.

The slouchy gray oversized tee?

The red-and-white Park City Soccer tee shirt Ben had given her last spring?

Her cell phone blipped, a text from Ket. Elin walked over to her desk and swiped it open, knowing she should stay focused on the task at hand.

Giiiiiiirl, where are you? Rosie says there won't be time for Sodalicious.

Elin swore under her breath, tucking the phone into her back pocket. She grabbed a white V-neck off her bed and pulled it over her head as she shoved her feet into a pair of flip-flops. She grabbed her mostly empty bag off her desk—she hadn't even bought a notebook. But Jenna was sure to have extra.

The dying cow honk sounded for a second time as Elin ran down her steps two at a time. "Do you want breakfast?" her mother called from the kitchen.

Elin didn't bother replying. Her mother would just assume she hadn't heard.

Rosie's car was idling at the curb. Teddy was hanging out the passenger side window. "Elin, move your ass!" he barked, but his eyes were twinkling.

Elin forced out a laugh. "I'm right here!" she said, putting a smile on her face and an extra sway in her step. "Hold your horses, Lawrence."

Teddy grinned at her lazily, shaggy curls hanging into his eyes. "Sorry," he said, not sounding sorry in the slightest. "But Rosie was about to honk a third time."

"I was not!" Rosie yelled from the driver's seat.

Elin tsked as she climbed into the back seat. "Living on the edge, Ro? A third honk and Mrs. Brown would come yell at us for sure."

Ket slid her bags aside to make room for Elin and leaned over the console. "Can we still stop at Sodalicious?" she asked. "I really, really need a dirty Diet Coke."

Elin sat cross-legged on the bench seat as she pulled her hair into a braid. She hoped Rosie wouldn't notice she wasn't wearing a seatbelt—Rosie was a stickler for safety. Rosie had driven their group to school since her mother got her the Trooper, an excuse to stop driving Rosie to her dad's house wrapped up as a gift.

Rosie drummed her fingers on the steering wheel, lips pursed, as they slowed for a stop sign. Elin glanced up at the rearview, checking Rosie's expression. She could practically see the calculation behind Rosie's eyes.

"Where are the others?" Elin asked, even though she knew the answer.

"Ben and Miles went early for conditioning and Jenna has tennis," Ket rattled off, right on cue.

The clock on the dash said that first period bell was going to ding in eight minutes. Rosie chewed her lip. Elin held her breath. The soda would make her feel better, but more than that, she felt stupid that it had been her indecision over a shirt that was going to make them late.

Teddy poked Rosie in the arm. "It's senior year, Ro," he said, half a smile on his face. "Does anyone really care if we're on time?"

Rosie sighed, but she was fighting a smile of her own. "Fine."

Rosie flipped on her turn signal and Ket grinned, flopping back on her seat and turning to look at Elin. Ket tilted her head to one side, toying with one dangling earring. "Rough morning?" she asked.

Elin paused, about to tie off the end of her braid. "No. Why do you ask?"

Ket nodded at her chest. "Purple bra, white shirt."

Elin glanced down. She made herself laugh, shrug. "Whoops."

"Oh Elin, I love your trainwrecked guts," Ket said, rifling through her purse. She pulled out one of a dozen lipglosses that were scattered at the bottom, tossing it to Elin.

"Thanks," Elin said, unscrewing the cap to apply it, barely even looking at the color. "I stayed up late on the phone with Ben. I slept in and grabbed the first outfit I saw."

"Ahh, young love," Ket said dryly, stretching out her long limbs and rolling down her window. Ribbons of her dark brown hair blew across her face.

In the front, Teddy was plugging his iPod into Rosie's auxiliary cable. The Talking Heads filled the cab, and Teddy drummed along happily. Teddy obsessed over musical trends.

Spring semester had been seventies rock, this summer was all new wave.

Elin wished they could just drive in silence for once. But she hated raining on anyone's parade.

Rosie raised an eyebrow at Teddy. "You're in a good mood," she observed, gazing at him over her Ray-Bans.

He shrugged, grinning at her sleepily. "Dirty Cokes, Ro. What else is there in life?"

Elin glanced at Ket, eager for a distraction, but Ket was deliberately not looking at her. Elin shrugged, pulling her legs up and wrapping her arms around them, pressing her cheek against her knee. Teddy's crush on Rosie—and Rosie's total obliviousness—had become a running joke between Jenna, Elin, and Ket last year, but Ket had begun to express less amusement over it.

They ended up second in line at the drive-thru—not bad for a school day. Rosie ordered four dirty Cokes, diet for Ket and Elin and extra lime for Teddy. They were going to be late, but for once Rosie didn't seem worried. Jenna had once told Elin that Rosie took too much responsibility for their friends. *Look who's talking*, Elin had thought at the time.

"So I can't drive you guys home until 4 o'clock today," Rosie said, passing out the drinks. "Elin and I have our first cross-country meeting after school."

Elin paused, cords around her stomach tightening. "I'm not doing cross-country this year," she said. "Or track."

Teddy and Ket were still comparing class schedules, but Rosie bent her rearview mirror so she could look at Elin. "What? Since when? Does Jenna know?"

Elin shrugged, peeling the paper from her straw. "My parents really want me to focus on my grades," she said, keeping her voice indifferent. Casual. "College applications and all."

Teddy finally tuned into their conversation as Rosie pulled back out into traffic. "Aren't extracurriculars good for college applications?"

Elin flashed him a sunny smile and took a sip of her soda. "You should talk. How many extracurriculars do you have?"

"Aikido is an extracurricular," Teddy said, feigning offense.

"And he's president of the comic book appreciation club," Ket added.

"*Graphic novel* appreciation club," Teddy corrected.

Rosie raised her eyebrows. "Since when?"

"Since today," Teddy said, knocking his paper cup against Rosie's. "Ro, we need to start that club or we aren't getting into college. Wanna be my treasurer?"

"Deal," Rosie agreed, her mouth quirking up in a half smile.

Elin leaned back in her seat, shoulders sagging against the cracked upholstery. She sipped her soda, the bubbles soothing her stomach, which was slowly unclenching as they got closer to school. For a week, she'd dreaded an argument from Rosie, a thousand reasons why she shouldn't quit cross-country. Jenna, if she'd been there, nagging her about being well-rounded. Teddy and Ket interjecting, trying to get Rosie and Jenna to back off. Ben, puzzled and torn between agreeing with Rosie and Jenna or Teddy and Ket.

But in hindsight, she should have expected this result.

Her friends tended to take her at face value.

5

Ket West-Beauchamp
April 18, 4:30 PM

Elin tugged on my hand. "Help me get into my dress." She gave me her best Secret Secrets smile and I grinned in return. She was back to normal—happy, laughing, mischievous. I grabbed another Red Bull and Jenna yelled something after us.

Elin and I ran down the hall, Elin glancing over the landing to check for Will. "You brought them, right?" Elin whispered.

"Duh, of course," I replied.

Even before the suicide thing, Mom Kim gave me and my friends serious side-eye. She read a lot of Jodi Picoult—you know, those books where teenage girls are always getting themselves into some situation that's half Lifetime Original and second-cousin to a very special episode of *Law and Order: SVU*?

Mom Kim was constantly wondering if I was pregnant, if I was convincing Elin to get pregnant, if I was cutting myself, if I was bulimic, if I had cancer and needed a kidney transplant. They really shouldn't let parents read those.

My older brother Adlai had been the perfect son—star soccer player, Eagle Scout, college scholarship. Pretty much the kid you'd want as the poster boy of gay parenting. He had never gotten the Jodi Picoult Stare of Soul Searching. I, on the other hand, was the kid the religious right would have you believe is the inevitable result of same-sex parents.

But was it really so bad that I'd stayed out too late, gotten caught copying bio homework, or flirted with Rosie's step-dad? Most of my bad behavior was usually just a joke taken the wrong way.

But being me has its benefits. Since Elin came back, I'd done my best to counter Rosie and Jenna's Special Brands of Crazy. Rosie hovered, Jenna overscheduled, but I brought the fun. Elin and I skipped class, went skiing, rented movies. My parents cut me a lot of slack, though if Mama Leanne's blowup about my calc grade was any indication, the Suicidal Friend Pass was running out of punches.

Elin shut the door to Rosie's room and pulled her dress out of her sleeping bag. "You think I can pull this off, right?" she said, her forehead crinkling with worry for the first time as she stripped off her tee shirt.

I snorted—not my most ladylike move—and unzipped my hoodie. "Ben has worshipped the ground you walk on since eighth grade. Yes, I think you can pull this off."

Elin grinned, shimmying out of her jeans. "I just want everything to go back to how it was," she said as she pulled her dress over her head. She smoothed the material down, twisting around to pull up the hidden zipper. "Just move *on*, you know?"

"Definitely," I agreed, stepping into my own dress.

I hadn't asked Elin why it had happened, figuring she'd talk about it if she wanted to. But she'd tossed enough vaguely loaded statements my way that I had a basic understanding.

We'd been sitting on a ski lift a few days after she'd come back to school, just us floating over a white expanse, snow-dusted black trees clinging to the mountainside marking the boundary between the ground and the stormy sky. Our skis knocked together, chunks of ice clinging to the sides, and my cheeks were numb.

Have you ever done something on a whim, and realized right away that you'd screwed up big-time?

Elin had looked small and impossibly young in her parka, two blond braids sticking out from under her hood, her blue eyes refusing to meet mine. Like I wouldn't get it.

I'd grinned and asked her if she'd like to meet this girl I knew, her name was Keturah West-Beauchamp. Doing things on a whim that I later regretted was my entire modus operandi. And Elin laughed, relieved.

I knew, intellectually, that downing a bunch of pills and cutting your wrist was not a *whim*, but I understood more than most the momentary comfort of a terrible idea. Rosie was convinced that Ben was to blame, and Jenna refused to speculate, but to me, it was super obvious.

Elin had never actually wanted to *kill herself*-kill herself. She'd just come up against the reality of a year's worth of Senioritis-induced bad grades and the fact that she never should have dumped Ben. She'd gotten drunk and done something stupid, but if she'd really wanted to kill herself, she would have waited until her parents had left for their weekend getaway.

It was total drama-llama, of course, so I could see exactly why she just wanted to pretend It Was All A Dream.

I checked out my reflection in Rosie's mirror. Elin came up beside me and sighed dramatically. "Promise that when I talk to Ben, you'll make yourself scarce?"

I rolled my eyes. "Like Ben would even glance at me with you in the room."

She giggled, slipping on her shoes. "Hey, don't forget my special delivery," she said, eyebrows raised.

"Oh, duh." I rifled through my bag until I found the condoms I'd snagged from Adlai's dorm. I tossed them in her direction.

She caught them and frowned. "I didn't bring a purse."

"Stick one in your bra," I advised. "Heck, stick two in there."

Did I know that if Jenna or Rosie caught wind of Elin's plan to woo back her ex-boyfriend tonight by looking amazing and putting out, they would *literally* have kittens? Yes.

But that's why it's good to have a friend like Ket in your corner.

I didn't judge.

6

Rosie Winchester
April 18, 4:45 PM

Elin burst into the bathroom, bouncing on the balls of her feet. "Tada!" she cried, throwing her hands in the air. My eyes went involuntarily to her forearm. Her wrist was encased in a wide silver cuff bracelet.

Ket whistled, appearing beside her. "That dress is amaze, Elin. Seriously."

"It really is," Jenna agreed, finally cracking a smile as I pinned her last curl in place.

Elin smiled, twirling in a circle. Her dress was a flowing Grecian cut gown, white with silver beading, toga-like straps over her shoulders. "Will you do my hair next, Rosie?"

"Sure," I said, putting down my drink. "Pull up a seat."

"Can you even believe that in four months, we'll be gone?" Jenna said, smacking her glossy-sticky lips together. "Have you decided yet where you're going, Ro?"

I squirted product onto my hands and ran my fingers through Elin's hair. "Not yet."

"I can't believe you're leaving," Ket said wistfully. "Can't you just stay and go to the U with me?"

I smiled faintly. "No can do. I can't wait to get out of here." (Only sort of true.)

My dad taught literature at the University of Utah, my mom was a big deal lawyer, but their real talent was hating each other. They divorced when I was two after my mom's affair with Will, whom my dad still calls "the intern" even though he'll turn forty next summer.

Over the years, Dad had gotten offers from different universities, but by court order neither one of them can move more than fifty miles from the other until I turn eighteen. So Dad lives in Salt Lake City, Mom lives in Park City, and they hate from a comfortable distance.

Part of me wished I could stay. Ket (and Teddy) were starting at the U in the fall. My dad's job would get me half-off tuition there.

I loved Utah. But if I moved to Eugene, or Tempe, or Boulder, or Austin, then we'd all—me, my mom, Will, my dad—be free.

I really loved the idea of freedom.

I zoned out as I wove Elin's hair into a messy braid. If my dad was right about my lack of literary talent (he called the only story I ever showed him "a touch juvenile" and followed up with, "Writing isn't for everyone") maybe I could go to hair school. Both parents would flip in unison then.

(That would actually be refreshing. . . .)

"You're wearing contacts tonight, Ro," Jenna said suddenly.

I looked over at her. She was rubbing some sort of shimmery lotion onto her face, refusing to meet my gaze. "What are you talking about?"

"Contacts," Jenna said, staring at her reflection, head tilted. "Can you see shadows under my eyes?"

"Shadows? No," I said. "What do you mean, contacts? I hate contacts."

"Doesn't matter," Jenna said, tapping a brush against a pot of pink blush. "That dress deserves contacts if I have to hold you down and shove my finger in your eyes myself."

"I'll help her," Ket said cheerfully, teasing up the back of her perfectly straightened hair.

"Seriously?" I said, twisting a lock of hair around the end of Elin's fishtail braid.

"Seriously," Jenna and Ket said simultaneously.

I pursed my lips but said nothing. When Jenna and Ket were agreeing (which was rare), there was nothing I could do to fight them. I focused on putting the final touches on Elin's hair, loosening strategic pieces.

One night. I could do this for one night.

For Elin.

"We've got to hurry if we're going to get to Fisher's by six," Elin said, adjusting the bracelet on her wrist.

I paused. "Fisher's?"

"Yeah, she invited us to her pre-party and after-party," Elin said, tugging her braid out of my frozen hand and leaning back from the mirror to inspect her reflection.

I glanced over at Ket, who raised her eyebrow less than a millimeter. Fisher? As in *Fisher Reese*?

Jenna stared at Elin. "Like, at *Fisher's condo*?"

Fisher Reese was probably the most popular girl in our class. Unlike the stereotypical teen movie villainess, she was not a bitch. She was genuinely friendly to most people, but she could hold a grudge, and she and Ket had disliked each other since freshman year.

Which meant none of us had ever been friends with her.

"Yes," Elin said patiently. "She invited us and it would be rude to be late."

This time, Ket, Jenna, and I all exchanged a glance.

Was it possible that Fisher knew why Elin had disappeared for two weeks? Elin's parents had told the school she had been sick. Jenna's parents had wrecked that excuse when they blabbed to the administration, but the Angstroms had upped the ante by threatening to sue any school employee who breathed a word other than "mononucleosis." And now Elin's parents weren't talking to Jenna's at all.

Still, rumors swirled, encouraged partially by Ket's jokes and innuendos. *If Elin doesn't want anyone to know the truth, it will be better that no one believes anything*, she reasoned. At this point, kids at school probably thought that Elin had an eating disorder, drug problem, dead grandparent, boob job, modeling gig, or none (or all) of the above.

Jenna cleared her throat. "You're being extra quiet, Ro."

Elin leaned over the sink, applying an additional layer of mascara to her lashes. "She's upset because she's not going with Teddy."

I glared at Elin. Tragic or not, that was uncalled for. "I am not."

Elin leaned back from the mirror, studying her reflection critically. "I didn't mean in the romantic sense. Like the, 'why hasn't Teddy gotten over it yet' sense."

Ket coughed. (Faker.) Elin glanced over at Ket, who raised her eyebrows meaningfully. Elin snapped her mouth shut.

Jenna sighed. "You shouldn't feel bad. Just because someone likes you doesn't mean you're obligated to like them back."

My cheeks flushed. "I know. I don't feel bad." (Lie.) "I just hate dances. The only reason I ever went before was because Teddy was there, hating the dance with me."

"Then why are you going to this dance?" Elin asked tartly.

Jenna, Ket, and I glanced at each other guiltily. The pause went on one nano-second too long. But finally Jenna cleared her throat and said, "Because I'm making her, duh. I didn't plan prom so one of my best friends could sit at home, moping about the boy next door."

5:20 PM

The four of us traipsed down the stairs. Elin and Ket were giggling. Jenna was being strangely silent again. I couldn't shake the feeling that we were better off just hanging out at home, watching trashy romantic comedies and ordering pizza.

For a second, I hesitated at the bottom of the stairs. I could suggest it—Will would buy us dinner. He'd probably even make us dinner. I opened my mouth, wondering how they would take the idea.

"Hey Ro? Could you come in here for a sec?" Will called from the kitchen.

I turned to the girls. "Just one minute," I promised as I walked into the kitchen.

Will was sitting on the counter, bare feet banging lightly against the cabinets, a bottle of beer in his hand. "So, you're going to be out all night?" he asked.

I shrugged. "That's the plan. We're going to end up at Ket's after the after-party, and then go to brunch. I'll probably see you sometime tomorrow afternoon."

"I'll make sure I'm home."

"You don't have to."

"I want to." Awkward pause, then Will cracked a smile. "I feel bad you won't let me take any pictures of you by the mantel."

"We don't have a mantel."

Will shrugged, dropping the smile. "I want to hear about how it went."

I squirmed, staring at my feet. Will had never pulled the "protective parent" act on me before. I really wish he'd never seen that email.

My therapist used to say that parents must exhibit two traits for children to feel secure: reliability and responsibility. Most people think those are synonyms. The difference is that you can count on parents who are reliable for your emotional well-being (Will) while parents who are responsible provide for your physical well-being (Mom, Dad).

It's not like Will had ever been a *bad* stepdad, honestly. He was a million times preferable to either of my ex-stepmothers. Before I got my car, he'd take me to the library whenever I asked and he would drop anything if I wanted to play video games. But he'd never enforced a rule and couldn't care less that I knew he smoked pot nearly every day.

Or he used to, anyway. All this suicide business had Will attempting to actually step-parent me.

He waited patiently for my answer. I sighed. "Sure, whatever."

Will slid off the countertop and straightened his posture. I could almost see him thinking, *Look fatherly*, and I felt a pang of affection for him. He didn't inspire fear, but I didn't want to disappoint him either. "Do you promise to call if you need anything?"

"Yup."

"Do you promise you won't . . . do anything crazy?"

I tried not to smile. The fact that Will couldn't even bring himself to get specific was why he scored so low on the responsibility side of the parenting rubric. "Yes, of course."

"No getting in cars with anyone who has had even one drink."

"I promise."

"Will you promise to call me if you need anything? Anything at all."

"Yes," I said. (Never going to happen.)

Will hesitated for a moment and then pulled me into a hug. I was surprised—my stepdad was not really a hugger. But after a fractional hesitation, I wrapped my arms around him. He rested his bearded chin on the top of my head. "I love you, Ro," Will said, his voice thick. "Please be safe, okay?"

"Of course," I said, blinking against an unfamiliar stinging in my eyes.

Will let go of me and took a step back. He flashed his usual wide smile. "You look damn cute, kiddo. Go break some hearts."

7

Jenna Sinclair
April 18, 5:30 PM

My pre-prom to-do list went like this:

1. Assign Hannah Larson a menial task she'd be incapable of screwing up.
2. Fill purse with emergency party supplies.
3. Buy snacks.
4. Pick up Elin.
5. New addition: Steal Mom's migraine prescription.

My headache hadn't gone anywhere all afternoon. I dug through my purse until I found my mom's pills. I swallowed one, closed my eyes, and resisted the urge to gag. Elin looked at me with a raised eyebrow and I forced a reassuring smile.

"Jitters," I lied, setting my purse down on the credenza in the foyer.

Elin smiled, flipping her braid over one shoulder. "It will be awesome," she said. "Everything you do is awesome."

I smiled, the words *thank you* rising to my lips automatically, but before I could speak, something in Elin's expression shifted, stiffened. Like she'd put on an Elin mask. I swallowed the words and put on a mask of my own. "Yeah, well," I said, shrugging and smiling.

Everything you do is awesome. Once upon a time, I would have deferred politely but secretly agreed. I knew I had no capacity to be chill, that I was too *into* everything I did, but I was usually good at pretending to be humble. Today, with Elin being fake, I was at a loss.

I leaned against the banister at the bottom of the stairs, closing my eyes. Ket and Elin were giggling about some stupid reality show and I could feel the throb of my headache behind my eyelids.

Interlocutor: noun, one who takes part in a dialogue or conversation.
"You okay?"

I opened my eyes. Ket was staring at me, eyebrows knit together. My gaze wandered to Elin. She resolutely avoided looking at either of us, fiddling with her silver cuff.

I forced a grin. "Good. I think my headache is almost gone." *Indefatigable: adjective, incapable of defeat, failure, or decay.*

Ket smiled and I felt a pang of pride. Ket and I were prone to bickering, but we hadn't even had a spat since . . . since. I'd done her makeup—"*Just* this *side of high class politician escort,*" she said, and I laughed—painting on dramatic cat-eyeliner, deftly applying long fake lashes, and dusting shimmery blush on her cheekbones. Ket's style might out-do mine any day of the week, but it took my special brand of OCD to properly wield liquid liner.

Elin stopped fiddling with her bracelets, crossing her arms impatiently. "What is taking so long?" she said, not even bothering to keep her voice down.

"Do you think Will's giving Rosie the *make good choices* talk?" Ket mused, checking her reflection in a compact mirror for the billionth time.

I shrugged. "That would be nice."

Ket snapped her compact shut and raised her eyebrows at me. "You think *Rosie* needs it, though?"

Rosie needs someone who gives a shit besides us. I smiled and shrugged. "Probably not."

Rosie appeared around the corner, snapping her silver clutch purse shut. She smiled, hers as phony as mine. "You guys ready to go?"

"Yay!" cried Elin, throwing an arm around Rosie's shoulders. I winced. If this pill didn't kick in soon, I didn't know what I was going to do for the rest of the night. Elin's voice was set to microphone squeal.

Rosie's stepdad came out of the kitchen waving his iPhone. "Just one minute for pictures? I gotta send this to Rosie's mom."

Elin and Ket laughed, vamping for the camera at the foot of the stairs, and Rosie and I exchanged a rueful glance. Anyone who had ever met Rosie's mom knew she couldn't care less about prom—her stepdad was just trying to pretend he wasn't sentimental. But we arranged ourselves next to Elin and Ket obligingly.

"Squeeze in," Will instructed, waving at me, and I forced my smile even wider as I leaned into Elin.

"Text me the good ones," Ket demanded as Will snapped a few pics.

"Not in a million years," Will said, never losing his good-natured grin.

Elin glanced over at Ket. "What would you even do with his number if he finally gave it to you?"

Ket laughed, shrugging.

Will handed his phone to Rosie. "Approve the ones you like, delete the rest."

We crowded around the screen, picking apart the images that Will had snapped. "I look bad in all of them," Rosie declared, and Ket shushed her.

I might have felt like crap, but at least I looked good. Rosie had put my hair up with a bejeweled headband *this close* to full-blown tiara. My gown had a sweetheart neckline and an enormous hot pink tulle skirt. Pink might not have been the best choice for my red hair, but I wanted the princessiest dress ever made. *Archetypal: recurrent as a symbol or motif in literature, art, or mythology.* I'd get my perfect photos with my perfect boyfriend, and then I'd hang them in my dorm room this fall. The capstone to a well-executed high school experience.

Unfortunately, the strapless top was a little loose—I'd bought it weeks ago, and between debate, officers meetings, and extra track practices, I must have lost weight. Thank goodness for double-sided tape.

The weird thing was, if you had asked me before, I would have genuinely thought prom was a quintessential part of high school. But getting ready in Rosie's mom's bathroom, unable to stop thinking about my best friend drowning in a tub, left me feeling like a balloon with its helium let out. None of my smiles in Will's photos reached my eyes.

So I studied my friends. Ket took great photos—if she weren't my friend, I'd be completely annoyed. It was like her expressions came pre-photoshopped. Elin looked perfect, her makeup all glowy, and I felt a swell of pride for helping her with her stupid parent scheme.

But it was Rosie who had knocked it out of the park. Not that she'd believe me if I said it—the girl had a serious *Carrie* complex. One compliment had her looking for the bucket of pig's blood. I pointed at the only shot where she was smiling. "That's the one," I said, and Elin and Ket agreed.

Ket and Rosie grabbed a few bottles of water from the fridge. I grabbed my purse and keys, trying to shake off my funk.

We made our way down the front walk of Rosie's house, careful on the cobblestones. I climbed into the car, tucking my tulle skirt before I shut the door. Ket claimed the passenger seat and immediately put an eardrum-bursting song on the radio. I ground my teeth together.

Rosie climbed into the seat behind me. I glanced at her in my mirror—she was propping her arm on the door and resting her cheek against her palm. I felt a rush of sympathy. Rosie was a fun-hater by nature. We'd all accepted that about her—the way she could laugh and joke in a small group, but shut down in a crowd, like an armadillo curling in on itself. She probably hated this prom plan even more than I did, but she was doing her best.

Still. If we were both this tired now, I had no idea how we were going keep up with Elin and Ket all night. I'd tried to nap after my run but had woken up in a panic after barely thirty minutes. *Pep up, Jen.*

My phone buzzed, emitting a cheerful *blip-blip!* that alerted me to a text message. "Would you read it to me?" I asked Ket as I pulled into traffic.

She pulled it out of my purse. "It's from Miles," she said. "He says, '*The dance is going to go great, J! See you at 9.*' Aww, and he added heart-eyes and a smiley poop."

"He's so sweet," Elin said.

I smiled faintly. "Yeah, he is," I said quietly.

I loved Miles, and when he said he loved me, I believed him. But I had a sneaking suspicion that, if he had any idea about how pissed off I always was lately, about everything, he wouldn't like me very much.

So I pretty much never told him.

8

Ket West-Beauchamp
April 18, 5:45 PM

We were going to prom. I was a senior. My friend wasn't dead.

That short list might have seemed a little shabby a few weeks ago, but today I felt like the Queen of the Universe.

Unfortunately, I was going to a party hosted by a girl who actually *was* Queen of the Universe, filled with people I could barely tolerate and a few I'd hooked up with—which wasn't much better.

[The things I do for friendship, man.]

My phone buzzed and I swiped open my text messages.

> **TEDDY:** *Have I told you lately that your heart is true?*
> *You might even say . . . you're a pal.*
> *I'd go so far as to say, a confidant.*

I slapped my hand over my mouth to avoid laughing out loud. Teddy was finally watching *Golden Girls*. Elin and I had started marathoning it after school—okay, *during* school when we wanted to sluff gym—once Elin got back from the hospital and needed a distraction. We had assumed it would be dumb, but it was actually kind of the shit.

I'm jealous of you right now, I typed as Jenna jerked along curving streets. She had insisted on getting a manual since that's What Adults Do but had yet to learn how to avoid stalling whenever she encountered a hill. Which, Newsflash, was basically all of Park City.

Elin tapped the back of my seat and I twisted around to face her. "You're excited to party, right?" she said, raising her voice over the beat of the music.

"Always!" I said with a grin.

"Good! You're the party mascot and you're being really quiet." She wagged a finger at me and I laughed, grabbing at it.

Three songs later, Jenna was pulling onto a skinny street loaded with cars. We found a parking spot a few doors down and walked to Fisher's, high heels clicking against the sidewalk. Elin and I clung to each other, giggling, as Jenna rang the doorbell.

Fisher opened the door and she and Elin burst into Hug and Squeal Mode. Rosie raised an eyebrow at me, and I shrugged, baffled. We stepped over the threshold, me checking out everything as subtly as I could. Fisher's party condo was exactly what I'd expected: granite countertops, leather furniture, giant flat screen, thumping stereo system. I scowled.

Standing in that "condo," which was probably bigger than my actual house, I couldn't help but resent Fisher Reese a little more. Mama Leanne was a nurse and Mom Kim taught preschool—it's not like we were broke, but we definitely only lived where we did because Mama Leanne had inherited our ramshackle little home from her grandma. And while it didn't bug me—much—that everyone around me seemed to have money to burn while my moms drove shitty cars and fixed broken appliances with Duct tape, people like Fisher Reese set my teeth on edge. Casually rich assholes getting richer renting out their extra houses to even bigger, richer assholes every Sundance, all the while acting like it was all No Big Deal.

Elin wandered off to gossip with Fisher, Rosie landed on the couch, and Jenna started drinking—*Jenna*.

I sighed, opening my purse to find my phone so I could text Teddy. Fisher appeared at my side, putting her manicured hand on my arm. I blinked, glancing up at her. "There's no smoking in my condo," she said, her smile corn-syrupy sweet.

I blinked, too stunned to roll my eyes. "Duh," I said. "I would never smoke in someone's house."

Fisher took her hand off my arm, and I couldn't help but notice the stupid diamond bracelet sparkling on her wrist. "It's just a really nasty habit," she said, blue eyes wide. Concern Trolling Level: Expert. "My grandma died of lung cancer."

"Thanks," I muttered, turning away.

I strolled into the kitchen and poured myself a drink as I mentally went through the comebacks I should have used on Fisher. I flirted with Sam Houston to make myself feel better. His ineffectually glaring date actually did boost my spirits.

Elin eventually found her way into the kitchen and grabbed a hard cider, winking at me as she wandered back into the living room. She wasn't supposed to be drinking, but she'd know better than me what she could handle. Besides, I had already screwed up in the Elin Department—not that she would ever know that, ideally—so I was inclined to give her basically anything she asked for. Hence the condoms and plotting.

Vaughn appeared at my elbow, leaning into my personal space. He brushed my outer thigh with his index finger. "Hey Beauchamp, haven't seen you in a while."

I sipped my juice, ignoring him. There were many reasons I had broken up with Vaughn—the fact that he refused to use my full last name fell somewhere around his insistence on calling me his "exotic princess" no matter how many times I told him it was gross.

Vaughn leaned against the counter, blocking me off from conversation with everyone else. I sighed, tossing my hair over my shoulder. "What do you want?"

He shrugged, offering a sly grin that I'm sure he thought was the Panty Dropper 3000. I kept my expression neutral, refusing to acknowledge that I'd succumbed to his charms once or twice before. "I don't know . . . you don't have a date, I don't have a date. I thought we could party."

"We are partying," I pointed out, turning to walk back into the living room.

Vaughn snaked one arm around my waist before I could take two steps, pressing himself against my back. Subtle. "I saw you staring at me before," he murmured in my ear. "There are empty bedrooms upstairs."

I paused for one second so he could think he'd won. I stepped forward deliberately, turning slowly to face him as I backed away. "I don't think so," I said with a Not In A Million Years grin.

Vaughn laughed. I had to give him one thing—dude knew how to let an insult roll off his back. "Come on, Beauchamp. I've missed hanging out with you." He waggled his eyebrows. Juuuust enough to hint that it wasn't my stellar jokes he'd been longing for.

I smiled despite myself. I had to admit . . . the thought was tempting.

I'd thought I was over Vaughn. He was selfish and douchey and he used way too much hair product. But looking at him standing there, and thinking about the prospect of a dateless prom hanging out with Rosie the Chaste, Jenna the Increasingly Inebriated, and Elin the . . . well, I couldn't think of a great moniker for her at that moment . . . I wavered.

Dude always was a good time, I thought.

And boredom always was my Sex-Kryptonite.

Vaughn smiled. "I know you, Beauchamp. You're just prolonging the inevitable."

I glanced over my shoulder. Jenna was drinking, Elin was moping, Rosie was *reading*, and this party officially sucked. "Give me thirty minutes," I murmured. "I have something I have to do."

9

BEFORE
Elin Angstrom
November 24, 6:30 PM

The knife slipped and Elin winced as blood dripped onto the marble countertop. Cat hissed involuntarily. "Be careful!" she scolded, rushing to grab a paper towel.

Elin scowled as Cat pressed the towel against her finger, which was sending painful throbs up to her wrist. "Thanks for the advice," she muttered.

Cat rolled her eyes, her meager caretaker instincts exhausted. "Go upstairs and clean that. I'll finish."

Elin could hardly argue, so she ran up the stairs, taking them two at a time. They were almost done making their salad anyway—the pies had been cooling for an hour.

Elin's family had been going over to Jenna's house for Thanksgiving every other year for as long as Elin could remember. The Sinclairs were the sort of family friends that were more family than friend. This year her brother Aron was spending the holiday with his boyfriend in California and Jenna's brother Blake was bringing his girlfriend home, but otherwise the traditional bi-annual Angstrom-Sinclair Thanksgiving was going exactly according to plan. The Sinclair house was the perfect holiday house. The armchairs were squishy, cinnamon-scented candles burned in every room, and Jenna's grandparents seemed like they'd popped straight out of a storybook. Her grandma wore hand-knit sweaters and offered hugs freely. Her grandpa would be wearing a Buckeyes sweatshirt and would make at least two jokes "forgetting" about Jenna's vegetarianism. Elin loved borrowing Jenna's grandparents for the day.

Elin took her time washing the cut, which was deeper than she'd thought. Unlike Cat, Elin had never been grossed out by blood. She studied it, wondering if it would need stitches. She supposed she could ask Jenna's dad. She sorted through her medicine cabinet, looking for Neosporin. She dabbed it on slowly, methodically. She wasn't any good at food prep anyway.

"Elin, hurry," Cat called from downstairs. "We're ready to go, and Mom's baked brie is getting cold!"

"Coming!" Elin called, wrapping her stinging finger with a Band-Aid and running back downstairs. Her parents and Cat were waiting, holding all the food they were bringing. How long had she been in the bathroom? It had only seemed like a couple minutes.

She had been looking forward to this day for weeks. Everything at school sucked lately. It was like the teachers didn't know that senior grades hardly counted. She and Ben had been bickering over her disinterest in classes. And it seemed like her friends were getting too busy for her. Cross-country had ended and now Rosie was spending more time at her dad's, arriving at school each morning looking exhausted from the drive. Teddy was spending even more time than usual practicing guitar. Jenna was always doing something for student council. And Ket was around, but hanging out with Ket solo required more energy than Elin had these days.

Thanksgiving was a reprieve, a break from the mundane crap that exhausted her.

The Angstroms lived a few blocks from the Sinclairs, so they walked, balancing pies and appetizers in the brisk autumn air. Jenna met them at the door with her red hair in two braids, glasses, no makeup. "We just put on *Princess Bride*," she told Elin, taking a pie from Elin's father. "Ooh, did you make the caramel apple one again?"

It was the perfect Thanksgiving. She, Cat, Holly, and Jenna had watched a movie in the basement while they waited for the turkey to finish roasting, the sounds of cheering coming from the living room where a football game was on TV. Jenna's grandmother had gushed over her blonde hair and heaped extra mashed potatoes on her plate. Lily snuggled between Elin's and Jenna's feet, waiting for Elin to feed her scraps of turkey, and Elin ate until she felt like she could burst. After dinner, Jenna's grandparents retired to their room for a nap while everyone else broke out the board games. Jenna and Elin's father battled fiercely for control of real estate on the Monopoly board until everyone else insisted they call it quits.

But as the night wore on, Elin fought a growing sense of disquiet. Which made no sense. She was so happy today.

So what was the problem?

Eventually it was time for pie. Elin helped herself to a slice of butter rum cream and pumpkin, hoping some sugar would cure her. Jenna's dad won the battle to pick the movie they would watch during dessert. He picked a subtitled kung-fu movie, a choice he must have regretted as he had to pause it roughly every ten minutes to explain what was going on.

"So Biyu has saved Po's life, which means she is now responsible for him," Jenna's dad said to Elin's mom.

"Isn't that Wookiees?" Jenna asked, not glancing up from her phone. She and Elin were sharing the oversized beanbag in the middle of the room. Jenna was texting with Miles, who was in California.

"No, if you save a Wookiee's life, the Wookiee owes you a life debt," Jenna's dad said patiently. "In kung-fu movies, if you save someone's life, you're responsible for them forever because you've changed their destiny."

"I'm not sure that's an accurate representation of Chinese culture," Jenna's mother said, waving a forkful of pumpkin pie. Holly and Jenna smirked at each other over their phones, and Elin felt a vague pang of jealousy. Holly and Cat had been best friends for even longer than Jenna and Elin had been best friends, and yet, Holly never left Jenna out of sisterly things while Cat always seemed vaguely irritated by Elin's presence.

"Probably not," Jenna's dad said, shrugging like that was irrelevant.

"It doesn't seem fair, though," Elin's dad remarked, his Swedish accent slightly thicker after a couple glasses of wine.

"Yeah," Cat said. "Why would anyone save anyone if it meant they had to watch out for them for the rest of their lives?"

"With great power, comes great responsibility. *Really* great responsibility," Elin whispered to Jenna, who choked back a laugh. Elin grinned—and then felt that growing sense of unrest again.

Jenna's dad rolled his eyes. "It's just a movie, people. Can we watch it already?"

"You should have picked something in English, Dad," Blake said from the loveseat, where he was entangled with his girlfriend, who was nodding off.

"Heaven forbid Americans read subtitles," Elin's dad said dryly. Elin's mother smacked his arm.

Dr. Sinclair sighed heavily, but it was increasingly obvious that he was losing the war.

"I'll watch it with you later," Jenna piped up, putting her phone away. "Just pick something different."

"The new *Star Wars*!" suggested Jenna's mom.

"Isn't that terribly long?" Elin's mother said, glancing at her watch.

Elin's stomach churned and her mouth felt sticky-sweet. She put her unfinished plate of pie on the ground next to the chair, unable to take another bite.

She finally knew what the feeling was. Tomorrow it was back to regular life.

10

Jenna Sinclair
April 18, 6:10 PM

Not five minutes into the party at Fisher's, Ket had wandered off to flirt with whatever hot loser she was hooking up with and Rosie had planted herself on the couch to ignore the party. Elin was on a tour of the infamous condo with Fisher, which left me to awkwardly stand in the kitchen by myself.

Awesome.

I loved my friends, honestly I did, but sometimes they were so inconsiderate I wanted to scream. Seriously, did they not know how rude it was? Elin especially. I was here, without Miles, because she wanted a "girls night" prom, and then she ditched me?

I realized I was staring at the running tap without getting myself a glass of water. I shook my head, trying to snap out it. I spied a tray of Jell-O shots, and before I could stop to think, I grabbed a red one and let it slide down my throat.

"Hey, check out Jenna," said Vaughn.

I glanced over my shoulder. Vaughn Hollis and his cronies—great.

Vaughn smirked at me. "Didn't realize you had no gag reflex."

I forced myself to smile, even though I wanted to slap his smug face. For one second, I allowed myself to visualize it—my hand hitting Vaughn's cheek with a satisfying smack, the impact rippling over his skin, the stupidly shocked expression he'd make.

The thought actually turned my smile genuine.

On my list of Park City High douchelords, Vaughn ranked number one. But since Ket had made the monumental mistake of dating Vaughn last quarter, I had to be nice or risk Ket being painted as some sort of vengeful, crazy ex-girlfriend. *Calumny: a false accusation of an offense.*

I reached for a can of soda. "Oh, hey guys. Where are your dates?"

"We should ask you the same thing," said Nolan Rhys, who was actually pretty cool. "Where's Miles?"

I shrugged, glancing over to the living room where one of my "dates" was absorbed with some *fascinating* app. "We decided to meet up at the dance. I wanted to hang out with the girls beforehand. Skip the photos-by-the-fireplace scene, all that."

In reality, Miles was not remotely interested in attending prom—he would pop in for our pictures, but he and some friends had been planning an all-night LAN party in Mr. Thompson's classroom for weeks.

Nolan smiled and nodded, obviously thinking, *What a cool girl.*

But Vaughn didn't seem impressed. "So Miles is just going to meet you on the dance floor, like some little lapdog?"

I grabbed a plate and started filling it with rice, beans, and lettuce, ignoring him. "So where did you say your dates were?"

I hated guys like Vaughn, the way they are so enamored with themselves even though they don't *do* anything worth admiring. A guy like Vaughn could get away with nearly any-thing—a sexist comment, a vaguely racist joke—and if any-one called him on it, he'd just flip the tables and somehow make *them* the ass.

A few months ago, I had no problem keeping my dislike of Vaughn under wraps because I believed—honestly, truly believed—that guys like him were the minority, that he'd either become a better person in college or peak in high school.

Now I was starting to wonder if I was naïve or just flat dumb about that. And it was getting harder and harder to keep my hatred at bay.

"I'm going stag," Vaughn said with a grin. "Gotta keep my options open."

Like prom is the same as clubbing, dumbass?

I smiled faintly, taking a bite of my salad. "What about you, Nolan?"

"Sings Praises," he said, popping the top of a Coke can.

"Oh, Sings Praises is so great!" I lied, smiling brightly. "She's been *so* helpful in planning prom."

Sings Praises—yes, *Sings Praises*—was not great and had been the exact opposite of helpful. She and Hannah were a two-person coterie of fail. Ever since I'd allowed them to design the prom tickets and they'd (1) chosen papyrus font and (2) failed to realize they'd spelled it "porm" before sending the PDF to the printer, I hadn't let either of them to do anything more important than pick up the committee's bagels.

I was used to dealing with worthless people. Any project you planned was bound of have some bailers—when I did Sub for Santa, Miles, my mom, and I ended up staying up until mid-night, wrapping all the presents ourselves when no one else showed. Stuff like that is annoying, but you can adjust for it.

But Hannah and Sings Praises were particularly egregious because they kept trying to take over. Even after the "porm" disaster—seriously, how hard is it to spell a four-letter word in an appropriate font?—they remained unaware that they'd be completely lost without me. Hannah thought I was a control freak and Sings Praises lived to validate Hannah's opinions. *Vituperate: to spread negative information.*

My phone buzzed and I glanced down. Speak of the devil.

HANNAH: *We have a situation.*

I bit my lip, resisting a smile.

JENNA: *Really? What's wrong?*

Her response appeared almost instantly.

HANNAH: *When are you going to get here?*

Normally this would have me fuming. The most annoying thing about Hannah was that the girl was allergic to answering a direct question. You could ask her for the capital of Romania and she'd respond with a snotty, *"Why do you need to know?"*

But this time, I felt nothing but smug satisfaction. I began typing out my response as Nolan and Vaughn and their friends returned to their conversation around me.

JENNA: *I don't know, 30 min, an hour.*
         Is it an emergency?

HANNAH: *Where are you?*

I couldn't help it—I burst out laughing.

Nolan glanced at me, pausing as he set cups out on the table for a drinking game. "What's so funny?" he asked.

I grinned at him. "You were in AP Geography last year, weren't you?"

"Yeah," he said, a puzzled half smile appearing on his face.

"What's the capital of Romania?"

"Bucharest," he replied automatically.

"Exactly," I said, barely suppressing a smile of my own.

Vaughn and his friends rolled their eyes at my weirdness, but Nolan just laughed. "Do you want to play beer pong with us?"

I paused. Did I?

I glanced around for my friends. Nowhere to be seen.

"Definitely," I said. "Give me just a second to take care of this."

I walked into the hallway to text while Nolan and the others started filling cups full of Bud Light.

JENNA: *Fisher Reese's condo.*

HANNAH: *WHAT?*
I was supposed to go to that party with Ben!
Why did u need me to recheck the lighting if u were just going to a party?

I suppressed a smile. I couldn't decide whether I should be more amused that Hannah hadn't figured out I'd already double-checked the lighting myself *and* password protected the program so she couldn't change it even if she needed to—or that after weeks of begging to be in charge of anything at all, she would rather be pre-partying.

> **JENNA:** *Because you're on prom committee, Hannah.*

This would make *her* fume. Hannah was one of those girls who could take offense from anything, and a condescending text would make anyone mad. This wasn't my typical MO for dealing with Hannah—usually I tried to placate her, just to avoid the hassle.

But right now? I was pretty much over everything.

Before she could respond, I sent another text, walking out into the foyer so I could pace in peace.

> **JENNA:** *I've done practically everything else for prom.*
> *So you're checking the lighting and I'm pre-partying.*
> *Just tell me what's wrong, is it something with the lights?*

> **HANNAH:** *Just find me when you get here.*

A slow smile spread over my face as I shook my head, staring at the text. I should have just let that be the end of it, but . . .

> **JENNA:** *Okie-doke!*

That was probably the first time I had said *okie-doke* since preschool.

I turned my phone over in my hands, warm satisfaction spreading through my chest like it was June and I was lying out in the sun. I would have done a victory dance if I wasn't sure people in the kitchen and living room could see me.

"Hey, have you seen Ben yet?"

I turned around. Elin was standing in the hallway, toying with the end of her braid.

My smile faded. "Uh, no, not yet. But Hannah is definitely otherwise-occupied."

Elin nodded, biting her lip, two lines appearing between her eyebrows. "But he's probably coming, right? I mean, Fisher said he was invited, and Hannah isn't coming . . ."

I hesitated, wrapping one arm around myself. "I don't know. I didn't even know *we* were invited to this party until an hour ago. Did you need me to make sure he was coming?"

What I did not say was, *You guys broke up.*

Why do I have to do everything?

Don't make me try to read your mind.

The two of us stared at each other in silence, the party bustling behind Elin in the kitchen. I felt my neck heat, prickling uncomfortably, and I knew my skin was turning blotchy. I looked down at my purse and cleared my throat. "You should have Ket text him. They're still friends, right?"

I slipped by Elin to rejoin the rest of the party, which had grown since I'd walked into the hall. I thought she might have whispered my name as I went past, but I didn't stop to be sure. My headache was roaring back to life. I spied another Jell-O shot—blue—and grabbed it. *Don't think about the horses*, I thought as I gulped it down. Which, of course, made me think about them even *more*, and for a second both Jell-O shots and the three bites of salad I'd eaten threatened to come back up. I winced, fighting the urge to gag in the middle of the party, and poured myself a cup of the nearest available drink.

Nolan raised his eyebrows at me, pausing just as he was about to toss his ping-pong ball across the table. Vaughn and some of the others had disappeared—bonus—so it was just him, Leni, Alex Kingston, and Sam facing off against each other. "You sure you can handle that, Jenna?" Nolan asked, a hint of a challenge in his voice.

I grinned weakly, raising my glass in a toast. "Gan bei, bitches."

I could hardly taste the flavor over the sound of them laughing.

11

Rosie Winchester
April 18, 6:30 PM

I wound up sitting on the couch at Fisher's, reading on my tablet. My standard party behavior—I can't believe Will was worried for a second.

Ket flopped down beside me, crossing her long legs and attracting more than a few glances. She handed me a can of Diet Coke and gestured to a group of boys standing by the fridge, holding red cups and arguing about something. "Check that guy out," Ket whispered, glancing back over my shoulder so she wouldn't get caught staring. "Do you think he's Fisher's date?"

There was one thing about Fisher Reese (aside from her model good looks, shiny hair, and loaded parents) that made her stand out in a high school crowd.

Fisher never dated a boy from our school.

Whenever Fisher attended a dance, she showed up with a guy no one had ever met—a sophomore in college, a guy from an opposing school who she'd bewitched after a swim meet, some boy she had met skiing. It would have been absurd if it hadn't been happening for four years.

I glanced over to the kitchen. "Which one?"

"Uh, the crazy-hot one, of course."

I sipped my soda, still not sure which guy Ket was talking about—until Leni Taylor stepped aside.

Then I knew exactly who she meant.

Fisher's date was precisely the sort of guy you'd expect to take a girl like Fisher Reese to prom. His black hair was cropped short in back and sides, but longer on top, falling over his forehead. His jaw was covered in stubble and he had a cocky smile, full of perfect white teeth.

I shrugged. "He's not that cute." (Lie. Filthy lie.)

"What's wrong with him?" Ket asked, sounding personally offended.

I racked my brain. "His stubble looks really calculated."

Ket raised one eyebrow.

"His eyebrows are way too thick. They look like caterpillars," I said. (Sexy, sexy caterpillars.) (Rosie, what is wrong with you?)

"They do not," Ket scoffed.

"He hails from Clan Douchebag," I said. "They're a proud and ancient people, known throughout the land for their body sprays."

Ket tapped her lower lip. "I don't know. He doesn't look like the bedazzled jeans type."

"Your douche-dar can't be trusted," I said, taking a sip of my soda. "You've hooked up with too many of their kind."

"Speaking of," Ket murmured, taking a sip of her drink and nodding at someone across the room.

I followed her gaze to where Vaughn Hollis was leaning against the wall. The sleeves of his white dress shirt were rolled up to highlight his (admittedly impressive) forearms and tattoos. "Ah yes. He's achieved the highest rank in Douche Society. You can tell because of his many misappropriated cultural tattoos."

Ket choked on her soda and I grinned. I didn't usually make Ket laugh. Vaughn glanced over at us, a scowl on his face. Ket waggled her fingers at him, not even bothering to hide the fact that we'd been making fun of him.

Elin flopped down next to us on the couch. "What is the deal with Jenna?"

"What do you mean?"

"She's done like, four Jell-O shots already. Does she not understand what's in a Jell-O shot? It's not just Jell-O."

I crinkled my brow. "Four? Really?"

"Well, she's done a lot. And she let Nolan mix her a rum and Coke."

I shrugged. "Well, we'll be at prom before too long, and then she'll be Miles's problem, not ours."

Elin crossed her arms, her lower lip jutting out. She crossed her legs, bouncing one foot, jittery. She'd done a one-eighty from the excited, happy girl she'd been at my house. I felt another creep of doubt about this prom plan. "She's being ridiculous. This isn't going to be any fun at all if she passes out before we even get to the dance."

"She's not going to pass out," I said, but I wasn't exactly sure. Jenna *never* did anything other than steal sips from other people. She'd once claimed to have gotten hungover after half a cup of watermelon Boone's Farm. "Look, we're going to leave in thirty minutes, and we'll stop at a 7-Eleven for coffee, just in case." (And please, some taquitos. Please.)

Elin studied her manicured nails. "Do you think Jenna's ever . . . had sex?"

"I don't think Jenna's ever pooped," Ket muttered.

"I'm serious. Do you think they're doing it, but she's just not telling us?"

I didn't even have to think about it. "No. Jenna's going to be an old-school virginal bride, and she'll text us the next day from the honeymoon suite about how magical it was. I bet Miles's never even felt her up."

Elin bit her lip. "I know it seems that way . . . but I think even Jenna has her secrets."

I shrugged. "I think Jell-O shots on prom night aren't exactly evidence of mysterious inner layers."

Elin huffed, and I knew we weren't playing along the way she wanted. "What do you think is wrong with her?" I asked, tucking my tablet under my leg so she knew she had my full attention.

Elin opened her mouth, shut it. She scrunched up her face, thinking. I studied her expression, the doubt I'd felt back at my house returning and taking up permanent residence underneath my ribs.

"Oh, come on," Ket burst out, impatient. "Jenna is getting drunk, which is crazy for her and annoying for us, but normal for life. There's nothing to be worried about."

Elin's expression smoothed out, unreadable. She nodded. I felt a flare of annoyance toward Ket but didn't say anything. Ket nudged Elin and pointed out a junior girl's shoes (Louboutins or knockoffs?) and I pulled my tablet back out.

Eventually Ket and Elin got bored with my party-pooper attitude and left me to return to my book—which worked fine for me. I loved my friends, but I didn't love that they were always trying to cheer me up. Teddy had always gotten that about me.

I was perfectly happy the way I was.

12.

Ket West-Beauchamp
April 18, 6:45 PM

Vaughn and I passed Fisher on the stairs as we headed to a bedroom. "I was just going to show Ket your dad's aquarium," Vaughn said innocently.

Fisher smiled, but the expression didn't reach her eyes. "It's something, all right," she remarked mildly, with an I Know What You're Really Up To tone that Mama Leanne could take notes on.

I couldn't resist—I paused on the steps even as Vaughn tugged on my hand. "Your condo is *so* awesome, Fisher," I said. "Thanks *so* much for inviting me."

Fisher's smile cracked, brittle as ever. "Glad you're enjoying yourself," she replied, continuing down the stairs without a backward glance. It was unfathomable to me why so many people liked her. I may have had a reputation for being a troublemaker who'd slept with too many boys, but at least I didn't have an icicle up my ass.

Vaughn tugged my hand impatiently and I giggled, racing up next to him. We found an empty bedroom and soon Vaughn had me pushed up against the door, his mouth on mine and one hand sliding under the hem of my dress.

Truth be told, Vaughn wasn't the best kisser—*way* too much tongue. I tilted my head back until his lips were redirected to my neck. I closed my eyes and smiled. *That* he was good at. "Don't get too riled up," I whispered, running my fingers through his hair before I remembered it was sticky from product. I tried not to grimace.

"Don't be a tease," Vaughn whispered against my throat.

"I'm serious," I replied as his mouth wandered along my collarbone. "We can hook up after prom, if you're good, but I don't want to mess up my hair before the dance." I pushed his hand out from under my skirt.

Vaughn groaned, kissing his way down to the neckline of my dress. "Seriously, Ket, what is the point of being with the school bike if you're going to be all hot-and-cold?"

And just like that, I wasn't turned on anymore.

I pushed him away, hard, and he was caught off guard long enough to stumble back against the bed. He stared at me, stunned, and I was pleased to see that I had ruined his stupid James Dean pompadour.

"The school *bike*?" I repeated.

"Yeah, you know," Vaughn said, his tone puzzled. "As in, 'everyone's had a ride.'"

"I know what it means, Vaughn," I said, my cheeks burning. "I just don't understand why you'd say that to me."

Vaughn sat back on the bed, hands on his knees, his forehead crinkling. "Because . . . you hook up with everyone. I didn't think you'd care."

That was not technically true. I'd only had sex-sex with five guys, and only two of them still went to our school. I had hit a few other bases with others, as well, which was probably the issue—every guy who'd ever touched my bra probably claimed to have visited Keturah's Promised Land. But that was beside the point. Vaughn was a far bigger whore than I was, and he was calling *me* the school bike?

And yes, I know there's a societal double standard when it comes to sex, and no, I'm not exactly interested in proving a big feminist point, but *Vaughn* calling me the school bike? VAUGHN? Where was the honor among thieves, dude?

"I care," I said, crossing my arms over my chest. "Don't ever say that to me again."

Vaughn flopped down on the bed. "Jeez, Beauchamp, I thought you were cool. Learn to take a joke," he said, the hint of a smirk on his face.

I hated that. Guys like Vaughn loved to make you feel stupid by pretending everything was a big joke, especially when it wasn't. Then if you insisted on treating something serious seriously, they acted like you were some crazy person.

From his smirk to the challenge in his eyes, Vaughn was daring me to be "crazy."

Challenge Accepted.

I scowled. "Forget about after prom. Ugh, I knew I should have been done with you."

Vaughn rolled his eyes, finally getting annoyed. "I'm pretty sure I dumped your ass, Ket."

"I'm pretty sure I was never your girlfriend, and therefore am, by definition, undumpable." I opened the door of the bedroom to leave.

Vaughn reached over my head to shut the door and leaned down to whisper in my ear. "If I wasn't your boyfriend, why did you come crying to me after Elin tried to kill herself?"

13

BEFORE
Elin Angstrom
December 31, 9:45 PM

It had been snowing all day, but it finally stopped.

Elin looked out the floor-to-ceiling windows, hoping the fireworks wouldn't be cancelled due to snow. Rosie's dad lived in the Avenues and had a view of the entire city, white and yellow lights twinkling under a fresh blanket of snow. Somewhere down there, her older sister Cat was partying. Elin shivered just thinking about it. Her eyes unfocused, the city blurring until all Elin could see was her own reflection, the reflection of the room behind her.

Rosie was sitting on the couch, sullenly flipping through channels, her lap covered with a ratty blanket. Teddy perched on the arm of the couch, his arms crossed over his chest, looking like a spring that was wound too tight. In the kitchen, Rosie's father and his girlfriend—Amber, maybe?—mixed cocktails.

Elin and Teddy had made the drive down to Salt Lake City to keep Rosie company. She'd been stuck at her dad's since Christmas morning, her IMs and texts becoming increasingly despondent.

"Are you sure you don't want to hang out with Ben tonight?" Teddy had asked when he'd picked her up that afternoon. "I can go by myself."

Elin had rolled her eyes, putting on her seatbelt and shaking the snow out of her hair. "I can hang out with Ben any night. Were you on this text chain? The one about him throwing out her copy of *Looking for Alaska*?"

Teddy nodded, sighing heavily as he pulled away from the curb. "I hate that douchebag."

"Amen," Elin said, buckling her seatbelt.

It was just the two of them. Jenna was babysitting her neighbor's kids, Ket was grounded. Elin couldn't even remember why—probably her moms making a pre-emptive strike against whatever shenaniganry Ket would get up to.

Elin knew why Teddy wanted to go to Salt Lake on his own. She felt guilty over keeping Teddy from a shot at the romantic evening he so desperately hoped for, but she really didn't want to spend New Year's Eve with Ben. It had been over three weeks since they'd had sex, and she knew he was going to want to do it. She couldn't use cramps as an excuse again, and she didn't want to talk about it, or worse, fight about it. Elin hated fighting with Ben.

Fortunately, Teddy never put his undying crush on Rosie ahead of his friendship with the rest of them. It was one of Elin's favorite things about him.

"I left money for you kids to order in," Rosie's dad called, wrapping a thick scarf around his neck, snapping Elin out of her thoughts. "Not pizza. Pick something with culture, okay?"

Rosie rolled her eyes so hard, Elin worried she might go blind. Teddy clenched his fists—he was not good with parents.

"Good night, Dr. Winchester!" Elin called before either Rosie or Teddy could say anything. Rosie's dad and his girl-friend waved as they walked out the door.

Rosie turned up the volume on the TV. "Don't call him doctor, he's not a real doctor," she muttered.

Teddy raised his eyebrows, some of the tension leaving his body. "Tell us how you really feel, Ro," he said, lips curling up in a smile.

Rosie's dad's furniture was crap, but every wall was filled with bookshelves, and his bookshelves were filled with various translations of Proust, Goethe, Anais Nin, Zola, Tolstoy. *"It's like he thinks he can get extra credit for only reading things that didn't originally come in English,"* Rosie had IM'd earlier that day.

Rosie had once told Elin that, when she was younger, she had believed she inherited her love of reading from him— her mother had no interest in fiction, said she got enough reading at work. But her dad didn't think much of the books Rosie liked to read. Mysteries, fantasy, graphic novels, horror, and definitely anything for kids—according to Professor Winchester, it was all trash.

At this point, it was like Rosie deliberately avoided the books he loved just because he took so much glee in disparaging hers. Of course, that did little to persuade him that he should help Rosie pay for college as long as she intended to pursue a degree in creative writing.

"You should stop coming here," Teddy was saying.

"They have joint custody," Rosie said, sliding down further into the couch and pulling her knees up to her chest.

"That's their problem," Teddy said, leaning over and resting his arm on the back of the couch, right behind Rosie. Elin felt a twinge of a smile, but Teddy's arm remained glued to the couch, hovering just a few inches above Rosie's shoulders.

If she'd thought for one second Rosie could be persuaded to return Teddy's affections, Elin would have given Rosie every reason she could think of that the two of them were perfect for each other. But Rosie needed someone who would sneak up on her. Elin just hoped Teddy had the patience to wait for Rosie to figure things out.

"No judge is going to make a seventeen-year-old with her own car go see her dad if she doesn't want to see her dad," Teddy said. "You're practically an adult, Ro."

Elin glanced over at Rosie, trying to see how she was receiving this. Her face was a stone. "My dad wants the child support," she said flatly. "And my mom hates paying it. If I didn't come down here anymore, it would just be a matter of time before one of them filed an order to show cause against the other. And I just can't. I just can't deal with that anymore."

Teddy caught Elin's eye over Rosie's bent head. His eyebrows were knit together, a flash of uncertainty in his eyes. Teddy got Rosie better than any of them.

It was unnerving when even he didn't know what to do with her.

Teddy tilted his head, gesturing toward Rosie. The look on his face said, *Do something,* as clearly as if he'd uttered the words. Elin lifted one shoulder, a half shrug, hoping she looked more nonchalant than she felt. Rosie was good at offering suggestions to their problems, but Elin had never been able to return the favor. It was just one more reason Elin was a subpar friend.

Let her talk, Elin mouthed at Teddy, and he nodded.

Rosie poured out her frustrations, Teddy glowered, and Elin stared out the window, wishing she were better at this. She tugged at a loose thread on her sleeve, wondering what

Ben was up to. She would text him, except she dreaded his inevitably understanding reply. She'd canceled on him right before Teddy had picked her up, and he'd been predictably kind. *Poor Ro. Tell her hi from me.* Shame had squeezed at her throat, making her ears burn scarlet.

But the exquisite relief she felt was stronger.

Elin told her girlfriends everything—part of everything, anyway. She had told them the first time she and Ben kissed, the first time Ben said he loved her, the first time they had sex. She told them it had hurt the first time, but not as much as she'd thought. She told them it had gotten fun by the fourth time they did it.

She was working up the courage to tell them—maybe Ket, since she'd had sex, or Rosie, who was the best listener— that it had stopped being fun. She could barely remember when it was fun.

But she would never tell them that sometimes she wished Ben were a little more like the guys Ket hooked up with. Less thoughtful. Less caring. Less inclined to stare lovingly into her eyes.

That way she wouldn't have to feel so badly about wanting it over with. That the vomit-y desperation, like she'd crawl out of her skin if it meant getting away from him, would go away for good.

I am a terrible person.

Sometimes, when Elin let herself think about how much luckier she was than most of her friends, she felt sick. It made no sense that she had such a hard time when she had everything she could have asked for. It was Jenna's mother's answer to every dilemma, every setback: *Count your many blessings.* And Elin had blessings to spare.

She was healthy and pretty and her parents would pay for her to go anywhere she wanted for college. Her family was happy. Her boyfriend was perfect. She loved Ben so much it sometimes physically *hurt*, a vice around her heart.

Nothing bad had *ever* happened to her. She lived the very definition of a blessed life.

The problem was, those blessings just made her feel guiltier.

Rosie and Teddy had almost no one. And yeah, maybe Rosie could be cold, and Teddy could be angry, but they were both *selfless*. They would never treat anyone the way Elin wanted to treat Ben.

"And I'm the only one he treats like this," Rosie said, her face icy and impassive, flipping through channels so quickly that Elin could barely tell what was on before Rosie had moved on. "Remember Amanda? She read tons of romance novels and he never once called her 'bordering on infantile.'" She made the air quotes with her fingers.

"He's just jealous because no one read his shitty book," Teddy said, taking the remote away from Rosie.

Rosie crossed her arms and said nothing. Elin glanced over at her. Rosie's shoulders were slumped, like a marionette with cut strings. "It's not shitty," she said sadly.

"You read it?" Teddy said, surprised.

"Yeah. I didn't tell him, he'd be too smug. I was hoping it would suck, but it didn't."

Elin and Teddy exchanged a glance—Rosie usually didn't express emotions like a normal person. They knew when she was upset because they'd known her forever, not because she ever *seemed* upset.

Now she seemed upset.

"He knows what he's talking about," Rosie said, eyes shining with unshed tears. "His book is so much better than anything I've ever written. Better than anything I've ever *thought* about writing. The words he chose, the way he put them together—it would never even occur to me."

"You're still in high school!" Elin protested, but her voice came out whispery-faint. It felt like her lungs could only half fill with air.

Elin was used to Rosie taking care of her, not the other way around.

"You're being too hard on yourself, your writing is awesome," Teddy said, his forehead crinkling, the anger melting out of his voice.

Rosie gave Teddy a scornful look. "You're my best friend," she said flatly. "Your opinion is not to be trusted."

Elin's heart pounded in her chest. Things were getting way too intense, and Elin didn't do well with intense. That was another Angstrom family trait: they preferred to look at the sunny side of life. She jumped to her feet. "There's too much sadness in here," she said. "I am declaring myself the Unofficial Ket of the Night, and as such, I think we need an immediate change of activity."

"Sorry I'm not being very fun," Rosie said glumly.

"Nonsense!" Elin said, grabbing Rosie's hands and dragging her into the kitchen. "Happiness is a choice. You're going to be fun any minute now, I can sense it. Teddy, did the good professor leave his booze unattended?"

Teddy glanced over his shoulder. "He sure did."

"And did this whole sorry affair begin when your dad tossed *Looking for Alaska* in the trash?"

"And poured a Coke on it," Rosie said bitterly.

Elin nodded. "Well, I think the only thing we can do is make an homage to Alaska Young and the Colonel themselves and get drunk, climb in the hot tub, and watch the fireworks."

Teddy uncorked the Patron. "'An homage,' huh?"

Elin grinned, feeling her cheeks ache from the effort. "Well, you know. Minus the tragic ending."

"Spoiler alert," protested Rosie.

"Oh, you weren't done?" Elin asked, reaching for the lime and knife that Rosie's dad had left on the counter.

"Not me!" Rosie said. "Teddy. I was re-reading, but he hasn't started it yet."

"To be fair, it's been out for a million years," Elin pointed out. "And it's John Green, so, you know."

"Stop!" Rosie said, pressing her hands against Teddy's ears. He squirmed away from her, but judging from his flushed cheeks, he had liked it.

"I don't mind spoilers," Teddy said again as he searched for salt and clean shot glasses. "I like knowing how things end."

Rosie rolled her eyes. "Don't I know it," she said, sounding slightly cheerier. "Okay, let me go find some towels and suits. Elin, you can borrow one of mine. Teddy, I hope you don't mind, but my dad has started wearing embarrassingly small European swim trunks."

"I'll stick with my boxers, thanks," Teddy said, pouring three careful shots of Patron.

Rosie turned down the hall, nodding at Elin. "Come with me, let's find a suit for you," she said.

"Don't start drinking without us," Elin instructed Teddy as she followed Rosie to her room.

Rosie's room at her dad's looked nothing like her room at her mom's. It was all white walls, plain furniture, a pink-and-yellow patterned comforter leftover from elementary school. Nothing indicated she even lived in it other than a pair of jeans tossed haphazardly on the floor and her beat-up laptop charging on the desk.

"So you finished *Looking for Alaska*?" Rosie asked, rifling through her drawers for swimming suits.

"Last summer."

"So what did you think of you-know-what?" she whispered, even though Teddy was on the other side of the house. "Do you think it was an accident, or . . .?"

"Accident," Elin said firmly, snatching Rosie's only bikini. "Only weak people try to kill themselves."

14

Rosie Winchester
April 18, 6:50 PM

Three books in, I was loving the Song of Ice and Fire series but reading it did have one drawback (aside from the murder and boob fixation): the extensive description of food. My stomach was practically eating itself.

I glanced over at the kitchen, where people were snacking on guacamole and chips, leaning over so salsa wouldn't drip on their dresses and ties. I bit my lip, considering. Fisher had told us to help ourselves. ("So there's Café Rio in the kitchen, sodas in the fridge, vodka in the freezer, and beer in the cooler. And there's Jell-O shots, but they're a little watery.") She had shrugged and tossed her hair, a golden curtain of perfect waves. Even when she was self-deprecating, girls like Fisher gave girls like me eating disorders without even trying.

But there was no way that Fisher intended for randoms like me to eat the food she'd bought. I wasn't actually friends with her. It was weird, the idea of eating the food Fisher had ordered for people she knew. People she liked. People who had RSVP'd.

I was not really a guest at this party. I was practically a lamp.

So when Fisher's date sat down beside me on the couch, I kept staring resolutely at my tablet. He was probably waiting for someone else anyway.

He cleared his throat. I glanced up, one eyebrow arched. (Ket and I perfected eyebrow arching after watching *The Little Mermaid* on repeat as first graders.) "What's up?" I said, my voice level.

"I just wanted to say hi," Fisher's date said. "What's your name?"

"Rosie," I said. I glanced around, not sure why Fisher's date was talking to me at all.

"That's a pretty name," Fisher's date said.

I stared at him blankly. "I'll let my parents know."

Fisher's date grinned and rubbed the back of his neck with one hand. "Yeah, good call," he said.

I realized I was staring. I glanced away before he got the wrong idea. I had played it cool (really cool) when Ket was drooling over Fisher's date. The boy was the cutest guy I'd ever seen. But boys were not my thing. The debacle with Teddy had made that abundantly clear.

I glanced back at him. He was staring at me, a faint half-smile on his lips. (Ugh, he looked like a damn Disney prince.) "Can I help you with something?" I said.

His smile grew larger. "I just wanted to say hi," he repeated. "You don't seem like you're having a lot of fun at the party."

"And you're going to change that for me?"

Fisher's Date raised one eyebrow and my heart beat a little faster. "I'm going to do my best," he said.

I flushed. I wished I hadn't said that. It sounded flirty and I was never flirty.

I'd never attracted much male attention. I'd never wanted to. I knew I was pretty-ish (which was nice, even if I didn't want anyone to notice) but I wasn't good at being friendly, much less flirtatious. Hand-holding, hugging, kissing? I was bound to be terrible at all of it.

Not that it even mattered, since I didn't *want* to be good at it.

I spent half my free time driving between Park City and Salt Lake City because of my parents' romantic misadventures. The whole boy-girl-kittens-and-squealing thing was not worth the effort when I couldn't even manage a part-time job. I wanted to move away from my parents, experience an unencumbered life. I couldn't do that and worry about someone else, too.

Part of what I had always loved about Teddy was that I had assumed he'd shared my opinions.

But here was this guy, already on a date with the prettiest girl in the room, staring at me in a way that made my heart pound in my chest. I wanted to look away, but there was something about the way he looked me right in the eye. I wanted to hate his smile. It was like his perfect stupid mouth was set on "perma cheer" for no reason.

"You don't like me," he said.

I shrugged, struggling to keep my face impassive and my panic tamped down. "Should I?"

He grinned—he didn't strike me as a guy who was turned down very often. "You've never met me. You should at least start me out with a blank slate."

I shrugged again. "You're Fisher's date, right? Close enough."

The smile faded from his face. He shifted closer to me. "Ah. Well, let me clarify—Fisher and I are just friends. I'm not the kind of guy who would be . . ."

"Would be what?" I said. I meant it to be sharp, but my tone came out softer. Too soft.

His eyes weren't really blue. They were a clear pale gray, like the sky before a storm. And they were locked onto mine. "Would be talking to a pretty girl when I'm on a date with someone else."

I felt a shiver run up my spine.

Fortunately, Ket flopped down on the other side of Fisher's Date. I had to give him one thing: he might have been talking up a girl who wasn't his date, but he didn't check out Ket's legs.

"I don't think we've officially met," Ket began.

"Ket, this is Fisher's date," I interrupted. "I've decided to call him FD. FD, this is Keturah."

Ket glanced back and forth between the two of us, not-so-subtly checking out the minimal distance between FD's thigh and mine. A slow smirk spread over her face. "That's not very catchy," she said, crossing her arms over her chest. "I think we should call him FDR."

For one second, I didn't get it. Then Ket raised one eyebrow and it clicked in my brain. She thought he had a crush on me—*Teddy and FDR.* I scowled.

FDR raised his eyebrows at us. "What's so funny?" he asked Ket.

I glanced over at FDR, refusing to acknowledge Ket's widening grin. For one second, my gaze tripped over Vaughn Hollis, leaning against the wall and smirking at Ket. (Ugh, Ket. Why do you make the choices you do?) I blinked, refocusing on Fisher's date and Ket. "How does FDR work for you?" I asked, determined to ignore Vaughn's creepy staring.

He shrugged, an amused expression on his face. He didn't look nearly so intense now that Ket was here. "Sounds all right by me."

"Not that you're terribly presidential looking," Ket continued. "But FD just isn't working for me."

"Well, you could always use my real name," FDR suggested.

"I don't think that will be necessary," I said, a little too sharply.

FDR glanced back at me and for once I was able to look away from him. I didn't know what was wrong with me—everything I said was coming out wrong.

Ket stood back up, tugging down her skirt to avoid indecent exposure, and grabbed my hand. "Pardon me for jumping in and stealing Rosie, FDR. Normally, I'd never block a cock—"

"Ket!" I cried, feeling my cheeks flame.

"—but I just need her for one minute. I promise, I'll bring her back."

"Promise?" FDR said, a grin spreading over his face.

Ket held up her pinkie. With zero hesitation, FDR hooked his pinkie around hers.

I smiled uncomfortably during their exchange—why couldn't I flirt so effortlessly?

(Not that I wanted to flirt with FDR.)

(I definitely didn't want to flirt with FDR.)

"I better go check in with Fisher anyway," FDR said, standing. He must have been over six feet tall—he towered over Ket in her heels. "But I'm going to find you later." His gray eyes met mine and another tremor ran up my spine.

"We're leaving soon, find us at the dance," Ket commanded as she pulled me down the hall. I couldn't help it—I glanced over my shoulder. FDR stared after us, a faint smile on his face.

"Jeez, what magic spell did you cast over FDR?" Ket whispered as we walked away.

"He's just goofing off," I muttered. "He's on a date with Fisher."

"Poor guy," Ket said, grinning. "No wonder he's looking for a different girl to hang out with."

I rolled my eyes. "She's gorgeous. I think he could do worse."

"She's boring and frigid and a giant snob," Ket retorted. "But think what you like. FDR is in *lurve* with you, I can tell."

"You think everyone is in lurve with everyone."

Ket twirled, watching the lights sparkle off her sequined dress. "Isn't that the best way to live, though?"

I refused to smile as I followed her into the hallway bathroom and she shut the door. I raised both eyebrows. "What, Ket?"

Ket lost the sly smile, putting on her serious face. "Ben is coming to the party. Promise you aren't going to say anything to him."

I crossed my arms over my chest. "What do you mean?"

Ket rolled her eyes. "Don't play dumb. Elin wants a chance to talk to Ben, and you've been guard-dogging her for weeks. Just . . . don't scare him off."

My cheeks flushed and I clenched my jaw. "Are you serious? He's probably the reason—"

"We don't know the reason," Ket said levelly. It was annoying that Ket was being so cool-headed about this. Normally it was me talking to her in an everything's-all-right voice.

"You don't want to know the reason!" I hissed. "Have you even asked?"

"No, because it's not my business," Ket said. "Have you actually asked, or are you just assuming it was Ben?"

"I know it was Ben," I said hotly.

Ket raised her eyebrows. "You don't know any more than I do. So will you just do me this solid, because we're friends?"

I rolled my eyes and refused to meet her gaze. Ket sighed. "What do you think could possibly happen in one conversation?" she asked, her voice softer, her expression suddenly sad, as if her previous happiness had been nothing more than makeup that she'd washed off. "Even if you're right. You can't keep Elin in bubble wrap forever."

I chewed my lower lip. "Fine," I said. "I will leave him alone. Tonight. But if it seems like he's upsetting her—"

"I will personally kick him in the tenders," Ket said, a wide grin spreading over her face. (How does she do that?) She squealed, wrapping her arms around me in a tight hug. I stiffened and Ket laughed. "I know I'm invading your personal bubble, but you've done so much growing I thought maybe you could handle it—"

"Okay, cut it out," I interrupted, squirming out of her grip. "Jeez. Why is everyone so touchy-feely today?"

Ket laughed. "It's prom, dude. How else are you supposed to act?"

We stepped into the hallway to rejoin the party. I kept an eye on the front door, my book momentarily forgotten.

I may have promised Ket that I would leave Ben alone, but that was only because Ben was dating Hannah Larson. Hannah was the baby sloth of girlfriends, always clinging onto whatever guy she was dating.

With Hannah by his side, there was no way that Ben would have a second to talk to Elin by himself, which meant Elin was safe.

Over in the kitchen, FDR was opening another bag of red Solo cups. He glanced at me and smiled. I quickly looked away, trying to forget whatever that *weirdness* had been on the couch. I positioned myself in the hallway, near enough to a group of other kids that I looked like I was part of their conversation.

7:15 PM

When Ben walked through Fisher's door without a date, I felt my pulse pick up. Where was Hannah?

Ben moved to the kitchen, helping himself to some chips and guacamole. Without Hannah hanging on Ben, Elin was a sitting duck.

I glanced over at where Ket was flirting with Vaughn in the hallway. She hadn't noticed Ben walking through the door, looking around like he was searching for someone.

I scanned the party. I didn't see Elin anywhere.

Sorry, Ket.

I jumped up and made my way into the kitchen, ending up across the table from Ben. "Hey," I said brightly, but not too loudly, as I reached for a chip.

Ben blinked at me, then smiled. "Hey Rosie," he said, sounding pleased but a little confused. After two years of being good friends, I had given him the cold shoulder ever since Elin had disappeared from school. I knew he'd been confused by my behavior.

That was what I was counting on.

"Want a beer?" I asked, grabbing his elbow and steering him toward the garage. "I think there's some Golden Spike out here."

15

BEFORE
Elin Angstrom
February 5, 6:30 PM

Rosie's ceiling had a spidery crack down its center. Elin could be doing anything in Rosie's room—studying, playing on her phone, flipping through a magazine—and always, always, always her attention would return to that crack.

Downstairs in the kitchen, Will was making stroganoff. Elin could smell the beef, onion, and garlic simmering in cream sauce. Her stomach wasn't growling, not yet. More like purring.

She was glad her appetite had made an appearance. For weeks and maybe even months, she'd popped Tums and Midol like candy, trying to rid herself of the aches that started deep in her hips and radiated out through her bones. Sometimes she could eat, sometimes she couldn't. Sometimes they kept her up at night. Her mother had taken her to a doctor, who had concluded she had growing pains and told her to stop taking so many pills.

"Dinner will be ready in twenty minutes, Ro," Will called from the hallway.

"Thank you," Rosie called back, not looking up from her work.

Elin much preferred Rosie's Park City house to her Avenues house, and not just because it was so much closer. Will, who worked from home, was always cooking something. Rosie's dad's place smelled like old takeout and bad perfume.

The two of them were supposed to be studying, but Elin was surfing the web for a present for Ben. Valentine's Day was around the corner.

Elin wasn't sure yet whether she and Ben would have another Valentine's Day together. But she wanted to be prepared, just in case.

Rosie sat at her desk and finished outlining their assignment. Elin loved being Rosie's partner on projects. If she partnered with Ket, they never ended up finishing. Jenna tried so hard to engage her, to inspire the same love of accomplishment that Jenna felt, and the two of them always ended up arguing.

Rosie just started working and, whether Elin contributed or not, put Elin's name at the top next to hers. It was a relief to not have to think, to feel badly about dragging another person down.

Elin shut her laptop, rolled over, and stared at Rosie's ceiling. That spidery crack down its center.

Elin was sure Rosie considered that a metaphor for her entire existence.

"Are you going to buy Teddy a birthday present?" Elin asked suddenly.

Rosie paused. Rosie was the loudest typer Elin knew—louder even than Jen. "No. Do you think I should?"

Elin shrugged, enjoying the feeling of Rosie's satiny comforter against her bare skin. Rosie and Will always ran cold, and whenever Rosie's mom was out of town—which was most of the time—they cranked the furnace. Elin had peeled off her sweater and was lying on Rosie's bed in a tank top and low-rise jeans, feeling like summertime. "He's turning eighteen," Elin said finally. "It's a pretty big deal."

That, and he's totally in love with you, and maybe you should throw him a bone?

"Yeah," Rosie said distantly. "What should I get him, do you think?"

Elin shrugged again. Teddy had been part of their circle of friends forever, and Elin adored him, of course, but Rosie and Ket were closest to him. Besides, who knew what to buy a boy? Elin barely knew what to give Ben for Valentine's, and they'd been dating since freshman year. He loved LEGOs, but she felt stupid getting him a toy. She'd ask Aron what cologne he wore, but then her boyfriend would smell like her brother.

I'll ask Jenna, she thought finally. Jenna was the best gift giver, always picking the exact thing that someone wanted but somehow no one else ever thought of—maybe not even the recipient.

Elin didn't know why she hadn't let Jenna decide on Ben's present in the first place.

"Is everything okay?" Rosie asked suddenly. Elin rolled over onto her belly. "What do you mean?"

Rosie pulled her book onto her lap so she could high-light and face Elin. She raised her eyebrows. "I can tell you want to talk about something."

Elin fiddled with the strap of her messenger bag, twisting it around her hands. "It's just that . . . well, remember how I told you that Ben and I slept together after prom last year?"

"Yeah," Rosie said, applying chapstick and smacking her lips together. Rosie had a habit of always doing two things at once—cooking and reading, running and texting, doodling and watching TV. But she always listened when her friends spoke.

"Well . . . we kept having sex after that, right?"

"That is generally how it works," Rosie said, one corner of her mouth quirking up. "What's the problem?"

Elin rolled over again, staring at the ceiling. That long, thin crack. Like lightning. "Well . . . I used to really like it, but lately . . . I don't know. I just don't like it as much. I . . . I kind of wish we weren't doing it at all, actually."

Elin didn't mention that it hadn't always been that way. After the first few awkward times, it was like Elin couldn't get enough. They had sex whenever they had the chance—Elin's house, Ben's basement, Ben's car, even once at Rosie's house while Rosie and Teddy were upstairs arguing over a movie.

And then something changed. She couldn't explain it.

But she didn't want to do it anymore.

She didn't even want to be touched, if she could avoid it.

Elin waited for Rosie to say something—to fill in the gaps of Elin's awkwardness with explanations, like she always did. But when Elin looked over, Rosie didn't have a thoughtful look on her face. Her expression was stormy. Elin blinked, surprised. "What?"

There was a battle raging in her brown eyes, concern and anger. "Is Ben . . . *making* you—"

"What? Oh, no, never!" Elin said hastily, cutting her off before she could even finish the idea. "Jeez, Rosie, it's not like that."

Her brow remained furrowed and she still seemed tense, but she nodded. "Well, what's the problem?"

Elin looked down, wracking her brain for a way out of this mess. *Could I suck more?* The strap of her bag was knotted in her hands. "I just . . . I don't know. It isn't as much fun as I'd thought it would be. I need to . . . you know, spice things up, I guess."

"Oh," Rosie said, her shoulders relaxing. "Well . . . jeez, beats me. Have you asked Ket? I am fresh outta sex tips, friend."

Elin laughed, harder than the joke deserved, but Rosie flashed her a faint smile and went back to their assignment. Elin felt her fake laughter melt away as she stared up at the crack in the ceiling. Her hunger was gone, replaced with a familiar nauseous feeling.

She prayed Rosie would not bring it up again.

Soon afterward Will called them downstairs to eat.

Elin barely managed to swallow two bites.

16

Ket West-Beauchamp
April 18, 7:05 PM

I stepped out of the bathroom, Rosie two steps behind me. I ran my fingers over my hair, making sure everything was still sleek and straight, and scanned the room for Elin. She was standing by the cooler, holding a beer, her face pinched like she had a stomach ache she was trying to ignore. Across the room, Jenna was sitting at the table, still playing Flip Cup.

Guilt shot through me as I glanced over at Elin. I knew I should go over and find out why she looked so unhappy. But the thought of looking Elin in the eye—in her wide, shiny, Bambi-esque eyes—made me feel ill. I glanced away before she could see me staring.

My phone buzzed in my purse and I pulled it out.

VAUGHN: *How much do you want me to keep my mouth shut about you-know-what?*

My stomach sank. Vaughn was a selfish dope, but not a malicious dope.

So why did that text seem so threatening?

Shielding my phone, just in case, I thought about my response. Jokey? Semi-Serious? Imma-Cut-You-Serious? I walked over to the hallway, hoping for a little bit of privacy.

Don't be a tease, I typed, deliberately echoing his statement from earlier. With guys like Vaughn, I'd learned it was usually best to pretend that nothing they said was serious. Usually they ended up feeling so dumb that they gave up.

My phone buzzed with a reply almost an instant after I hit send. I jumped, but it was only Teddy.

TEDDY: *Be honest. You and Elin and Jenna and Rosie plan to retire together down in Florida someday without me*

I shut my eyes, feeling sick—not my normal reaction to a Teddy Text, which was usually a painful sort of delight. To think that Teddy was finally joking around again and I was sitting here, trying to figure out a way to keep Vaughn's mouth shut about Elin. If Teddy could see the mess I'd landed myself in, he'd never talk to me again.

DAMN. IT.

I closed his text—I would think of a reply later.

My phone buzzed again.

VAUGHN: *I think you'd do anything.*

I paused.

There was no denying it now—Vaughn was threatening me.

Instinctively, I looked over at the couch where Rosie had been sitting. Jenna would be more likely to know what to do, but Rosie would be less prone to shooting me judgey looks.

But for the first time all night, she wasn't t
she was off making out with FDR. I cracked an involun...,
smile at the idea.

I strolled over to the couch that Rosie had vacated, focusing
on looking Indifferent To It All in case Vaughn was watching. I
sat down and crossed my legs at the ankle like a Good Girl.

KET: *What do you want?*

Hoping the answer was something I'd be willing to give.
It took him all of ten seconds to reply.

VAUGHN: *You know what I want.*
Get ready for your closeup,
Beauchamp.

I shut my eyes and resisted the urge to groan. For one
second, the world seemed to stop. I opened my eyes, and
everything restarted.

Over in the kitchen, Jenna was doing shots.

And Elin was standing alone in the kitchen. Looking miserable.

And effing Rosie had still not made a reappearance.

I had never taken a naked picture of myself and sent it
to someone. Of course, I had received Dick Pics O'Plenty,
mostly from Vaughn himself. They didn't do anything for me
and in most cases they made me uncomfortable, but I could
almost always laugh them off. When asked to reciprocate, I
always declined, usually with a grin or a joke or a kiss.

But despite all my best Avoidance Strategies, Vaughn
wouldn't let it go. And what he really wanted, what he'd regularly begged for, was a Full-On Sex Tape.

Something told me this time a joke wouldn't get him to back off.

I chewed the inside of my cheeks—the one nervous tic that just looks like you're practicing a selfie face—and turned my phone over in my hands.

It wasn't just that I didn't want to send a guy a naked picture. Mama Leanne and Mom Kim's Lectures on the Permanence of the Internet had sunk in even when most other Lectures had not. But even if I did feel the urge to document my current level of hotness, who would I send it to? I didn't trust anyone enough to believe it wouldn't get passed around. And if a picture was something I didn't want to do, a sex tape was Something I Didn't Want To Do. A whole other magnitude of Not Want.

But what did I risk by promising now, and maybe defaulting later? If Elin had a good prom, then I could deal with Vaughn later. Hook up with him one more time, but weasel out of the Audio Visual portion of the evening. It's not like I hadn't done that before.

And even if Vaughn told people about Elin's suicide attempt on Monday, with Elin happy and confident and back with Ben, who would believe him? A few people, sure, but some people already believed Elin had gone to the Cirque Lodge and shared a room with some coked-out Disney star. And yeah, Elin would be pissed, but not nearly as pissed as she'd be if he started running his mouth before she had a chance to get back with Ben.

So I didn't need Vaughn to shut up for the rest of our lives, or even until graduation. I just needed him to shut up until Elin and Ben had a chance to smooth things over and hopefully have some sweaty prom night sex in Ben's car.

I bit my lip and then typed out my response before I could chicken out.

KET: *Deal.*

17

Rosie Winchester
April 18, 7:20 PM

I stepped out onto Fisher's porch, arms wrapped around myself, wishing I'd worn a coat. (Wishing I had someone to tell me to put on a coat.) Goosebumps broke out over my exposed back and I rubbed my arms, willing some warmth into my skin. I sat down gingerly on the cushion-less porch furniture, wincing as the cold of the metal seat seeped through my skirt, biting into my skin, and settling into my bones.

This stupid dress. Why had I even bought it? When we'd stepped through the door of her legendary party condo, Elin had gushed over Fisher's dress, a one-shouldered gown that looked like a painting—splashes of orange, blue, purple, and green on a white background, cinched with a gold belt that made her waist seem reed-thin.

Fisher had shrugged off the praise. "I snagged it at thrift shop." She'd probably spent fifty dollars to look like a character in a movie, and I looked like a total try-hard.

I opened my borrowed clutch, looking for a stick of gum, my stomach sour and churning. I should have gotten something to eat, or at least had more at my house than a can of Red Bull. I took a deep breath, held it. Let it out.

Inside, someone had turned up the stereo. The bass thumped through the closed doors and windows, and for some reason that made me want to cry. I blinked furiously, refusing to let any tears fall, and touched my cold cheeks with my fingertips. Instinctively, I reached under the glasses that I'd forgotten weren't even on my face tonight.

I should have just met my friends at the dance when I found out about Fisher's party. Parties were not my thing. I wasn't like Jenna or Ket—I couldn't make small talk with people I wasn't friends with. I wasn't like Elin, finding the positive in any situation.

(Elin isn't like Elin anymore.)

Some people were all sunshine, some were all shadow. I was miserable at parties.

(And more miserable, knowing that a normal person would not be miserable.)

The air smelled like metal and wood smoke. The sky was ominous, gray clouds hanging low. Threatening a storm on Jenna's perfect night. My cheeks burned in the cold, the tips of my ears numbing.

I just wanted to go home. I could take off this dumb dress, take out these stupid contacts, and climb into my mom's bed. Will would order whatever food I wanted and we could watch old episodes of *Adventuretime* until I wanted to sleep. Then I knew Will would let me have the bed for the night.

I could finish reading my book.

I could play *Call of Duty*.

I could write. (I haven't written since Teddy stopped talking to me.)

Whatever I did . . . it would be so much more fun than this.

And he'd never say it, but Will would be so relieved. (Would he?) (He told me to go have fun.)

I opened my flip phone, closed it. Opened it again.

He would come to get me, no questions asked.

(You promised Jenna. For Elin.)

(You promised Ket something, too, and you just broke that one.)

I closed my phone. Put it back in my clutch.

I didn't want to be here. I didn't want to see Ben, to feel *guilty* about everything I had just said when he was the one in the wrong. I didn't want to miss Teddy and wonder if we were ever going to be okay again. I didn't want to watch Ket roll her eyes because she wanted to dance and I wanted to hover at the edge of the room. I didn't want to see FDR, wonder why the hell he was even talking to me. I didn't want to be the raincloud on Jenna's big night. I didn't want to worry about Elin.

My phone blipped with a text. I flipped it open. From Elin: *Where are you? I want to go to the dance. Jenna's drunk, are you good to drive?*

I let out a long breath. Bit the insides of my cheeks.

Closed my eyes.

Counted to five.

Opened my eyes.

And typed back, *Of course. Let's go.*

18

Jenna Sinclair
April 18, 7:45 PM

If this is what being drunk was like, I didn't know why I wasn't drunk all the time. Ket's jokes were better, Rosie's annoyance was funnier, and Elin finally, *finally* wasn't bugging me. What was to stop me from just being this way, all the time?

Liver cirrhosis, probably.

I snorted at my own silent joke and Ket glanced over at me, an amused smirk on her face. We pushed open the double-doors to the gym and Elin gasped with surprise. I grinned, my brain swimming with endorphins.

Elin wrapped her arms around me in a hug. "It looks awesome, Jen!"

My headache roared back to life, but I made myself hug her back. "I've gotta go take care of prom committee stuff!" I yell-lied over the music. "I'll be right back!" Rosie looked at me, disappointment etched across her face, but before I could start to feel guilty, Ket grabbed her hand and Elin's and dragged them to the dance floor. I ran off to find Miles or Hannah—whoever I located first.

Everywhere I turned, kids were dancing, taking selfies, laughing, and I couldn't keep the grin off my face. For the first time since my morning run, I felt energized, adrenaline running through my veins. Prom might have been a bit silly, and definitely more trouble than I had expected, but this—*this* was the reason I'd busted my ass for two months.

People had been bitching for weeks that we weren't able to rent out a hotel ballroom for prom. Last year's seniors destroyed several rooms and a hot tub at the Yarrow after the dance, and no hotel wanted to deal with us without a hefty deposit, but I was not easily foiled. As senior class vice president, I had planned every detail of senior prom. From the flavor of punch—cucumber lime, much harder to spike and way less stain potential—to the trays of refreshments scattered around the gym on long banquet tables. I ordered the warm white Edison bulb lights we strung across the ceiling—LED twinkle lights look terrible in photos—and planned the light sequence for the dance floor with some of the AV kids. I ordered black draperies to hide the brick gym walls and filled enough balloons with helium that you couldn't even see the ceiling. It was a still a gym, but at least it was a gym that looked expensive.

I gave the DJ explicit instructions to stick to Top 40 dance remixes with non-explicit lyrics, ballads, and a healthy dose of country for the girls, and limit the playlist to no more than two unironically ironic songs each hour. I'd even emailed him a list of twenty acceptable songs that kids wouldn't be embarrassed to dance to, in case he couldn't think of any.

He'd written back, *"I like your style, kid."*

The theme of prom was "Starry Night." Usually prom committees picked a sappy country song to close out the dance ("Amazed," "I Hope You Dance," and "It's Your Love" being traditional favorites), but I liked the generic.

My phone buzzed and I fished it out of my purse.

HANNAH: *WHERE ARE U???*
We have a problem.
Meet in the east girls room.

Normally a demanding, zero-explanation text from Hannah would have my blood boiling. This time, though, I was struck with a case of the giggles. I was pretty sure I knew exactly what had set her off—and it wasn't the light check.

There were six dances every year—Homecoming, Halloween, the nondenominationally titled "Winter," Novelty, Sadie Hawkins, and Prom. Since freshman year when my sister Holly demanded I join student council, I had helped on every single one of them. I'd sat at crepe-papered tables selling tickets during lunch, gone on snack runs for upperclassmen, designed advertisements, and fantasized about when I'd be the one calling the shots.

Ket liked to joke that I should skip college and just go into party planning, but that was never the appeal. It was one of those things I wasn't supposed to say out loud, but it wasn't even the dances that I liked—it was hanging out with other kids who took things as seriously as I did.

High school is made up of little overlapping worlds. My best friends world, boyfriend world, tennis and track worlds. And I loved my friends, and Miles was the perfect boyfriend, but I needed student council in a way I couldn't explain to any of them. Teddy and Rosie didn't want to join anything and Ket made fun of everything. Miles was perfectly happy with basketball and videogames. Even Elin, before what happened had happened, didn't understand why anyone would do more than the minimum.

But student council was full of kids who high-fived when projects came in under budget and took it personally when the student paper criticized an assembly. Kids who understood that there was nothing wrong with wanting perfection.

Yeah, there were Josh Bowmans too—popular people who had never volunteered for anything before but needed a résumé line like "student class president" for college applications. Last year, I'd thought about running against Josh for president. My sister, ever the realist and last year's senior class president, talked me out of it. I was *just-popular-enough* to win the VP position, and to be entirely honest, that wouldn't have even happened if Holly hadn't helped me. Sometimes I think popularity can be genetic—I inherited most of mine. *Nepotism: the practice of those in power favoring family and friends.*

At least Josh knew he didn't want to work hard. As long as he got some credit, he stayed out of my way. But Hannah Larson was a different story. The junior class president, a tremendous brat, and a Grade-A pain my ass, Hannah had actually suggested that we hike the price of prom tickets twenty dollars to raise money for next year's prom and get back into the world of rentable hotel ballrooms. When I pointed out the obvious problem with that—*Why should this year's seniors subsidize next year's dance?*—she just stared at me, like, *"So?"*

But as much as I'd love to blame her, it wasn't Hannah's exhausting antics that had sucked the fun out of finally being in charge of prom.

I knew I should just get this Hannah business over with, but I took my time wandering up to the bathroom, tracing my fingertips along the rows of metal lockers. The halls were shadowy and my dress made little whispery sounds against the tile floor, my heels clicking softly, making the school seem almost regal. Why didn't we wear ball gowns all the time? I felt like a fucking princess.

I loved this school—if I weren't leaving it for even *more* school, I might have been upset at the prospect of graduation. I hadn't taken every AP class I could fit into my schedule just to pad my résumé. Learning something new about how the world worked, whether it was macroeconomics or comparative government or psychology, made my pulse pound with more excitement than watching a tennis ball fly off my racket, sailing just inside the line, my opponent miles away from being able to return.

When I got to the bathroom in the east wing, Hannah and Sings Praises were already waiting for me. I almost laughed when I saw their faces. How long had they rehearsed this little confrontation?

At least twice, I'd imagine.

"What's up, ladies?" I said cheerily, glancing in the mirror to check my hair. Still perfect, thanks to Rosie.

"We have a problem," Hannah began.

Querulous: whiny, complaining.

"Oh?"

"The prom queen results are . . . off."

I furrowed my brow, not even caring if I was overacting. "I thought no one was supposed to know the results until Josh opened the envelope at crowning?"

Hannah paused and she and Sings Praises exchanged a glance, caught. I peeked another glance in the mirror—my face looked perfectly innocent. That alone was enough to make me want to laugh.

"Irregardless," Sings Praises began.

"Regardless," I corrected automatically.

Sings Praises pursed her lips and paused as a couple of sophomores walked into the bathroom. "Regardless, we feel that there must be some mistake with the results."

"Oh?" I said, injecting as much innocent confusion as I could into my tone. "How so?"

"Elin Angstrom was elected prom queen," Hannah said flatly, apparently indifferent to being overheard.

I smiled. "Well, that's nice!"

Hannah curled her lip in disgust. "Give it up, Jenna. We all know Elin is your best friend and there's no way she won. You did something and I'm going to prove it."

Sings Praises glanced at Hannah uncertainly and I raised my eyebrows—it would seem that Hannah was going off script.

Not that I was surprised. The girl was pathologically incapable of following directions—apparently, not even her own.

"A computer program tallies the results of the voting," I said, all studied patience.

"No one is going to believe that a coke whore like Elin got the most votes," Hannah snapped.

My cheeks started to burn and I felt my resolve to stay calm start to crack. "Well, if the computer says she won, she won," I said, dropping the smile and putting my hands on my hips. "And if you want to cause a big scene about it, be my guest."

Of course Elin hadn't really won. Hell, I'd gotten more votes than she had. But while I was a firm believer in democracy for countries, I'd never been that impressed with the democratic process in high school. Fisher Reese had won, but she'd already been Homecoming Queen and hadn't seemed particularly delighted with that honor, so why did she need this one?

Elin deserved to be prom queen—that way, she'd look back on her senior year and have something to think about besides hospitalization and bad grades. But I'd like to see Hannah or Sings Praises, who dropped Computer Science after a whopping two days, prove that shit. I'd programmed the app for prom royalty voting in class last quarter and simply gone back and re-coded it so as long as no candidate won a majority of the vote, every candidate who got less than ten percent of the vote registered as a vote for Elin.

Hannah crossed her arms over her chest. "I'm going to tell Josh that we need to skip the crowning," she threatened.

My cheeks were probably well on their way to matching my dress in color, but I didn't care. I took a few steps toward Hannah and Sings Praises, and they retreated, pressing back against the stalls. "Crowning is prom tradition, Hannah," I said, my voice low. "You *can't* forgo it. Besides, if you talk to Josh about this, he's just going to ask me what to do, so what is the point?"

Hannah's resolve was starting to crumble—I could see the defeat in her eyes.

A lightning bolt of pain shot through my skull.

The sophomore at the sink was still washing her hands, listening to every word we were saying. My face twitched. "Could you finish washing your hands and turn that water the *fuck* off, already?" I snapped, turning to the mirror and pulling the bobby pins out of my hair. This hairstyle must be pulling my scalp too tight.

The sophomore jumped, and Hannah and Sings Praises stared at me as I discarded bobby pins on the floor. I felt a twinge as she hastily turned off the water, her face red with embarrassment. But my regret only made me angrier—*she* was the eavesdropper, not me.

"This *is* a desert and we *are* in the midst of unprecedented national drought," I snapped as the girl walked out of the bathroom. Why was I the only person who cared about water security? Ugh. Now I was going to have to find her and apologize and I had no idea what her name was. I imagined making the announcement during PSAs on Monday: *Snoopy blonde sophomore, please report to the office. Jenna Sinclair would like to say sorry. And tell you about the dangers of desertification.* I choked back a giggle. Oh damnit, they were back.

"What is wrong with you?" Hannah asked.

I bit my lip, trying not to burst out laughing. "Nothing."

Hannah took a step toward me and gave a deliberate sniff. "Are you *drunk*, Jenna?" she asked, eyes wide and gleeful.

I pulled a tube of gloss out of my purse, reapplying carefully, focusing on the task as the urge to laugh subsided. I pursed my lips critically. "It's prom, Hannah. Unbunch your panties."

"You're senior class vice president!"

I ignored her faux outrage, running my fingers through my hair, untangling stiff hairsprayed curls. "And you're embarrassing yourself. Elin won, get over it."

"I'm going to tell Vice Principal Seelig," Hannah threatened, eyes shining with glee.

I paused, slowly unwinding a red curl to tuck it back behind my ear. *Tell Seelig?* Yesterday, this would have made nausea rise in my throat. Getting caught drunk at school would mean suspension, which would mean no competing at state, no graduation with high honors, no senior party, no volunteering on a campaign before I moved to New Jersey, no *China*.

But as I studied Hannah and Sings Praises' reflections in the mirror, I realized something important: that was yesterday.

Tonight I was just in no mood to be fucked with.

I raised one eyebrow, willing to give Hannah one last chance to save herself—knowing she'd turn it down. "I'd be careful. Threats are beneath the dignity of the institution of *prom*."

She rolled her eyes. "I have never met anyone who cared as much as you do about everything. So take your pick, Jenna. Prom queen or suspension?"

I shrugged, a half smile quirking up the side of my mouth. "It's up to you. But if you get me suspended, I'll tell everyone you gave Josh a hand job after we cleaned up the pep rally last week. I bet Ben will be *super* impressed."

Hannah jerked back like I'd slapped her. Sings Praises' jaw dropped, her judgey little ferret face now registering her disapproval at Hannah instead of me.

I ran my fingers through my hair one final time and retied my headband. "I don't like you, Hannah, but here's some advice," I said, never taking my eyes away from my own reflection. "If you want to fool around, fool around. Just pick a guy who's more discrete than Josh Bowman. And then don't bait other girls with words like *whore*."

I turned to go find my friends before the crowning, and I could practically hear Hannah's heart break into a million itty-bitty pieces.

And I couldn't help but grin a little.

19

Ket West-Beauchamp
April 18, 7:55 PM

I don't know what I expected prom to look like. Magical, I guess. But when we stepped through the tulle-wrapped archway and into the gym, my first impression was mild disappointment. Jenna ran off immediately, presumably to do Important Jenna Things, leaving the three of us to circulate around the dance floor and me scrambling for an excuse to jet myself.

Rosie looked around, chewing her lip, clearly wishing she could disappear. I knew I should stay with Ro, try to ease her into this totally normal experience that she was treating like joining the Marines, but I had to act fast if I was going to convince Vaughn to keep his mouth shut. "I'll be right back!" I yelled to Rosie over the music. "I left something in the car!"

Then I grabbed Elin. "Talk to Ben ASAP," I hissed in her ear before I ran off, leaving her in Rosie's Ever-Capable hands.

On the ride to the dance, Elin had chattered nonstop. If she was angry with me after our conversation in the bathroom at Fisher's condo—in which I had Ever-So-Delicately explained that I'd shared a Few-Too-Many details of Elin's spring with Vaughn—she was hiding it well, and I matched her joke for joke. Jenna laughed until she snorted and even Rosie cracked a smile or two from behind the wheel.

I had expected Elin to be hurt or angry when she found out, but she was hyperfocused on her Ben Plan. To be fair, I had stressed how positive I was that Vaughn would keep his mouth shut, and she seemed to believe me, even though I had glossed over the Why of it all. But I worried that if Elin had a chance to stew for too long, she'd realize Vaughn was a potential time bomb and that she should rightfully be pissed at me.

Which meant I had to keep this up for the rest of the night. It was finally feeling like the way it had been last fall, before everything had fallen apart.

If someone had been Sex Blackmailing me last fall. And Rosie regularly wore makeup. And Jenna only made eighty percent as much sense.

So . . . maybe not quite like things used to be.

I pushed my way out of the double doors to the gym that we had just come through and glanced both ways. Random kids were loitering in the halls but there wasn't a teacher in sight. I hurried down the hall, hoping no one I knew saw me and would want to gab.

One of the good things about being friends with a pair of Super-Losers like Rosie and Teddy, bless their hearts, was that I knew all the good hideout spots in the school. Ro and Teddy had spent nearly every high school dance and many an assembly hanging out in the big, soundproofed practice room in the band department.

With Rosie in the gym behaving like a real teenage girl and Teddy moping at home, that meant I had the perfect hookup spot available. I just had to make sure it was still unlocked and then decide when—if—I was going to use it.

And if Vaughn ended up in there, waiting for me for, oh, say forty-five minutes, then I would just remind Vaughn of all the times he'd left me waiting back when we were hooking up.

I didn't know how I got myself into messes like this one. Like, I remember joking with Teddy once about his love life—or lack thereof. We were sitting on his grandparents' porch, just the two of us because Rosie was at her dad's house, and it was one of those moments where we were pretending that we didn't know that Teddy had been hopelessly in love with Rosie since sixth grade.

"I'm literally going to be a forty-year-old virgin," Teddy said, just enough bitter edge to his tone that I knew he wasn't entirely joking.

And because I am Keturah West-Beauchamp—Sexually Adventurous and Ever-Ready with a joke—I immediately bumped his shoulder with mine and said, "Oh Teddy. I'll seduce you before it comes to that."

Do you know those times in life when there seem to be two of you because you've done something so monumentally DUMB, not even you can believe what you did?

That's what that moment was for me.

Outer Ket lifted one eyebrow at Teddy's initially shocked expression and giggled with him when he burst out laughing. Outer Ket kept running her mouth, teasing him with gloriously dirty details of his inevitable deflowering.

Inner Ket wanted to die.

Even as Outer Ket was gleefully detailing how she would fulfill any and all of his sexual fantasies—even if she had to dress up as Ronald McDonald, because she was just That Good of a Friend—Inner Ket was thinking, "*Shiiiiiiiiit. Why did I have to say that?*"

As Teddy was gasping for air because Outer
So Damn Funny, Inner Ket wanted to run home and ~~bury~~
her face under her comforter for a week.

As I'd hinted to Rosie on more than one occasion, Teddy
Lawrence was the sole unattached unicorn in our high
school—a boy who was funny and respectful and loyal, a
boy who possessed the exact same level of maturity as all the
girls around him. Teddy was possibly the only such mythical
creature in Summit County, excepting maybe Miles Brooke
and Ben Holiday.

If Rosie never pulled her head out of her ass, Teddy
would go off to college and find some girl with a French
name who loved manga and volunteered at a homeless shel-
ter and who'd never even been kissed. They'd have sex and it
would be instantly magical because when mythical creatures
bang, that's just how things go.

[Guys like Teddy Lawrence did not end up with girls like
Ket West-Beauchamp, girls who lost their V-card at fourteen
in a burst of lust and curiosity.]

Telling Vaughn about Elin had been like that moment.
Outer Ket just needed someone to listen while she cried, and
kind of liked that it was Vaughn—who was usually sort of a
dick—being extra nice about it.

Inner Ket was like, *I think I just made a massive mistake.*

Inner Ket can be such an insufferable know-it-all.

I hurried down the stairs to the basement band room,
glancing around to make sure no one was watching.
Surprisingly, there were no band nerds making out in the
stairwell—which just goes to show you, private spots are
wasted on the dorky. I reached for the knob of the band
room, closing my eyes and hoping for the best.

Success.

I slowly opened the door. The band room was partially lit, the lights in every practice room on and glowing through the windows, the main lights off. I shut the door behind me softly, creeping over to the largest practice room and opening the door.

Teddy looked up from his iPad, grinning at me. "Hey, Ket."

20

BEFORE
Elin Angstrom
March 9

Her mother had brought her favorite sweatshirt, slip-on canvas shoes, and a pair of jeans so she'd be comfortable when they checked out. She tucked her hands into the kangaroo pocket, trying to keep warm as she stared out the window of her room.

Not her room anymore. The room. She was leaving today. Going home to recuperate with her parents.

As soon as the final details were ironed out.

Elin figured she wasn't in any position to bargain, but she really wished her mother had remembered her makeup. It may have made her feel a little more grownup while the grownups argued over her.

"She needs to be around other kids," her dad snapped. "Look, doctor, I respect your expertise, but I know my daughter. This is not her. It's not. She's a happy kid who's been having a few bad months. It's her senior year and the pressure is getting to her. And you know teenagers, they're always so dramatic."

"She broke up with her boyfriend," Elin's mother added helpfully. It was probably the third time she'd mentioned that since Elin had woken up in the hospital.

"Yes!" her father agreed eagerly. "The boyfriend, and her grades, and all her friends are getting into excellent colleges and it turns out she missed the application deadlines. Senior year stress, I'm surprised this doesn't happen more often."

"It does happen often, actually, Mr. Angstrom," the doctor replied softly. "Which is why I would strongly urge you to find a therapist for your daughter, so she can continue to get well."

"She doesn't need therapy," her mother said, her voice gaining strength. "She needs to go back to her routine."

Elin stared out the window. The sky was flat and gray, like brushed nickel.

If Ben were here, he would know the name of the clouds.

"We want her to feel normal," Elin's dad said firmly. "You've given her the prescriptions, we're going to make sure she takes them like clockwork. But what she needs is normality."

"Normality," Elin's mom repeated.

The doctor sighed. "How would you feel about a support group?" he said finally.

March 14

Elin's parents had done their best to keep her ensconced safely in the house, after she came home from the hospital. When Elin asked when she was going back to school, they exchanged glances and said, "Soon."

She wanted to fight them about that, but she could hardly stand to look at them. The way they seemed to have aged ten years in two weeks. Even if she hadn't meant to, she'd done that to them, so she said nothing.

So Elin spent the week in her room, her phone and lap-top practically useless because her parents had turned off the wifi in an effort to—who even knew. Rewind the clock to the 1980s, when everything was awesome? She watched movies and slept. Ket and Rosie and Teddy texted her, and she texted back appropriately reassuring things.

She should have expected Jenna to just barge in without asking.

"Hey, can I come in?"

Elin glanced up from her book to see Jenna standing in the doorway, her messenger bag slung over one shoulder. Oh, it was a Friday afternoon—Jenna must have just finished school. Elin had lost track of the time and the days.

"Sure," Elin said, putting down her book and feeling self-conscious. She hadn't changed out of pajamas, and Jenna was wearing a white button up under a blue sweater, jeans rolled up past her ankles, her red hair up in a messy-cute topknot, her makeup perfect. Like always.

Jenna dropped her bag on the floor and sat on the edge of Elin's bed, kicking off her shoes. "You're coming back to school on Monday?" she asked, tucking one leg underneath herself. "Your mom said you were."

Elin raised her eyebrows. "Apparently." And apparently Jenna was able to get a straight answer out of her parents even when Elin could not.

"That's good, you've missed so much school," Jenna said, sounding relieved, as if Elin had simply had mono and was finally well.

"Yeah, I know," Elin said warily. She picked up her book, thumbing aimlessly through the pages, just to give her hands something to do.

For the first time since she'd come in, Jenna looked uncomfortable. "I know you know," Jenna said, biting her lip and glancing out the window.

They sat in silence for a moment, and it wasn't like the silence they'd lived with their whole lives. This silence was heavy, uncomfortable. Like they both knew it had to end eventually, and neither one of them liked what they were about to say.

As expected, Jenna broke the silence first. "Your parents are really pissed at mine," Jenna said, still looking out the window.

Elin felt a rush of defensiveness toward her parents—her poor parents, who had gone through hell for the last two weeks. "Well, your parents had no business telling the school anything," Elin said.

Now Jenna met her gaze, her eyebrows knit together. "Of course they did," she said, sounding baffled. "The administration isn't going to say anything; there are privacy laws against that. But they had to know. Besides, my parents had to excuse my absence."

Elin stared at Jenna incredulously. "*You* missed school?"

"Well . . . yeah," Jenna said. "Just last Monday, but, you know. I was really upset."

Elin could feel her heart pounding in her chest, her breath getting shallow. "Not everything is about you, Jen," Elin snapped.

Jenna blanched, and Elin knew she should feel bad, but she didn't. It might have been wrong—it *was* wrong—but she had to protect herself. Had to banish the panic that was threatening to overwhelm her.

"I didn't say it was about me," Jenna said quickly, but Elin suddenly knew that was why she had come over without calling.

So they could talk about it.

And Elin didn't want to talk about it.

Not now, not ever.

"This is something I am going through, Jen," Elin said, and even she was shocked at how icy her voice sounded. "And when and if I feel like talking about it, I will let you know. But until then, I would expect that, as my friend, you respect that."

Jenna stared at her, eyes wide and unblinking. For a second, Elin thought she would argue, but instead she nodded. "Okay," she said simply, standing. She grabbed her shoes and bag. "See you Monday."

Elin watched her go, wishing she could call her back, talk to her about everything she was missing at school, hear about all the gossip.

But the relief with her gone was too great.

March 17

The first day back at school went as well as she could have anticipated. She dressed for school carefully, like it was a chance to do her first day over. She braided her hair and put on a cute outfit—but not too cute, she didn't want to stand out—and did her makeup. Her mother drove her but she arrived at the usual time, walking in with her friends like she had come from the same parking lot as them.

But there were little reminders, everywhere, that things were different.

Every time she walked in a room, it seemed like people stopped talking and she tried to pretend she didn't notice.

Girls who generally gave her the barest of glances in the hallway went out of their way to flash her tentative smiles. Ket spent their lunch period talking a mile a minute, planning a shopping trip to the outlet mall—Ket to the max. Rosie sat silently, reading a book, when she usually engaged at least a little—Rosie dialed even further down. Jenna and Miles sat across from them, and if Jenna was still mad, she didn't show it—but she wasn't overly friendly, either, when she usually did her best to split her attention equally between her friends and boyfriend.

Like always, Elin found herself glancing around everywhere she went, looking for Ben. But somehow, on this day, she couldn't find him anywhere.

After they'd broken up, Elin had taken care to remain friendly, but Ben didn't want to be friends. The old, *I love you, but I'm not in love with you* speech had that effect. After years of him eating lunch with Elin, Rosie, Ket, Jenna, Miles, and Teddy, suddenly Ben only ate with the soccer team. If his eyes locked with Elin's in the hallways, he always glanced away first. When Elin waved, his response was always fractionally less enthusiastic than hers.

Eventually, Elin remembered that the plan had been to let him go, so she started to avoid him just as much as he avoided her. But she still saw him everywhere, from the corner of her eye—running up a hallway when she was coming down, sliding into a seat in class just as the bell rang—and that was sort of comforting in a way.

Except on that first day back. She didn't see him a single time that day.

Finally, after last period let out, she found him standing by her locker. He was leaning against the row of lockers, arms crossed, eyes cast down. Elin's throat felt like it was going to close, and she prayed, really prayed, that her medicinally influenced emotions would not betray her with a crying jag or giggle fit.

The hall was nearly empty when she'd gotten to her locker. She spun the combination on her locker, not even bothering to pay attention to the numbers. *What was he doing here?*

Finally, he spoke, but his eyes remained glued to the floor. "How have you been?" he asked.

Elin paused, trying to focus on the numbers. *What's my combination?* Ever since the hospital, she'd had foggy moments. "Fine," she said. She stopped trying to open her locker and turned to face him. "How have you been?"

Ben shrugged, eyes still glued to the ground. In that moment, Elin couldn't have figured out whether he was trying not to cry or kicking himself for even talking to her. "Are you going to tell me where you were?"

Elin ran her fingertips over the grate on her locker. "Umm. I just needed to get away from school for a while. It's a long story."

Ben looked up and met her gaze, and her breath caught in her throat. Ben wasn't a tall boy, an inch taller than Elin's five-foot-six, and his eyes looked directly into hers. They were red-rimmed, which made his irises look even bluer. "I'll listen," he said.

Elin didn't know why she hadn't just told him right then. She'd wanted to.

But instead she'd just forced a smile, something she'd gotten extremely good at before the meds, and nodded. "Sure. I'll call you sometime, okay?"

As soon as the words left her mouth, even she could hear the dismissal in her tone.

There was an awkward pause. Something in Ben's open expression changed. His shoulders relaxed slightly, his jaw tightened almost imperceptibly.

It was like Elin could see him physically closing himself off from her.

"Sure," he said, his voice casual and easy. He tapped her on the shoulder, like she was one of his soccer buddies. "See you around, okay?"

Her throat closed up, so all she could manage was a soft "Mmhmm" as she turned back to her locker, blinking back tears.

Later, Elin had decided that when he'd said, *I'll listen*, he meant it as an open-ended offer. If she had done anything, said anything, to let him know that she *wanted* to take him up on it, she was sure he would have waited patiently until she found the words.

But she hadn't done anything. And the longer she went without doing anything, the more impossible it seemed to explain.

The next day at school, and the next, and the next, Elin watched as Ben would offer her a faint half-smile. That up-nod guys give their friends. And she'd wonder, *"Does he think he got me pregnant, and I never told him? Does he think I lost weight because I was bulimic or something?"*

She told the girls at session about it one night. Half of them thought Ben sounded like a jerk and she should forget about him. The other half thought that she needed to give him a chance, to see if he really would listen.

Elin couldn't decide which faction was right. So she kept doing nothing.

And she never mentioned Ben to the group again, even though girls asked.

Instead, she fantasized about scenarios in which fate would lead her and Ben back together. Elin's car broken down on the side of the road in the rain, Ben coming along to rescue her. Ben getting injured in a soccer match and waking up to Elin sitting by his bedside.

And prom. Always prom.

That would put her life back together.

March 23

A code existed among the troubled teenage girl set: don't talk about each other outside of the group.

It was like Alcoholics Anonymous, or Fight Club. It just wasn't fair to repeat what a girl might say in the group. First, no one really understood the way they understood, so it would probably get misconstrued. Something that sounded totally crazy to a non-troubled person kind of made sense during group, which is why it was safe to talk in the first place.

And second, and perhaps more importantly, it was like that thing during the Cold War: mutual assured destruction.

Dr. Shumacher held the meetings in Salt Lake City on Sunday and Wednesday nights. Girls came from as far as Park City and Orem and Layton. While they probably wouldn't run into each other in real life, finding a girl online was as easy as a Google search.

It never even had to be said—*if you ruin me, I will ruin you.*

At first, Elin didn't know the rules. The first time she walked into session and saw a familiar face, she froze. But the other girl merely glanced at Elin and gave her a little nod, looking away without any other acknowledgment. As Elin took her seat in the circle, she realized that the other girl—*Genevieve*, according to her nametag—was never going to say a word about seeing her there. That Genevieve trusted Elin to give her the same courtesy.

After that, that little nod and the flick of her head as she looked away, Elin felt confident that, at least with this group of semi-strangers, her secrets were safe.

But one Sunday night after a particularly uneventful session, the other girl sat beside Elin on a bench while Elin waited for her mom to pick her up.

The two of them sat in silence as Elin wondered what she wanted. If she wanted to talk about therapy, she was breaking the rule. If she wanted to extract a promise that Elin wouldn't blab about her secrets, well, she was undermining the rule.

Finally, she spoke up, peeling her nametag off her shirt. This time it said *Clara*. "It's been awhile since you mentioned your ex-boyfriend."

Elin shrugged, uncomfortable with this intrusion. She preferred to keep her crazy life and her real life separate, and while group therapy had only ended fifteen minutes ago, it had *ended*. "I guess."

Clara glanced at her watch. "I'll get out of here before your mom shows up. She doesn't know I go here, does she?"

"No," Elin said quickly. "Of course not."

Clara nodded, relief etched across her face. "Good."

They sat in silence until Elin couldn't stand it anymore. "Why did you come over here?" Elin asked. She wanted to ask, *Why do you write a different fake name on your nametags every session?* But she suspected that was the question Clara expected her to ask.

The wind blew strands of blonde hair across Clara's face and she tucked them behind one ear. "I just wanted to say . . . if you wanted to get him back, I think you could."

Elin glanced over at her sharply. "What makes you say that?"

"I know a thing or two about a thing or two," Clara said, cracking a smile for the first time.

March 31

The second time they spoke after session, it was about *Twilight*.

They were both standing on the corner, waiting for their rides. "Eloise" was getting one from her cousin, she said, peeling her fake nametag off and folding it in two. He wouldn't mind swinging by Elin's house, too.

Elin declined, saying her mom was on her way. It was only a little because she didn't want to meet Eloise's cousin, to let separate worlds collide.

Elin didn't mention that she had given her mom the wrong time on purpose the last three sessions, just in case the two of them were both stuck waiting again.

Elin should have known then that she wanted to be her friend.

Eloise tossed her cigarette on the ground, not bothering to crush it beneath her sole. Elin stared at the glowing ember, emitting a pathetic little stream of smoke.

"God, I hate sheep," she said finally.

Elin blinked. "For reals?"

She hitched up one shoulder, twisting her mouth to one side. It was fascinating, watching this side of her. She was all jerks and quirks, like a different person than Elin had known before.

Which made sense. After all, wasn't Elin different here, too?

"I mean, all that shit in there," Eloise explained. "Candace talking for ten minutes about how unhealthy *Twilight* is. For 'girls like us.'" She made air quotes with fingers like talons.

"Oh," Elin said, a little puzzled. "I zoned some of it out, honestly."

Eloise sat on the bench, resting her chin in her palm, elbows on her knees. Her hair was pulled back in a sleek ponytail, not a single flyaway anywhere.

"It makes me sick when people can't come up with an original thought," she said, as if Elin hadn't said anything. "Like, everyone hates Coldplay, right? Except Coldplay sells tons of songs, so not everyone hates them. Same with *Twilight*. Okay, if you didn't like it, whatever, but it's just so trendy to shit all over it. And please, if you finished *Twilight*, it's because you liked it. Everyone who didn't like it stopped before Bella goes on her first date with Edward, because frankly, that beginning is a little hard to get through."

"You read *Twilight*?" Elin asked.

She rolled her eyes. "Duh, who didn't? I'm just saying, if you're going to hate something, hate something original. Like *Harry Potter*."

Elin's eyes widened. "You hate *Harry Potter*?"

She waved her hand, impatient. "Of course not, *Harry Potter* is the shit. I'm just saying, if you want to hate something, pick something that everyone loves, not something that everyone already loves tearing apart." She raised her eyebrows at Elin, but Elin had nothing to say. "Are you seriously this little lost lamb in the woods?" she said finally.

Elin cracked a smile. "Are you seriously this passionate about *Twilight*?"

Eloise laughed, standing up and pulling her pack of cigarettes from her purse. "Come on," she said. "There's a diner around the block, we should wait where it's warm."

Elin followed the other girl as she clicked down the sidewalk in her four-inch heels, like a tide to the moon. "How come you never share at troubled teenage girl club?" Elin asked suddenly, accusingly.

She turned and walked backward to face Elin, smoking her cigarette like a pinup girl in an old French movie. "You call it troubled teenage girl club? That's funny," she said, and Elin wondered how long she could walk backward in stilettos. "I call it the clinical cryfest, but I like yours better. Why don't *you* ever share at troubled teenage girl club?"

Elin shrugged. "I don't have anything in common with those people."

She snorted. "Don't you? Okay then. What about your boyfriend? You never told me why you stopped talking about him."

Elin felt her cheeks flush. "There's nothing to say. He's not my boyfriend. We broke up."

"And you aren't getting back together?"

Elin hitched her bag up tighter on her shoulder. "How do you know so much about me and Ben?"

She shrugged, turning back around, waving her cigarette in the air. "We've been in school together since we were twelve. Who doesn't know about you and Ben? You guys are like ... Hazel and Gus, Katniss and Peeta without all the murder. You always seemed like a legit couple. You can't really say that about many high schoolers."

Elin blinked. "Well . . . yeah. I thought so, anyway."

"So why did you break up?" she said, pushing open the door to the burger joint. A wave of salty, greasy air hit Elin and her stomach growled involuntarily.

"Umm . . ."

She stopped so abruptly that Elin ran into her and she stumbled. She turned and Elin expected a scowl, but she was amused. "Watch out," she chided gently.

The girls ordered. Even though she hadn't been hungry five minutes before, Elin was suddenly starving. She ordered onion rings and a cheeseburger with a Diet Coke. Eloise got zucchini fries and a chocolate-banana milkshake, paying for both of them.

"You'll get me next time," she said as they sat down at a booth to wait for their food.

Elin smiled, puzzled. "Why have we never hung out before?"

She shrugged. "If we had, it wouldn't have been like this."

Their food arrived and they ate in silence for a moment.

"So why don't you try to get back with Ben?" Eloise said, licking milkshake from her spoon. It was like she had completely forgotten that she'd asked Elin why they'd broken up and that Elin hadn't answered. "I mean, I know he's dating Hannah Larson, but he doesn't seem that into her. I bet you could get him back."

Elin stole one of Eloise's zucchini fries, resisting the hope that was blooming in her chest. "How do you know that?" Elin asked, dipping the fried veggie in the watery ranch sauce.

She shrugged, licking shake off her straw. "Like I said. I know a thing or two about a thing or two."

21

Ket West-Beauchamp
April 18, 8:05 PM

"Why do I get the feeling you aren't so happy to see me?" Teddy asked, his half-smirk revealing that one dimple in his left cheek, legs stretched out in front of him as he leaned against the wall. A blazer was tossed in the corner next to him—houndstooth. Probably his grandpa's.

I wouldn't have thought it was possible, but he had actually gotten cuter in the last few hours.

"I ... I totally am!" I said. "What are you doing here? I thought you were going to watch *Golden Girls* all night!"

He held up his iPad, which was streaming Blanche and Dorothy in all their crinkled chiffon glory. "I have been. But I was thinking about what you said, and ... I don't know, you're right. I miss you guys, too. I figured I'd just hang out here until the dance was over and then tag along with whatever you did afterward."

I forced a smile. "You won't believe this, but I think we're actually going to Fisher Reese's party."

Teddy whistled. "Seriously? How did you guys pull that off?"

I shrugged. "No clue."

My phone buzzed and I jumped. Teddy raised his eyebrows. "Stressed out about something?"

"Ha, not really," I said, swiping open my phone.

Just trying to deal with a sexual psychopath.

VAUGHN: *So where are we going to do this thing?*
I'm leaving Fisher's in a minute.

I scowled. I didn't see him looking for a solution to the problem, did I?

KET: *I'm assessing the situation.*
Patience.

Patience was not Vaughn Hollis' strong suit.

Neither was empathy, tact, or common sense.

Homeboy was kind of lacking in *a lot* of essential areas, I was realizing.

"Ket?" Teddy asked. I glanced up. Teddy stared at me, puzzled.

"Sorry," I said after a too-long-pause. "It's . . . Jenna. She got drunk at Fisher's party, I was looking for a place she could sober up."

Teddy's eyebrows shot up. "Our Jenna? The Jenna who made us spend a whole Saturday delivering nonpartisan campaign signs for a city council race?"

I laughed. "The one and the same."

What was it about Teddy that made all my stress melt away? I felt like I could sit here and joke with him for the rest of the night.

Except, if I did, Vaughn would definitely blab.

And Elin would never talk to me again.

Vaughn might not remember exactly why we stopped hooking up, but I do. I remember every detail of our Non-Relationship Relationship. He was the conquest I'd worked toward all winter. While Jenna applied for ten thousand safety colleges, Elin did piles of make-up work for all the classes she was failing, and Rosie's parents dragged her into one last mediation to determine who got her for the final holiday season of her childhood, I pursued Vaughn Hollis.

Vaughn was desirable for many reasons, all of which seemed stupid to me within days of our breakup.

He was one of the hottest guys in our class.

He had his own credit card and took the girls he dated to great restaurants and concerts.

He made the National Ski Team earlier this year. He got into events and received free gear from sponsors—he even gave me a sweet pair of goggles that he didn't want.

And he was allegedly great in the sack—which turned out to be true only seventy-five percent of the time. I didn't think I'd ever experienced anything as frustrating as hooking up with someone who DEFINITELY knew what he was doing—a rarity among the guys I'd hooked up with—but sometimes just couldn't be bothered to make an effort.

We successfully hooked up at a party right before New Year's Eve—I broke curfew so badly I ended up grounded on the actual holiday. I couldn't have cared less. We dated for the next two and a half months, and I felt like I had really achieved Something. I wasn't sure what, exactly, just that when Rosie told me that Teddy had confessed his True Love, it wasn't the searing stab of pain I had expected. More like a slow constriction of my airways.

Being with Vaughn was fun and unsettling, like going to a great party when you should be studying for a final.

And then, one day, the party ended.

It was a Thursday, about a week after Elin's parents check-ed her into that facility. Vaughn's parents were out of town and he wanted me to come over, but I was going to Teddy's aikido match. "There's always tomorrow," I said as we walked to the parking lot after school, kicking up fresh drifts of snow.

Vaughn rolled his eyes. "You're ditching me for that fag?"

I stopped and turned to stare at him. "You can't say that to me," I said.

Vaughn held up his hands, as though he were apologizing, but the smirk never left his face. "Sorry, I forgot about your moms. My bad."

"Not just that," I said. "You can't use that word and you can't talk shit on Teddy, either. He's one of my best friends."

Vaughn rolled his eyes. "Fine, fine. I'm sorry. Tomorrow?"

"Tomorrow," I agreed, but I'd already decided to blow him off. With that one comment, I stopped caring that I'd lusted after him for months. I was done, a switch flipped somewhere deep inside me, and I didn't really care what he had to say about it. That was one advantage to him not being my boyfriend—I very literally did not have to take his feelings into account.

At first, Vaughn acted like he didn't care, which didn't surprise me. After all, there were plenty of girls lining up to try out Vaughn's sexin' skills and get themselves a free pair of goggles.

I should have guessed he hadn't really let it go. He didn't like the word *no*.

Teddy stretched out his back like a cat. "Well, where is our little felon? We can't have her getting caught on her big night."

"I don't think underage drinking is a felony," I said.

"I don't think there's a word that means 'person who commits misdemeanors,'" Teddy countered.

I grinned despite myself and slid down to sit beside him. "You know who would know if there was? Jenna."

22

Rosie Winchester
April 18, 8:00 PM

Elin and I wandered by the edge of the dance floor. Brightly colored dresses whirled and bounced and flickered to the pulse of the music, living confetti among all the dark suits. Silver, magenta, baby blue, rich violet, and gold under ever-changing lights. I felt a flash of longing, but I didn't dance. "Are you having fun?" I asked Elin, raising my voice over the deejay

Elin turned and smiled, but her expression looked wan and brittle. "Totally," she said.

I raised my eyebrows, but she turned her attention back to the dance floor. I decided not to push it. I watched people dancing, feeling weirdly disconnected. Where were Jenna and Ket? What was the point of coming to the dance together if they were just going to run off?

"How bored are you?" Elin yelled over the music. "On a scale of one to ten?"

I forced a smile. "I'm not bored."

I peeked at Elin from the corner of my eye to see if she knew I was lying, but she wasn't paying attention. She was staring out at the dance floor, eyes shining. I followed her gaze and scowled—Ben dancing with Jamie Nelson, a girl from track. The words bubbled up before I could stop them. "That douchebag? Still?"

"He's not a douchebag, Ro," Elin said, softer. If I hadn't been watching her, I might have missed it.

I gritted my teeth and refused to respond.

It didn't take a genius to add up the facts preceding Elin's suicide attempt. She and Ben broke up a few weeks before. And before that, she'd admitted to me that she didn't even like having sex with him. She denied that he was pressuring her, but she was hiding something.

The fact that she relentlessly defended him now was just more evidence against him.

Elin couldn't tear her eyes away from him. Any guilt I felt over telling him to get lost and leave Elin alone at Fisher's party evaporated. He was not the guy I'd thought he was.

I glanced around, searching for a sparkling rose gold mini dress, a poof of hot pink. Where were Jenna and Ket? Seriously, why did Jenna even want all of us to come to this dance if she wasn't even around? "If you're not having fun, we should ditch prom," I said suddenly. "Will gave me his credit card; we can call a cab and go do something else. *Anything* else."

"Maybe," Elin replied, but it was her maybe that meant, *I don't think so.* She glanced over at me. "So you really hate this, right?"

I opened my mouth, shut it. "Kind of," I admitted. "It's just not my thing." (I wish it were my thing.)

One corner of Elin's mouth turned up. "Jenna's making you?"

I grinned. "Maybe."

Elin shook her head, the hint of a smile on her face. "Let's get some pictures and spend at least an hour dancing, and then split. My dad gave me cash this week for a spa day, but we can go blow it on sushi. If Jen needs to stay until the end, we can come back for her. Deal?"

It felt like an invisible weight had lifted off my shoulders. "Deal," I said, relieved.

"I'm going to go find Ket," Elin said, heading toward the doors. "She thinks I'm mad at her."

23

Jenna Sinclair
April 18, 8:30 PM

"Miles!" He turned, his smile lighting up. He wore dress pants and a white shirt tucked in, but he had rolled up his sleeves and discarded his jacket and tie somewhere. I should probably make him put them back on before our picture, but at that moment he looked like a black teenaged James Bond.

Oh my gosh. They should *totally* make that movie.

"Hey, J," Miles called, walking toward me. "I've been looking for you—I just saw Elin but I haven't run into anyone else yet. Is everything going great up in the gym?"

I picked up my skirt and ran toward him, slipping a little before slamming into him. I couldn't stop giggling. "It looks so pretty! I can't wait for you to see it," I said, grinning. At least, I hoped I was grinning—I could barely feel my cheeks.

Miles wrapped his arm around my waist and bent to whisper in my ear. "What is with you tonight?"

I wrapped my arm around his neck and stared up at him, my giggles evaporating into a sense of calm and peace. Damn, I loved Miles. I should have found him as soon as we got to the dance—I could be at my most raw-nerve anxious, and he'd find a way to make me feel like myself again. *Panacea: a cure for all difficulties.*

Not for the first time, I wished I had told him about Elin when it all happened. But I hadn't. I'd kept it a secret, and now it was too late to explain. At first, I'd told myself it was because Elin's parents wanted it that way, but that wasn't it.

It was because Miles thought I was perfect. And if I told him one piece of it, I knew the whole thing would come tumbling out.

And there's nothing less-perfect than being unable to handle the effect your friend's suicide attempt had on *you*.

"Everything set up for your LAN party?" I asked, tracing the outside of his ear with one fingertip.

Miles laughed and pulled me closer. "I guess I just figured out what got into you," he whispered. "You might want to snag some gum, my crazy little ginger."

I clapped my hands over my mouth. "No! Serious?" I leaned back and laughed. Miles tightened his grip around my waist so I wouldn't fall.

This was what I wished my friends had. Someone to keep them on their feet. Elin used to have it with Ben. I'd hoped that Rosie would find it with Teddy—but I'd since revised my opinion on that.

Miles grinned, his forehead pressed against mine. "Yeah, you gotta learn to be sneakier."

I relaxed into Miles. *Ebullient: joyful and full of energy.* "Did you see the gym? Doesn't it look pretty?" I said, wrapping my arms around his neck. "Did you get some refreshments?"

"It looks great," Miles said, tightening his grip around my waist, and I sighed. "Hey, you won't get any drunker than this, right?" he asked.

I smiled, shaking my head. "Promise. I overdid it at Fisher's party, that's all." I'd even checked an online BAC calculator on my phone to see when I'd be sober again. Five shots—or was it six? probably just five—plus a rum and Coke that I hadn't even liked that much and a beer added up to full sobriety at 3:30 a.m. Ta da!

"Don't get me wrong, you're kinda cute drunk," Miles teased. "But if you don't feel good, come find me and I'll take you home."

"You can't take me home drunk, silly," I scolded. "Promise me you won't take me home if I'm drunk. Even if I ask you to."

He laughed. "Fine, I'll let you sleep it off and then I'll take you home."

"Miles, you're up in five minutes, dude!" called Rob Jackson, who I noticed *had not* dressed up for prom. Ugh.

"I'll be right there!" he called. He leaned in to kiss me and I leaned back, blocking my mouth with my hand. "What?"

"My bad breath," I whispered, my fingers forming prison bars over my lips, but my whisper was way too loud. A couple kids turned and snickered.

Miles laughed, kissing me on the forehead. "It's not bad, it's just boozy. And I'd want to kiss you anyway. What time do you want me for pictures?"

I paused. "You know what? Let's just take some on our phones later," I said. "The photographer is totally overpriced."

Miles grinned. "You are *really* drunk."

I wrapped my arms around him, resting my cheek on his chest. "And *you* are really the best," I whispered.

He kissed the top of my head. "Right back 'atcha. Now get back in there, tiger."

24

Rosie Winchester
April 18, 8:35 PM

Someone tapped me on the shoulder and I turned around. "Would you like to dance?" FDR asked, holding out one hand, a half-smile on his ludicrously handsome face.

I didn't even bother hiding my scowl. "Seriously? Didn't you get the message at Fisher's party?"

He grinned, putting his hand in his pocket. "Has anyone ever told you that you're kind of mean?"

"All the time," I lied. (People would have to talk to you to know that you're mean.)

"Well, Mean Girl, I remember our conversation going differently. It seemed to me like you were warming up to me a little bit when your friend pulled you away."

I shrugged noncommittally, glancing around. Where were my friends? FDR seemed like he was flirting with me, which was a little (a lot) out of my area of expertise.

The silence between us stretched into an uncomfortable length. Finally I forced myself to look back at FDR. His faint smile hadn't faded. "It's just one dance," he said lightly. "And you don't seem super busy."

If someone else had said it, I would have taken it as a slight—but something in FDR's tone made it seem like a kind observation. I couldn't stop the rueful smile that spread across my face. "Sounds good, FDR."

He laughed and took my hand. "Are you going to call me that all night?"

I pursed my lips, resisting a smile as we headed to the dance floor. "That's the plan."

FDR wrapped his arms around my waist. I couldn't help but shiver when his fingertips brushed my bare skin. I hesitated one second before gingerly placing my hands on his shoulders, stubbornly resisting wrapping my arms around his neck.

"Why do you dislike me so much?" FDR asked, as casually as you might say, *So where are you going to college next year?*

"I don't dislike you," I said, glancing around the room as we swayed to the music.

"Liar. You disliked me from the first second I tried to talk to you."

"No. I just wasn't interested in flirting with another girl's date," I said, meeting his gaze.

A smile flickered across his face, and I glanced away again. "I told you, Fisher and I aren't dating. I promise."

"Umm, have you missed the part where I've been calling you FDR because you're *on a date with Fisher*?"

He laughed. "Yeah, I noticed. But what I mean is, Fisher and I are just friends."

I felt a pang and wondered if Fisher knew that. As a girl who had wound up on the misleading end of *just friends* before, I was sympathetic to Fisher Reese for the first time in my life. In fact, it might have been the first time in history that anyone had to sympathize with Fisher Reese about anything.

I looked up into his eyes. They reflected pinpoints of light, like they were full of tiny silver stars. I swallowed. "Why do you like me?"

"What makes you think I like you? I barely know you." His lips curved up as he said it.

"But you've been bugging me all night."

"Since when is asking a pretty girl to dance *bugging her*?"

"Since she's made it perfectly clear that she would prefer you left her alone."

He took my hand from his shoulder and spun me in a slow circle. Somehow at the end of my turn, I ended up a little closer to him than when I began, my arms squarely around his neck. He offered me a half-smile. "I was kind of just hoping that was Katherine Hepburn–style banter."

"Katherine Hepburn? What, are you a film major?"

"German major, linguistics minor."

"Bold choice. I assume you're prepared to make a lot of lattes in the future?"

FDR laughed, tightening his grip around me ever-so-slightly. I swallowed, trying to keep my face impassive. "Come on, if that wasn't Hepburnesque, I don't know what is."

"So does that make you Spencer Tracy?"

"It makes me *trying* to be Spencer Tracy."

I laughed—I couldn't help it. He grinned down at me. "I'm growing on you, aren't I?" he said, one eyebrow lifting slightly.

I pursed my lips, struggling to ignore the electricity shooting up my spine and racing over my scalp, sending tingles through each strand of my hair. *Stop it, Rosie! He's on a date, and even if he weren't, you are not the dating type.* "Your dancing is growing on me."

"Close enough, Kate."

My smile faded. "Seriously though. Even if I believed you about Fisher . . . you don't want to grow on me. I'm kind of a disaster."

One corner of FDR's mouth quirked up. "I doubt that."

I broke my best friend's heart. I shrugged, glancing away. Thinking about Teddy usually made me want to cry.

But dancing with FDR was making it really hard to think about Teddy at all for some reason.

8:45 PM

I felt a tap on my shoulder. I turned and saw Jenna, a satisfied smile on her face. "Sorry to interrupt," she said as FDR and I stepped apart. "I just have to borrow Rosie for one quick second."

I touched my hair self-consciously. For one second when Jenna interrupted, I felt *disappointed.*

(Stupid.)

"I better go check in with Fisher anyway," FDR said, letting go of my hand. "But I'm going to find you later."

"Jeez, is it me, or is Fisher's date super into you?" Jenna whispered as we walked away.

Whatever warm feeling had swept over me while we were dancing dissipated. "He's just goofing off," I muttered. "He's on a date with Fisher."

"Fisher doesn't date, she's *escorted* places," Jenna retorted. She wrapped her arm around my shoulders. "Where's Elin? I've got a surprise for her."

"What?" I asked, glancing around for her. "She went to go look for Ket, I think."

"Never mind. You'll see her in a minute," Jenna sing-songed.

I wriggled out of her grasp. I'd had no idea that drunk Jenna was so affectionate. She stumbled and I grabbed her arm. "Seriously, Jen, how are you still this drunk?" I whispered, careful not to let everyone around us hear. It was probably obvious, since Jenna was practically falling out of her shoes, but I didn't want to be the one who busted her.

Jenna rolled her eyes. "It's prom, Rosie. Stop mothering everyone all the time. This is why you have no fun."

I blinked, letting go of Jenna's arm. "Seriously, Jenna? You're being a giant bitch tonight."

Jenna groaned. "Oh, don't be like that. I just want you to loosen up a little. I did."

I clenched my jaw but didn't reply.

"One, two, three. Can everyone hear me?"

Up on stage, Josh Bowman stood at the microphone, an envelope in his hands. The music faded and people began shouting and whooping. Josh raised his hands, directing everyone to hush. "Welcome to prom, Park City High!" he yelled into the microphone, and the screeching sound of feedback filled the gym. "Yikes, sorry about that," Josh said, grinning a cheesy politician grin. "All right, I don't want to take up too much time, so let's just get to the main event— your prom court!"

Kids cheered. I tried not to yawn. I knew this was Jenna's bag, and I was intellectually proud of her for pulling it all off. But honestly, who gave a crap?

I zoned out as Josh announced the attendants and prom king. Jenna poked my arm. I flinched. "What the hell, Jenna?" I asked, irritated.

"Listen!" Jenna snapped.

Up on stage, Josh was opening a second envelope. He paused and, for one moment, a look of hesitation crossed over his face. "And the prom queen is ... Elin Angstrom!"

My eyebrows shot up. I turned to look at Jenna, who had a smug smile on her face. All around us people clapped, but there were murmurs of confusion. "Did you do this?" I whispered, bringing my hands up to clap for Elin.

Jenna shrugged, smiling. "Maybe."

I glanced around. People seemed vaguely confused by the announcement but not disbelieving. Elin was pretty and likeable. It wasn't outside the realm of possibility that she'd be prom queen.

Aside from the fact that she didn't exactly have a ton of friends left to vote for her.

And had disappeared for some mysterious reason last month.

I saw Fisher from across the room. She was clapping for Elin. She didn't seem annoyed by the fact that she had just lost prom queen—she was smiling faintly, glancing around. It only took me a second to realize who she was looking for.

Up on stage, Josh was smiling, squinting and shielding his eyes against the spotlight, scanning the crowd. "Elin? Come up to the stage."

I leaned toward Jenna. "Where is Elin?"

All around us, people were whispering the same thing.

25

BEFORE
Elin Angstrom
February 26, 1:20 AM

The carpet of Elin's bedroom floor was covered in dirty clothes and dust bunnies. Elin stared at a clump, wondering if the lack of neatness in her room was making Jenna twitch.

Probably.

"I don't know how you managed to forget about a final paper," Jenna muttered for what must have been the fourth time.

Elin said nothing. There really wasn't anything to say.

Elin's grades had been tanking all year, even though she had quit all her extracurriculars. She had always struggled a little in school, but it seemed like the more time she spent on just homework, the further behind she fell.

Yesterday, Ms. Crawford had called Elin's parents, explaining that she was going to get an Incomplete—no good old C or D or even F for Elin Angstrom. Ms. Crawford was giving Elin one day to turn in her paper and salvage her senior year. Elin's folks had hit the roof, and still Elin had been indifferent to the idea of not graduating on time.

Elin had heard her mother on the phone, calling someone as soon as she'd hung up with Ms. Crawford. "I don't know what we're going to do with her," she had said, voice quavering.

For one second, Elin had thought her mother was calling her sister or Mrs. Sinclair for advice. But then Elin's mother had said, "That's so great, Jenny," and Jenna had appeared after dinner, acting as if she just conveniently wanted to hang out.

Elin should have been annoyed. Offended, even. What kind of mother called her daughter's best friend for parenting advice? Would Sarah Angstrom be meeting up to go shopping with Ket next? And what sort of best friend conspired with a girl's *parents* behind her back?

She should have thrown a fit. Screamed at her mother. Given Jenna the cold shoulder. She might have, if she thought Jenna would have bought it.

That was one of the most annoying things about Jenna. When Elin was this tired, it was all she could do to force herself to behave like a normal person, which was hard enough around Ket and Rosie and Teddy. Had been hard enough with Ben. But with Jenna, who had known her since before either of them could speak in full sentences, it meant fending off Jenna's questions and quizzical looks.

And that would have taken more energy than Elin had to give.

Jenna rubbed her eyes. They had been working on Elin's paper for hours—it hadn't helped that Elin hadn't bothered to read *Their Eyes Were Watching God* or *Things Fall Apart* and Jenna had to summarize both before they started. From years of experience, Elin knew that Jenna was prepared to type every word of Elin's paper, improve her grammar and syntax, but that she would flatly refuse to invent the words herself. Jenna despised cheating, but she despised the idea of Elin failing even more.

"So how would you say Okonkwo and Janie reacted to conflict? We need three similarities and three differences to fill five more pages," Jenna said.

Elin sighed. She knew she should try. Try for Jenna, if no one else.

But she was so sick of trying.

"I don't know, Jen. Just . . . let it go."

Jenna clenched her hands. "You have to give me something, E."

"No, I don't," Elin said. "It's my grade and I didn't read the books. I'll just have to live with it."

Jenna turned in her desk chair, staring at Elin like she had just spoken in some imaginary language from the books that Rosie and Teddy read. "What do you mean, you'll *just have to live with it*?"

"I mean, it is what it is."

"Ms. Crawford will fail you," Jenna said, her voice rising.

Elin shrugged, turning her attention back to the mess. If Elin wasn't already in serious danger of failing out during her senior year, her parents might have said something about the state of her room.

Elin heard a soft sniffle and glanced back up at Jenna. Jenna was staring at Elin, her eyes filling with tears and not even bothering to hide it. "Elin, I just told you *everything* you need to know about both books," she said, her voice trembling and her lower lip jutting out. "I have been here all night, and you're just going to sit there and say . . . nothing?"

Elin swallowed thickly. She had never seen Jenna cry. Rosie and Ket, yes, but never because of something Elin had done. And never Jenna. "Jen . . ."

"What the fuck is wrong with you?" Jenna said, her voice cracking and tears spilling over.

Later, Elin would realize it was the swearing that did it. She had seen Jenna cry maybe once or twice, but she had never heard Jenna swear before. Something shifted inside her head and she searched for an answer to her question. "Okonkwo ... tries to control his family members? And Janie rebels against hers?"

Jenna opened her mouth, shut it again. Forced a smile. "That's good, I'll write that," she said, wiping her cheeks with both hands and turning back to the computer screen.

Elin ran her fingers through her hair. "Were you there when Ms. Crawford announced we were studying *Things Fall Apart* instead of *Tess of the d'Urbervilles*?" she asked suddenly. "She looked right at Miles the whole time. It was so awkward."

Jenna laughed, even though this was old gossip. Miles had told this story, rolling his eyes, over a month ago. "Poor Ms. Crawford," Jenna said, giggling and wiping her tears. "She tries so hard, and it's so gross."

It took until dawn, but Jenna managed to coax Elin into writing a ten-page paper comparing and contrasting themes in *Things Fall Apart* and *Their Eyes Were Watching God*. By the time they finished, they were both punchy and snickering over jokes that didn't make sense. Mrs. Angstrom poked her head in Elin's room, her eyes bleary with sleep, and mouthed *thank you* at Jenna when she thought Elin couldn't see. Jenna packed up her stuff so she could get an hour of sleep before she left for early morning tennis conditioning.

Downstairs, Elin's mom began frying bacon and scrambling eggs, the first time she'd made breakfast in as long as Elin could remember.

Elin showered, dressed, and came downstairs to eat breakfast across from her parents, silently, before she went to school.

None of them said anything. Elin assumed they felt bad about screaming but also justified since their rage had prompted her all-nighter.

Outside, Rosie honked her horn. Elin grabbed her bag and ran out the door. Her parents didn't say goodbye.

In second period, Elin remembered that she had left the paper on her desk.

26

Jenna Sinclair
April 18, 8:50 PM

For a second when everyone was glancing around, wondering where Elin was, I briefly thought she was playing a trick on me—Elin of last summer, gleefully yanking my chain before she'd burst out of her hiding spot, snickering at my expense.

Up on stage, Josh scratched his head theatrically. "Well, I guess Elin disappearing on us is no surprise!" he joked. The laughter in response was automatic and I blinked, snapping back to reality.

Beside me, Rosie was frozen. I grabbed her hand. "Come on," I said, sharper than I'd wanted, and turned to stomp off the dance floor. My heart pounded in my chest, my breath coming rapidly, my head swimming. If I was going to lose it, I didn't want an audience when it happened.

I pushed the double doors to the gym open with more force than was needed, and they banged against the walls. One of my high heels slid out from under me and I stumbled briefly before Rosie caught me. Stupid shoes.

"She's got to be here somewhere," Rosie said, her voice even. Anyone who didn't know Rosie—which was most people—wouldn't even realize that she was as worried as I was. "She told me she was going to find Ket."

Why didn't I just tell Elin she had to be there for the crowning? *Haughty: arrogantly superior or disdainful.*

Inside the gym, the deejay resumed the dance track. Josh must have abandoned the idea of crowning Elin. All the way out in the shadowy lobby, I could feel the bass pounding my ears. My skin felt hot and too tight.

The rational part of myself—the part that always argued for the simplest solution—said that Elin was simply off in the school somewhere, maybe sneaking a cigarette with Ket.

But the primal, lizard brainy part of me knew that wasn't it. Whatever Elin was doing right now, whatever she was up to, it wasn't harmless fun. And someone was going to pay for it.

Most likely me.

For one second, my imagination went to the darkest possible place. Elin's face, white and still and waxy as a doll's. A razor blade on the edge of a sink. Empty pill bottles scattered on the floor. Red ribbons rising through water, like strands of smoke from a candle flame. My heart pounding, about to fall over the edge and into a chasm of panic, not knowing what to do.

I took a deep breath and shoved all that aside—buried it deep inside my brain, slammed the door and locked it. Elin's doctor had sent her home, which meant none of that was a possibility.

"Where is she?" I whispered, half to myself.

"I've been texting her, I'm not getting any reply," Rosie said, biting her lip, her eyes glued to her phone. "Ket says she's not with her."

I pressed the heels of both my palms to my forehead and shut my eyes, wishing the situation away.

"What's going on?"

I turned to see Ket and Teddy—Teddy?—walking toward us, emerging from the dim hallway. I could barely see the expressions on their faces.

"Where have you guys been?" Rosie asked.

Ket and Teddy glanced at each other. "In the band room watching *Golden Girls*," Ket said after a long beat, and a look of hurt flashed over Rosie's face.

I shook my head. No time for Teddy-Rosie drama right now. "We can't find Elin," I said. "She's not answering texts, either."

Ket blinked, her mouth hanging open—and for some reason, her surprise justified my own. "Well ... what do you think happened?"

Rosie shrugged, wrapping her arms around herself. "Beats me! She said she was going to look for you. Did Ben say something to her?"

"I don't think so," Ket mumbled.

I ignored her and turned to Rosie. "Why would you think Ben said something?"

Rosie glanced away, silent as always.

Teddy was glancing between the three of us, concern washing over his face. He might not have known exactly what we were talking about, but Teddy had always been a good listener. "Guys, what's going on?"

Ket cleared her throat. "I, uh, may have an idea of what happened."

I raised my eyebrows. "Care to share with the class?"

Ket glanced at Teddy, who raised his eyebrows. "Why are you looking at me?" he said. "I don't know what's going on."

Ket grabbed my arm and Rosie's, propelling us down the hall. "We'll be right back, it's a girl thing!" she called over her shoulder.

I tried to put on the brakes when I realized Ket wanted us to head into the bathroom. "Hold on," I snapped, my heart thumping wildly in my chest. "Just tell me what you think is happening already."

Ket looked around, glancing over her shoulder. She obviously wanted the potential privacy the bathroom would offer, but I couldn't handle another unnecessary bathroom visit tonight. "No one's listening," I hissed impatiently.

Ket leaned against a row of lockers, shoulders hunched as she faced me and Rosie. She bit her lip. "I told Vaughn about what happened. To Elin."

For one second, I couldn't believe what I was hearing. Then Rosie cursed under her breath and I snapped back to myself. I let out a long breath. *At least there's a logical explanation.* And that was what mattered.

"I know it was stupid, so don't lecture me," Ket said. "But I'm sure he won't tell anyone. The problem is, I told Elin at Fisher's party and now she's pissed."

"But she's not pissed," Rosie said, forehead crinkling in confusion. "At least, I don't think she is."

Ket threw her hands in the air. "Why else would she run off when she's been looking forward to prom for weeks?"

"I don't know, but the last thing she told *me* was that she was going to look for *you*," Rosie said. "She was talking about getting sushi! Did Vaughn say something to her?"

"No," said Ket.

"How are you so sure?" Rosie said.

"I know," Ket said firmly.

"*How* do you know?" Rosie insisted.

Didactic: excessively instructive.

Ineffable: unspeakable, incapable of being expressed through words.

Wo tingbudong: I don't understand.

"He's not even at the dance yet!" Ket snapped.

"Stop," I said finally. "There's no point in arguing. We need to split up and look for her. She's probably just moping in a classroom somewhere or fixing her makeup."

As expected, Ket and Rosie didn't argue with me. They nodded. "What are we going to tell Teddy?" Ket asked, her eyebrows tilted miserably.

"Why is Teddy here, again?"

Ket's gaze flicked toward Rosie, who glanced away. "I think it was a last-minute decision."

"Well, yeah, he's wearing jeans and a suit coat he probably stole from his grandpa," I muttered, rubbing my temples. My brain was swirling.

Rosie nudged me. "Who's down there with Teddy?" she asked, peering down the darkened hallway.

Ket swore under her breath. "It's Fisher and FDR."

"And *Ben,*" Rosie said, her tone acidic.

She and Rosie started down the hall toward Teddy's shadowy figure. I stood rooted to the spot for a moment. "Who the hell is FDR?" I said finally, picking up my tulle skirt to hurry after them.

Fisher Reese and her date were standing with Teddy and Ben when we returned to the lobby, all wearing identical expressions of concern. "Hey, is Elin okay?" Fisher asked, her voice hushed.

I scrunched up my nose. "Fisher, when did we become friends?"

Fisher flinched. "Jenna," Ket hissed under her breath.

I was puzzled. It was a genuine question, I didn't mean to be rude. Since when was Ket the arbiter of what was right and proper? And since when did Ket stick up for *Fisher?*

"Sorry, Fisher," I said, confused. "But for reals, are we friends?"

Fisher blinked and a smile spread over her overly ortho-donted face. "Of course we're friends, Jenna. We've known each other since we were little."

"Oh, okay," I said, even though knowing someone for a long time was not the same as being friends. It's not like it was a syllogism or something.

"We don't know where Elin is," Ket confessed. "We're going to split up and search the school for her before it becomes a thing."

Weirdly, Fisher didn't ask any questions. She nodded. "I'll tell people she wasn't feeling well and she went to my condo to take a nap," she said. "If you find her before the after-party, no one will ever know she split."

I blinked. That was . . . a surprisingly good idea. "Okay," I said. "That's a good start. So we were her ride, which means she's still on campus somewhere. Let's split up and search, we're bound to find her."

Ben blew out a breath from between his teeth. "Fine. Where should we start?"

I furrowed my brow, trying to think of a polite way to point out that if Ben ditched Hannah to go look for his ex-girlfriend, Hannah would do everything she could to make the situation worse. *Truculent: defiantly aggressive.*

But Rosie beat me to it.

"I think we'll be fine without your help," Rosie said coolly.

Ben scowled at her, his jaw clenched. "Seriously, Rosie, what is your problem? You have been the biggest bitch to me lately."

"Don't call her a bitch," Teddy and Ket snapped simultaneously.

Ben glared at Rosie and, for one second, he legitimately looked like he hated her. Sweet, kind Ben glaring down Rosie, who was glaring right back.

What the hell was going on? *How drunk am I?*

"You tell me at Fisher's party to stay away from Elin—"

"Wait, what?" Ket interrupted, turning toward Rosie, whose cheeks were flushing scarlet. "Did you lie to me? You promised you'd leave Ben alone."

Rosie glanced away. "Look, can we talk about this later?" she asked.

"No, we're going to talk about it now," Ket said, her voice rising and dark eyes flashing. "Because I think I just figured out what really pissed Elin off."

I put my hand on Ket's arm. "We don't have time for that," I said. "We have to find Elin, and we need all the help we can get."

Fisher's date spoke for the first time. "Well, at least half of us should head outside."

"In this?" Ket asked, gesturing toward the doors. Snow was falling steadily.

"We saw her outside when we arrived," Fisher said.

"I gave her my coat," Fisher's date added. "It wasn't snowing yet, but she looked cold."

Rosie nodded, turning to me. "Fine. So everyone who wants to help look"—her eyes skittered toward Ben and then away from him—"should split up. If you find her, text the others. Otherwise—"

"There is no otherwise," I interrupted. "We're going to find her."

Rosie met my eyes and I remembered who I was dealing with—Rosie Winchester, Eeyore personified. She couldn't resist finishing her sentence. "Otherwise, meet back here in thirty minutes."

27

Ket West-Beauchamp
April 18, 9:20 PM

We had searched everywhere and we had no idea where Elin was. Every call and text went unanswered.

Rosie swallowed visibly. "I think we need to call the police."

Jenna whirled around to face her. "What? Why would we do that?"

"Why do you think?" Rosie hissed, glancing over at Ben, who was listening to our every word. "Our friend . . . who is not very *responsible* right now . . . has disappeared."

"Don't you think that's extreme?" Teddy asked, his face unsure. "I mean, you guys got in a fight and she left prom. That's not irresponsible, it's just dramatic. She'll apologize tomorrow."

Rosie ignored him, her eyes glued on Jenna. "We need to call the cops," she repeated.

"I don't know, Rosie," I said, glancing between the two of them. "If the cops come, she is going to be so embarrassed. And pissed."

"Totally," agreed Jenna. "We just have to find her ourselves."

Rosie's lip curled in disgust. "You just don't want to get caught being drunk at school."

Jenna flushed. I couldn't tell whether it was from embarrassment, anger, or the alcoholic content of her blood. I felt a rush of defensiveness on her behalf. "That's not true, Ro," I said, trying to channel as much Mama Leanne as I could. Authoritative Calm. "If we thought Elin was really in danger, Jenna would be calling 9-1-1 already. But I think that's a really aggressive step at the moment."

Rosie folded her arms across her chest, glaring at the two of us. Jenna's face was still red, her jaw clenching. I cleared my throat, hoping to avert disaster. "I think we need to continue this conversation in private," I said, glancing pointedly at Ben and Teddy.

"What? Again?" said Teddy, sounding annoyed. We ignored him and headed off to the girls' bathroom.

"Not the bathroom," Jenna protested, but I shoved the door open and pulled her inside. A handful of sophomores in juvenile dresses hovered around the sinks, reapplying lip gloss and mascara in front of the mirrors.

Oh, to be a pathetic sophomore again.

"Out!" I bellowed. The sophomore vacated the bathroom post haste. I glanced under the stall doors—no one.

"We have got to call the cops," Rosie whispered, even though we were alone.

Jenna turned to Rosie. "If this is how Elin reacts when she thinks *one person* knows about what happened, how is she going to react when *the entire school* knows? Besides—" She snapped her mouth shut abruptly.

"What?" Rosie asked, her jaw clenched.

Jenna glanced at the door, avoiding our stares. "Elin's parents don't know she's here."

Rosie and I stared at her. "Wait, what?" I said.

Jenna shrugged, playing with the ends of her wavy hair. "Elin's doctor thought she should go to the dance, but her parents didn't think it was a good idea. So she asked me to cover for her. They think we're at a sleepover at Ket's."

My jaw dropped. "And you didn't think you should tell me?" I asked.

Rosie said nothing, just glanced back and forth between the two of us. For the first time, she looked uncertain. "But . . . I mean, who cares how she'll feel if she's . . . off somewhere . . ."

"She's *not*," hissed Jenna, wrapping her arms around herself. "She went to the hospital and the doctors let her go, and they don't let you go if you're still like that!"

"Adults don't know everything, Jen," Rosie said softly.

"Doctors *do*," Jenna snapped. "She's *fine* and you're being dramatic."

I glanced back and forth between their faces—Rosie's solemn, Jenna's incensed.

Rosie bit her lip and leaned back against the sink. "Okay. We won't call the cops, or tell Elin's parents. *Yet*," she added when Jenna let out a sigh of relief. "We'll keep looking for her. If we can't find her by midnight, we have to call the cops and tell her parents. Agreed?"

"Totally," I said, and Jenna shot me a look.

What really bugs me about the party-girl stereotype is the implication that I'm a bad friend. There's always an episode in any medical or cop show where a bunch of girls were partying, one ends up with alcohol poisoning and/or is kidnapped, and all the other girls just giggle and deflect while the doctor or detective tries to get some Damn Answers Already.

I mean, please. If Rosie, Jenna, Elin, or Teddy had alcohol poisoning, I would be the *first* person to haul them into the ER and tearfully confess every sin and mistake from my entire life.

But in this case, I didn't think Elin was really in trouble. She was obviously super pissed at either me or Rosie or most likely both of us. Which meant calling the cops and making it worse would be a monumentally big mistake.

I blew out a long breath, frustration bubbling up inside—frustration at myself for trusting Vaughn, frustration at listening to Jenna. Frustration at Rosie for lying to me. But none of that was going to help us, so I said nothing.

We stepped out of the bathroom. Ben had disappeared, presumably off to find Hannah, but Teddy was still waiting, wearing an expression of annoyance and disapproval. And now FDR had joined him, his eyebrows knit together with worry.

"We've got a problem," FDR said. "My car is missing."

28

Rosie Winchester
April 18, 9:30 PM

Ket and I stood outside, Ket smoking and me resisting the urge to call Will and ask him what to do. (Not that he'd even know.) FDR was calling his GPS provider, trying to get a location on his car, which presumably Elin had since he'd left his keys in the pocket of the coat he'd given her. Ben had disappeared, probably pissed off, or at least scared of pissing off Hannah. Jenna was sitting on the curb a few yards away, head between her knees. Teddy sat beside her, arms resting on his knees, earbuds in as he resolutely ignored me. His breath puffed white in the cold air, but even without a coat in the falling snow, he didn't shiver.

"What are we going to do, Rosie?" Ket said finally. "If we can't find her?"

I chewed on my thumbnail. "I don't know. Call the police. Something. Find Elin, then pretend none of this ever happened."

But even I wasn't so sure about the police anymore. It was one thing when we just had a missing friend. Now we had a missing friend who had committed *grand theft auto*.

Ket wrapped her arms around herself, holding her cigarette off to the side, her wrist cocked artfully. "Don't you think that's the problem, though? I mean, Elin wouldn't be okay if her parents hadn't come home early. And we never talk about it."

Jenna groaned and Ket and I turned to study her. She didn't make any more noise—I assumed she wasn't going to barf.

I leaned my cheek against my knees and wrapped my arms around my legs, hoping to conserve as much warmth as possible. (Stupid, stupid dress.) "What is there to talk about? We know what happened."

"Do we?" Ket asked.

"Yes," I whispered, keenly aware of Teddy's presence, earbuds or no. "Elin had a breakdown, probably because of Ben—"

"You don't know that," Ket interrupted, sounding annoyed.

"—and then her doctors released her," I hissed, jerking my head toward Teddy so Ket would remember to keep her voice down. (I didn't want to talk about this.) "Jenna's drunk, but she's right about that. They wouldn't have let her go if she wasn't better."

(I hoped.)

Ket eyed Teddy. "He didn't hear anything," she said finally, but her voice was lower.

I shivered violently and wished FDR would hurry.

"What do you think your parents would do?" Ket said suddenly. "If they found out about tonight."

"Nothing," I said, no hesitation.

Ket took a long drag on her cigarette. "You never worry about what they think," she said, sounding vaguely amazed.

I shrugged. "I worry what Will thinks. Sometimes."

"Do you think Will and your mom will ever get divorced?" Ket asked.

I chewed on my thumbnail. "Probably. I think my mom only married him so she could have a built-in babysitter. I have no idea why Will married her. They don't even seem like they like each other that much."

"Because your mom is hot for an older lady, and because she's loaded," Ket said, half her mouth turned up in a wry smile.

I scuffed the toe of my shoe against the pavement and Ket bumped me with her shoulder. I glanced up at her. Her smile had faded. "Maybe Will married your mom for the money," she said. "Or, I don't know. Will is weird. Maybe it seemed like an adventure at the time. But whatever it was, he stays married to her for you."

I swallowed, my eyes stinging in the cold. "If they get divorced, we won't even be related anymore," I said softly, my voice thick. "He'll just be another ex-step-parent."

(I'll never see him again, just like I never saw Amanda or Marianne again.)

(He'll probably get remarried and have a real kid.)

Ket rolled her eyes. "Don't be dumb. Whether they get divorced or not, he's going to cry like a bitch when you move away for college. I'll bet you cash money."

I cracked a smile. "He can be super sappy."

"Exactly," Ket said.

I shook my head, trying to clear my thoughts. "What were we talking about?"

"Parents, and the multitude of ways we disappoint them."

I frowned. "Are you worried about your parents? You didn't do anything."

Ket shrugged but didn't say anything, the corners of her mouth turned down. I felt a pang. Ket so rarely seemed sad. "You didn't do anything," I repeated. "Jenna helped her lie to her parents. I was with her when she ran off. You told Vaughn, but . . . I don't know. Vaughn is such a dick, but I think most people would tell their boyfriends. Jenna told Miles, didn't she?"

Ket tossed her cigarette on the sidewalk, but despite the cold, we didn't stand to go inside. We stared, fixated on the little stream of smoke curling up from the still-burning ember. "That's not the point," she said finally. "It's just that, I know my moms wish I were more responsible. As if my whorey ways are some kind of reflection on their same-sex parenting, and it's my obligation to be, like, the model child instead. I mean, no offense, but if you got in as much trouble as I do, at least people would say, *Well, she comes from a broken home.* When things like this happen, maybe it's not really any-one's fault, but I know they think, *They're going to blame us, the lesbians who raised this batshit daughter.*"

I snorted. "That's ridiculous."

"It's not," Ket insisted. "Adlai was so perfect. I bet he'll be mad at me, too."

"You're jumping to conclusions," I said. "And why would Adlai even care?"

But it was like she wasn't even listening to me, staring out at the parking lot as I studied her profile. "This night is going to ruin my life," she whispered, eyes shining.

My heart thumped a little harder. "We're going to find her," I insisted. "No one's life is getting ruined."

Ket stood suddenly, stomping her feet on the sidewalk. "You must be freezing," she said, her voice shaking. "We should wait inside."

I stood, stiff from sitting in the cold so long, my brain still trying to follow all the unexpected turns of my conversation with Ket. I opened my mouth to ask, *What aren't you telling me?* But the stormy look on her face stopped me.

(Coward.)

Teddy glanced up at us and pulled his earbuds out. "You guys heading in?"

"Yeah," said Ket, her voice returning to normal.

Teddy nudged Jenna and she opened her eyes slightly. He helped her to her feet and wrapped his arm around her waist, steadying her as they headed for the school.

My eyes stung as I watched them, him helping her like he would help his sister. My throat clenched and I swallowed, hard, forcing myself to come back to neutral.

(God, I miss Teddy.)

(Worry about that tomorrow.)

I hung back with Ket, hoping she would say something—anything—about why she was so upset.

But she followed them without another word.

9:45 PM

Most people become less awkward over time.

I get worse.

If Ket hadn't befriended me in kindergarten, thanks to an alphabetical order seating arrangement . . . if Teddy hadn't moved next door when I was eight . . . if all three of us hadn't met Jenna and Elin on the first day of middle school and became inseparable the way slightly nerdy kids tend to band together to face sixth grade . . . I would probably have no friends at all.

They were the people I loved most in the world, and yet, if we had all met today instead of years ago, I worry we wouldn't even bother with each other.

(They wouldn't bother with me.)

But it wouldn't take a more socially attuned person than I to realize that all of us standing around after FDR returned with a location on his car, trying to decide who would go after Elin and who would stay, was the definition of awkward.

"So I think you should give Fisher a ride back to her party," Ket said to Teddy, glancing at me with puppy-dog eyes. Like *I'd* be able to come up with something.

Teddy stared at Ket, refusing to look at me at all. My stomach felt queasy-greasy. I felt preternaturally aware of FDR's presence, his lanky frame just a few inches from my side. Teddy's lip was curled ever-so-slightly—his disgusted face. "Yeah, sure," he muttered.

"I'm sorry," Ket said, glancing up to meet his gaze for the first time. "I know I told you to come to the dance, and I'm so glad you did—"

"Whatever," Teddy said, tucking his hands into his back pockets. He was trying to look bored, but I knew—and I was sure Ket did as well—that he was pissed. "Where is Fisher?"

Ket trailed off, biting her lip.

"She's waiting in the front circle," FDR supplied helpfully. (At least one of us was determined to ignore the awkward vibe.)

Teddy's gaze flickered over to FDR and I scooted a few inches away from him. "And Elin took your car?" he asked.

"Pretty sure," FDR said, a smile still plastered on his face.

Teddy rolled his eyes. "Glad that's sorted out," he said, his voice laced with sarcasm.

"You should stay at Fisher's party," Jenna suggested suddenly, snapping out of her drunken stupor. She had been

164

leaning against her car during the entire discussion, eyes squeezed shut. I hadn't even realized she was listening. "We can still hang out after the dance, once we find Elin and bring her back." She beamed, swaying slightly on her feet.

I felt a wave of relief that Jenna was fixing this, but Ket cleared her throat. All eyes turned to her. She pursed her lips. "Well . . . maybe we should just meet up tomorrow instead?"

Teddy blinked, hurt flashing over his face, and I stared at Ket. *What the hell?*

Teddy looked at me for the first time. I knew every expression Teddy's face ever made, but not this one. Annoyed? Pissed? Had I really lost my ability to read Teddy in two months of not talking? His eyes darted over to FDR standing at my side and then back to me.

Jealous?

"No, you should come to Fisher's party," I said, taking a deliberate step away from FDR. This was the first time in weeks that Teddy had willingly spent more than five minutes in my presence—I wasn't letting the opportunity pass me by. "Or wherever we end up. I'll text you, okay?"

Teddy's expression was unreadable. He glanced over to Ket one last time. "Yeah, sure," he said finally.

I felt my heart sink. I knew that Teddy was going to ignore that text message. Just like he'd ignored every other message I'd sent since his birthday.

Ket's mouth was hanging open, like a confused guppy, as Teddy stalked off to the school. I felt a flash of annoyance toward her. Why was she making it so weird for Teddy?

"Let's get this over with," I said, grabbing Jenna's keys from her hand.

10:00 PM

Finding a parking space was nearly impossible—we may have reached Main Street in ten minutes, but every second we spent circling blocks, *not* finding Elin, the knot in my stomach grew tighter.

In the back seat, Jenna had her forehead pressed against the cool glass of the window and Ket was texting frantically. I wasn't sure what she thought she'd accomplish there—Elin hadn't answered any of our messages so far, so why would she answer these?

Beside me in the passenger seat, FDR kept up a steady stream of inoffensive commentary. I knew he was probably trying to keep us calm. Well, *me* calm, since Jenna and Ket weren't paying attention—but it wasn't helping. I opened my mouth more than once to ask him to shut up, but the words caught in my throat.

"There!" shouted Jenna, too loudly for the enclosed space. I winced, but I saw what she meant—a space to the right, almost too narrow to fit. If we had any more time, I would have waited to find something better.

We squeezed out of our doors, holding them carefully to avoid hitting the neighboring cars. "Where did the GPS say your car was?" I asked FDR.

"They could only narrow it down to a four-block radius," FDR said.

His eyes flickered down for a moment, and for one second I saw a crack in his relentlessly cheerful exterior. Neither of us were saying what we were worried about.

That we would find FDR's car but not Elin.

(Don't even think that.)

We hurried down each street as quickly as we could. All around us, people were huddled on patios with tall heating lamps, walking in and out of bars and clubs and restaurants, laughing. My eyes stung. I wasn't a crier, but I was getting as close as I ever got.

"There it is," FDR said, jogging over to a red Subaru Forester. I was surprised—then annoyed that I'd thought about it. I expected Fisher Reese's date to drive an Audi or Volvo or ... I didn't really know cars, but something nicer than a Subaru.

His pace slowed as he got closer to the car, and it only took me half a heartbeat to understand why.

No Elin.

29

Ket West-Beauchamp
April 18, 10:10 PM

I stared at the draft of a text message to Teddy, written but unsent. *I am so sorry, dude. Please let me explain tomorrow?*

Of all the times for Teddy to listen to me, to try having a good time, he had to pick the night that I was planning to hook up with Vaughn again?

COME ON, UNIVERSE.

Ahead of me, Rosie and FDR were asking randoms if they'd seen a girl in a long white dress and next to me Jenna was swaying on her feet. People were responding with dumb jokes about runaway brides.

And this was literally the best plan we had.

Total. Disaster.

Meanwhile, I had to figure out a time and a place to hook up with Vaughn again. The longer we didn't find Elin, the more obvious it was to me that I needed to do my part to eliminate the one problem I could control.

But even though I'd been into the idea of hooking up with Vaughn again just a few hours ago, I couldn't shake the feeling that trying to negotiate with Vaughn on this point was a Very Bad Idea.

Forget the taping for a minute, I heard Jenna's voice say in my head—which was ludicrous, because if Jenna knew about Vaughn threatening me, she would be googling "DIY Castration Techniques."

But imaginary Jenna was full of practical ideas. *Take this problem one step at a time*, suggested Bizarro Jenna. *Couldn't you have sex with Vaughn again to save Elin's reputation? Just one itty-bitty time?*

Bizarro Jen was right—it's not like I hadn't had sex with Vaughn more times than I could count. I closed my eyes and tried to visualize it—but the second Vaughn's imaginary lips wandered past my imaginary collarbone, I felt my skin start to crawl.

The Bizarro Jenna in my imagination shook her head, disappointed in my Lack of Commitment to Excellence.

A snort escaped my mouth. I clapped my hand over my lips to stop myself from breaking down into hysterical laughter. Rosie turned to stare at me, eyebrows knit together. *What is going on?* she mouthed, looking a combination of pissed and worried.

The Rosie Winchester Special.

I just shook my head, tears stinging my eyes from the effort of holding back. *Get it together, Ket.* Rosie stared at me for a moment longer and then turned away.

Good old Rosie. You could always count on her to avoid a conflict.

I scrolled over to my texts with Vaughn, re-reading them over and over, hoping I could think my way out of this mess.

VAUGHN: *Why aren't you in the bandroom?*
I hope you're not playing me.

KET: *Something came up, you gotta give me some time.*
Go back to the dance, I'll see you at the afterparty?

VAUGHN: *Losing patience, Ket.*

KET: *Are you shitting me? You're sex-blackmailing me over a suicidal girl and you're talking about patience?*

VAUGHN: *I'm not blackmailing you.*

KET: *What do you think this is? The only reason I am even CONSIDERING this is because you are threatening me.*

VAUGHN: *Protest all you want, but we both know you want to*

KET: *Yes, because saying "no" totally means "let's ruin our future employment prospects."*

VAUGHN: *I'm not going to spread it around! I just want to keep it in my personal spank bank. For when we go our separate ways.*

KET: *Gross, dude*

VAUGHN: *You know, if you just want to let everyone know about Elin, that's fine with me.*

KET: *Fuck you, dude. Seriously.*

VAUGHN: *Soon enough, babycakes.*

My stomach churned. *Babycakes.* He got that phrase from me and my friends—that's what Jenna called her dog whenever she was being silly, and now we all said it all the time. And now *Vaughn Hollis* was saying babycakes.

For some reason, that disgusted me most of all.

I stared at the draft I was thinking of sending to him. *Does it not bug you at all that I really do not want to have sex with you tonight, much less tape it?*

The fact is, I wasn't sure what I had planned to do if I had found Vaughn down in the bandroom. Try to talk him out of this, probably. Delay, definitely.

But with each text he sent me, it became clearer that there was no getting out of this.

Jenna was leaning against a lamppost—I couldn't believe she'd gotten so wasted, so fast. Rosie and FDR were flailing, stopping any stranger who would stop to listen to them, which wasn't many.

It was a lost cause. Elin wasn't going to be found unless she wanted to be found. And yeah, taking FDR's car was pretty bananas, but considering Elin and Fisher were apparently *such good friends* all of a sudden, maybe she thought she could get away with it. At least she'd left the poor guy's coat and scarf on the driver's seat for him to find, the keys in the ignition.

Elin was going to reappear exactly when she felt like it. I wasn't worried about that.

I was worried about what was going to happen after she reappeared.

The Elin Aftermath: Part II.

I bit my lip, wondering if I had any chance of excusing myself from the Save Elin Brigade long enough to go hit it and quit it.

"Have you guys seen a blond girl? White dress, braided hair?" FDR was asking a group of fratbros crossing the street. Most of them ignored him. One stopped and raised his eyebrow. Tall, shaved head. Romance-novel-cover good looks.

"Yeah, I saw a girl," the guy said. "Short, pretty? Silver thingies on her dress?"

"Yes!" Rosie cried. "Where did she go?"

The guy laughed, nudging his friends. "She and her friend were hot," he said.

"What friend?" Rosie asked, wrapping her arms around herself.

"Another blond girl," the guy said, shrugging. "Taller. She wasn't into me."

"Why would she be?" snickered one of the other guys, and the guy hit him half-heartedly on the shoulder. I opened my phone, scrolling through my pictures. I held one up of Elin and me that we'd taken back at Rosie's house. "This girl? You saw this girl?"

The guy squinted blearily at the pic. "Yeah, definitely. That girl with another girl. What's her name?"

"Elin," I muttered, shoving my phone back in my purse. Who the hell was this other girl he was talking about?

FDR stepped forward, a bland smile on his face. "Do you know where she is? We really have to find her."

"No, man," the guy said, running his hand over his buzzed head. "I wanted to take off, head to this other party, but her friend split and then she said she had to go and caught a cab.

That was, I don't know, maybe twenty minutes ago? Thirty? Was she eighteen, man? How did she get into that club?"

"I don't know," FDR said mildly. "She's definitely in high school. Did you buy her drinks?"

"No," the guy said, and for the first time he seemed to focus on me, Rosie, and Jen. His eyes skimmed over my legs shamelessly before fixing his gaze on Rosie. "You girls all with this guy? Do you wanna come party?"

FDR slung his arm around Rosie's shoulders, and to my surprise she didn't squirm away from him. "Did you see which way the cab went?"

"Come on, dude!" one of the other guys called.

"Stop dicking around," added another.

The guy nodded and turned to follow them. "Sorry, can't help you, man. Hope you find your friends!"

30

Jenna Sinclair
April 18, 10:40 PM

My parents always wanted my siblings and me to give back to our community, to have an awareness of the world around us. They took us to documentaries about land mine victims and bought tickets to Hunger Banquets. When I was ten, they took us to El Salvador and we helped build an orphanage.

The problem with telling kids that they can save the world is that, if you go by my family's experience, one out of three of them will believe you. I'd sit in those darkened movie theaters between my mom and sister, watching films about suffragettes and female scientists and think, *I could do that*. I'd go running, my feet pounding along to the rhythm of the *Hamilton* soundtrack—or even more embarrassingly, *Newsies*—and fantasize about operating immunization clinics in Ghana or making civil rights arguments at the Supreme Court or thwarting terrorist plots.

Of course I never said anything to anyone—who tells people that you fantasize about being the main character in the biopic of your own amazing life? Which was good, since it had become spectacularly obvious that I was not as awesome as I'd previously thought.

It wasn't just that I never doubted whether I'd do something heroic or wonderful with my life. It was that, until recently, it didn't even *occur* to me to doubt it. *Erratum: error in printing. Solecism: grammatical mistake in speech or writing.*

What was the word that meant, *making a grave error in world view?* I bet the Germans had one.

I pressed my palms into my eyes until I saw stars. "Look. We aren't going to find Elin if she doesn't want to be found. What we need to do is give her a reason to come back."

"What are you talking about?" Rosie said, her voice rising shrilly.

"Ben," I said, my eyes still closed. I rubbed my temples, trying to clear my head. "She wanted to talk to Ben, she didn't get to talk to Ben. What we need to do is get Ben in a position where Elin can talk to him. We need to wingman Hannah back away from him."

I opened my eyes, expecting Rosie and Ket to be staring at me in relief.

Thanks, Jenna.

Way to solve our problems again, Jenna.

Instead Rosie's lips were pressed together, white with anger, and all of Ket's attention was focused on her, not me. "That is the most ridiculous thing I have ever heard," Rosie said.

Abjure: to reject or renounce.

Acrimony: bitterness or discord.

My temper flared, but I held on to it. "Look, Rosie, I know you're not a Ben fan, but Elin is. She wanted to talk to him all night. All we need to do is get him to call her, and she'll answer."

Adumbrate: to sketch out in a vague way.

"We don't know that!" Rosie exploded. "And why would we want to expose our friend to that . . . that . . ."

Anathema?

"Asshole?" Ket supplied.

I glared at her and she glanced away. "Just trying to help," she muttered, staring at her cell phone screen.

Rosie put her hands on her hips. "Yes, *asshole*," she said. "What we need to do is just *find her* and forget about him!"

"Where do you suggest we start looking, Rosie? She's not here," I said, gesturing around. "She left and now we really have no idea where. We need to just do what we can, and that means getting Ben to find her."

Ket blew out a long breath. "I agree with Jenna," she said finally.

"Fine!" Rosie shouted. "I will go find Elin myself. You guys go back to the dance."

Ket turned to her, eyes shining, but Rosie was already striding down the sidewalk. "Rosie, we're not just going back to the dance," she called, raising up on her toes like that would help her words carry further.

I slumped to the sidewalk. "Let her go," I mumbled. "She's not going to be happy unless she can be unhappy about something."

31

Rosie Winchester
April 18, 10:45 PM

I stalked down the sidewalk, furious with Jenna. Furious with Ket.

I heard footsteps behind me. "Hey, where are you going?" FDR called.

I whirled around. "We've found your car, you can go back to the dance."

"And leave you wandering around here by yourself? No way."

"I don't need your help."

(Yes, I do.)

"Maybe not, but I'm not leaving," FDR replied, matching me step for step.

I wrapped my arms around myself and turned away so he wouldn't see the tears springing into my eyes. Even still, I could feel him standing just behind me, in my blind spot. People streamed around us, like we were stones in a river, and they couldn't care less that I'd let my friends get us into the biggest mess of our lives. "I just don't know where she could have gone," I whispered.

I didn't hear a reply. For a second I thought that FDR had left, leaving me standing alone on a sidewalk in the middle of the night. Then the weight of a warm suit jacket appeared on my shoulders. I ducked my head, ashamed.

Was it really possible that the only person who was ready and able to help me find Elin was some stranger who I had been horribly rude to all night?

I turned around, expecting FDR to be wearing his confident, crooked grin. But his brows were knitted together, his eyes solemn. "We can find her," he promised, his eyes searching mine. "We just have to think like she thinks."

I tugged his jacket tighter around myself, gripping the lapels in my fists. "What do you mean?"

"Well, we have to figure out why she drove to Main Street in the first place, and then figure out why she would have left," FDR said. "It shouldn't be too hard to figure out where she would have gone after she left, if we know why."

I nodded slowly. That made sense—even if it did leave out the most obvious part. How would we figure out *why* she came here if she wasn't around to be asked? I bit my lip. "If I were Elin . . . and I wasn't having fun at the dance anymore . . . I'd just go home. But if she went home, why did she come here first? And why wouldn't she just call us? And who was she hanging out with, who is this other girl?" My mind spun as I remembered one other thing. "And she *can't* go home, not until morning, or her parents will know that she lied about where she was going tonight."

"So she didn't go home," FDR prompted. "But why would you think she would?"

I bit my lip, staring at my feet. "Because . . . whoever this other girl was, that guy said she left first. And if Elin was done partying, and she was alone, she would want to be somewhere familiar and comfortable."

"So other than her house, where would be familiar and comfortable?"

I racked my brain. "She loves ... the outdoors. She loves skiing and running."

(Except she quit doing both ...)

"But it's too cold to hang outside," FDR pointed out. "And she left my coat in the car. Is there anywhere else she might go?"

And just like that, the answer was right in front of me. I glanced up and met FDR's gaze. "I think so," I said.

32

BEFORE
Elin Angstrom
The Week of March 6

Elin Angstrom planned every detail of her death. And she channeled her three best friends when she did it.

Like Jenna, she considered every potential outcome. She picked two different methods—drugs and slitting her wrists. She knew when her mom got her Valium refilled and she took them all with her dad's leftover Vicodin from his knee surgery, then washed it down with a glass of red wine. She didn't even like wine, but the warning labels on the pill bottles said not to drink with them.

Like Ket, she didn't bother with excuses. She wrote a simple note and left it on her bed, right where it would be found.

Like Rosie, she made sure to take care of the people she loved. She picked a night that she knew her parents wouldn't interrupt—her dad had put a weekend stay at Stein Erickson Lodge on his calendar weeks before. She would be found by the maid service that came on Saturdays, but better them than her parents. The maids would call the police, who would clean up before her parents had to see anything.

And then she took care of everyone else she loved.

She broke up with Ben so he wouldn't think it was anything he'd done.

She made sure she wasn't fighting with her friends, but she didn't do anything that would tip her hand, either. She'd seen that video on signs of the suicidal teen and she wasn't interested in that sort of predictability. But she did make sure that she did little things so they would realize later that she'd been saying goodbye.

On Monday, she dropped off cupcakes to Ket and her moms to thank Mom Kim for showing her how to make buttercream frosting. Ket, Elin, and Mom Kim had shared three, watching an old episode of *The Simpsons* until Mama Leanne had come home from work. Ket's mothers had insisted Elin stay for dinner, and for two hours no one asked her about homework or college. The four of them laughed the whole evening. She hadn't felt so light in weeks.

Rosie was tough—she resisted when people tried to do nice things for her, like a cat that struggled to get away from a snuggle. The Tuesday before, they had done their homework after school as Will rolled out dough for pizzas in the kitchen. When Rosie took a bathroom break, Elin had said, "Hey, Will?" without looking up from her homework.

"Yeah?" Will asked, throwing dough on the pizza stone.

"You watch out for Rosie, right?" Elin said, pretending to look at her homework but really keeping an eye on the hallway Rosie had just walked down. "Because her real dad is such a douche. And no offense, but her mom couldn't give a shit."

Elin glanced up. Will was staring at her with his red-rimmed, slightly stoned eyes, hands unmoving in the dough. For a second, Elin thought he would scold her for criticizing his wife—Rosie's mom was a bitch, but she was still an adult—but instead he said softly, "I know."

"I know you love her," Elin said, her eyebrows knit together as she studied his face. "But you have to do better."

Will leaned against the counter, his forehead wrinkling in concern. "Is she okay?"

"Oh yeah," Elin said hastily. "It's, you know, the writing thing. And Teddy. And the tuition thing."

The tension in Will's shoulders relaxed. "Gotcha," he said.

"So you'll do better?" Elin insisted. Will could be too mellow for his own good—for Rosie's own good.

He nodded, his face serious and steady. "I'll do better."

On Wednesday, she stayed in with her parents, offering to cook dinner. She picked vegetable stir-fry, which she knew neither one of them were terribly fond of—no sense in ruining favorites like chicken piccata or grilled salmon for them in the future. Her parents seemed to think that she was about to ask for something. She caught the surprised glance they exchanged when she told them goodnight.

She collected all the books and DVDs she had borrowed from Teddy over the years in a box and labeled it *Teddy Lawrence*, just so her parents would know what to do.

For Jenna, Elin couldn't do anything particularly out of the ordinary. They studied together at Elin's house on Thursday night, the night before, like always, except for one thing. Elin loved studying with the television on in the background, a habit Jenna barely tolerated. That night, without saying why, Elin turned off the TV as soon they opened their textbooks. Jenna glanced up at her, a pleased but puzzled smile on her face. Elin shrugged, smiled, and turned back to studying.

And then she went through with it.

Elin remembered staring at the ceiling of the bathroom, during, and feeling like time was slowing down. Every blink took an eon, her lids heavy. *They're the top of my coffin*, she thought dreamily, and the thought repeated itself in her brain. *Top of my coffin, top of my coffin.*

The water was warm and kind of pretty. Pink, with a growing red cloud by her left wrist. Just one wrist, because when she took the razor blade in her other hand, she was already too dizzy to finish. It didn't hurt. It felt like someone else's arm.

Her mouth tasted bitter from the wine, and she wished she'd thought of mouthwash, but she was too tired to stand up and get some, and the taste was fading anyway.

Elin smelled lilacs, the candles she'd lit. Her favorite smell. She'd heard in science once that the sense of smell is the oldest, evolutionarily-speaking, and the last to go. She didn't know if that was true or not, but if it was, she wanted her very last thought to be lilacs.

Elin didn't remember the door to the bathroom opening.

Elin didn't remember if she screamed or gasped or simply sprang into action.

She just remembered the paramedics.

After.

33

Ket West-Beauchamp
April 18, 11:00 PM

You would think, as the only daughter of a lesbian couple, that I would be well-versed in the ways of Ladyhood. Not so. Neither of my moms ever covered how you're supposed to sit on a dirty sidewalk in a sequined mini and keep your lacy delicates under wraps. I sat on the edge of the curb, trying to minimize the damage to my dress, ankles crossed to the side and thighs locked together like my life depended on it.

Jenna leaned on my shoulder, nearly passed out.

It was hard to stay mad at someone who was barely conscious, but I'm a trooper. I stared straight ahead, waiting for our ride and refusing to talk to her.

After Rosie and FDR decided to continue their wild goose chase looking for Elin, I stayed with Jenna, waiting for a ride to take us back to prom. Where Jenna would work her magic to get Hannah away from Ben for the evening so Elin could finally talk to him.

And then I would work my magic on Vaughn.

Listening to Jenna's semi-snores as my ass went numb had done wonders for my resolve. The more the minutes ticked away, the easier it was for Outer Ket to rationalize our actions to Inner Ket. I was a liberated woman, right?

I knew how birth control worked. And if Vaughn did break his word and our little tape found its way into the Big, Wide World, well. Screw the haters, right? Sex Positivity, Freedom of Expression, and All That?

Sure. That'd work.

The only trouble with this rationale was the person I'd had to call for a ride. Because even though Jenna's car was still right-freaking-here, it hadn't occurred to me until it was too late that Rosie—the only other person in the world I knew who could drive stick—had just run off with Fisher's date.

Teddy's car pulled up to the curb right as Jenna finally passed out, her head slumped onto my shoulder. He rolled down the passenger side window. "Are you guys okay?"

"Yeah, I think so," I said, eyes on the sidewalk as I wrapped my arms around Jenna's waist and tried to hoist her up. She slumped limply, her eyes slitted and glazed. I ground my teeth and resisted kicking her. "Scratch that. Could you help me?"

We were able to get Jenna settled into the backseat, belted in as best we could. I tried twisting around to inspect the state of my butt before climbing into the passenger seat, but the cat-calling from the bar's patio told me I was better off just climbing in the car and conducting my derriere inspection in private.

"So you guys still have no idea where Elin ran off?" Teddy asked as he buckled himself in and started the car.

I glanced at my cell phone. My last two texts to Rosie had gone unanswered. "Not yet," I said. "But I'm sure she'll turn up soon."

"Yeah, I'm sure," Teddy said, his voice tense.

I glanced over at him. His eyes were glued to the road, but the dim neon of the dash revealed his jaw was clenched.

I glanced down at my lap, ashamed. "Teddy, I'm seriously so sorry."

"What the *fuck*, Ket!" Teddy burst out, the muscles in his forearms corded as he gripped the steering wheel. "You beg me to come to prom, and then the first chance you get you send me off to play chauffeur for *Fisher Reese*?"

I leaned my elbow against the car door, propping my head against my fist. Teddy wasn't an idiot, so I had two choices: tell him the truth, that I couldn't stomach the idea of him being around while I planned to sleep with Vaughn again, or give him an excuse he would believe.

I wished I was a good person, the sort of person who wouldn't have the perfect lie pop right into her head. But I wasn't a good person, and I knew exactly what I could say to get Teddy off my back.

Rosie likes FDR and I was trying to wingman for her—she wouldn't have even smiled at him with you around.

Simple.

Believable.

Heart Shattering.

In one sentence, I would save myself—and undo two months of bridge-building I'd been doing for Rosie and Teddy.

Which was no choice at all. I couldn't hurt Teddy or Rosie.

But the thought of Teddy finding out about Vaughn . . . unbearable.

The silence between us stretched into an eternity. "Would you believe me if I promised to explain everything tomorrow?" I whispered, voice cracking.

I thought he would yell but nothing came from his side of the car. For ten minutes, we drove back to school in silence.

"Do you hear that?" Teddy asked suddenly as we were stopped at a red light.

I turned in my seat to check on Jenna. "Jen? You okay, dude?"

She mumbled something incoherently, one arm thrown over her face like she was blocking out the sun. She raised the other and knocked it into the back of my seat.

"Is she reciting SAT words?" Teddy asked incredulously.

I rolled my eyes. "Probably." I twisted back around. "Jen, is there a word that means 'person who commits misdemeanors?'"

Jenna groaned, and for a second I thought she wasn't going to answer. "Misdemeanant," she said finally, voice raspy and thick. "Why do you need to know?"

Teddy and I looked at each other. Teddy's lip twitched as he tried to hold back a smile. He glanced up at his rearview mirror, twisting it down so he could see her. "I'm not impressed until you translate that into Chinese," he said.

"Fuck off, Lawrence," Jenna muttered.

Teddy snorted, choking on laughter. The light turned green and he accelerated, turning the radio on low. He glanced at me out of the corner of his eye and nodded. I smiled, relief spreading through my chest as we drove the rest of the way to school.

Finally we arrived back at the dance. Teddy put the car in park, but he didn't shut the engine off. We sat in the idling car, listening to a check cashing company commercial, neither of us saying a word.

"I wish you guys would tell me what is going on," Teddy said, softly, so just I would hear over the music.

I turned to stare out the window. "It's not our secret to tell," I said finally.

And then Teddy did something he had never done in almost ten years of friendship.

He reached across the console and took my hand.

My breath caught in my throat. Teddy laced his fingers through mine, his skin rough and warm. I broke out in gooseflesh when the base of his palm pressed against mine.

He's just being a friend. He's in love with Rosie.

Yeah, tell that to the Naughty Tingles in my loins.

I swallowed, hoping that he couldn't tell how much his stupid hand in mine affected me.

"How big is the trouble that Elin's in?" Teddy asked softly.

I bit my lip. "Big," I admitted.

"Then you can tell me tomorrow."

34

Rosie Winchester
April 18, 11:00 PM

I stared out at the passing buildings. The roads glistened under lamplights, the only evidence of the snow that had fallen earlier in the evening. Elin had left FDR's car unlocked, keys in the ignition, and for once I was grateful for her natural flakiness. I gripped the handle above the window nervously, flipping my phone open and shut with my other hand.

"Who still has a flip phone?" FDR joked, breaking the silence. "Is that thing an antique?"

I stopped flipping my phone open and shut. "I'm on my dad's cell phone plan."

FDR glanced over at me. "That's not an answer."

I shrugged. "My dad gave it to me. My mom wanted me to have an iPhone, but he said they were too expensive. He thinks my mom is materialistic and that I'm always on her side, so I acted like my flip phone was the coolest, even when all my friends were getting smartphones."

FDR smiled faintly. "That's kind of a sweet story."

I shrugged again. "Not really." I stared at the dash of FDR's car—red and blue neon lights, glowing like a spaceship.

"How so?"

I paused. I had never told anyone the rest—not even Teddy. But FDR was a stranger, a guy I would never see again. I felt the words bubbling up and out of my mouth. "Two years ago, my dad got an iPhone for himself and one for his new wife. The upgrade for my number, actually," I said, turning my phone over in my hands.

"He never even said anything, never explained why it was materialistic when I wanted an iPhone, but normal when his wife did. I was so pissed, but whenever I get pissed, he says I'm acting like my mother. My mom said she would buy me whatever phone I wanted. She said it was to cheer me up, but really she wanted to . . . spite him, I guess. So I asked for a tablet so I could still get online and play music and read, but kept this phone for calls and texting."

FDR said nothing. I flipped it open, flipped it shut. Gone this far, might as well finish. "I wanted to be the one to spite him," I said finally. "Keep the shitty phone he gave me until it broke."

"That's messed up," FDR said finally.

I felt heat creeping up my neck and into my cheeks. "I know."

"Not you," he said. "Your parents. That's messed up."

The knot in my chest loosened with relief that he understood, followed by a familiar wave of shame.

The more I talked about how horrible they were, the more I was like them.

(It's inevitable that I will be like them.)

I tucked my phone into my clutch. "I don't really want to talk about this," I said. "Can we just focus on finding Elin?"

"You got it," FDR said as he pulled up to the curb of the library and turned off his car. Sitting in silence, we stared at the old building. *Elin, are you in there?* I wondered.

Ever since she was a kid, Elin had had a thing for this building. When other kids were having birthdays at McDonalds or Lagoon, Elin's parents rented out the children's reading room. Pictures of Elin and Jenna, standing side by side from ages five to eleven, were tacked on the walls in her room at home. Even now that she was older, she liked to meet up on the front steps for frozen yogurt in the summer and hot chocolate in the winter.

If the lawn had been blanketed with fresh snow, we'd be able to see the telltale sign of footprints and know we were on the right track. But none of the snow that had fallen earlier had stuck, and the building was surrounded by dead, raffia-looking grass and heaps of crusty, gray snow. Anyone could have passed by here and we'd have no way of knowing.

For a second, I wished that it were Jenna here, tackling this problem. She never hesitated in the face of a problem. It was truly some sort of cosmic joke that she was drunk and I was here.

Sighing, I opened my car door. (Pretend you're braver than you are.) FDR and I ran across the grass to the library. We crept along the side of the building, checking each window to see if one was open. Part of me hoped that none of them were, that this was a wild goose chase, and I could finally just call the police and have someone else take over.

"Hey," whispered FDR, a few yards down from me. "This one is open."

So much for the wild goose chase theory.

FDR shoved the window open and then both of us stared at the opening, just slightly higher than I could vault into myself.

A beat went by with neither of us saying anything, and then FDR grabbed me around the waist, lifting me without asking. I sucked in a sharp breath. He set me on the windowsill, and I gathered the skirt of my dress around my knees so it didn't catch, swinging my legs into the building. FDR boosted himself up and landed lightly beside me.

I squinted, trying to adjust my eyes to the darkness. We were in the children's reading room. Dr. Seuss cutouts plastered the walls, Sneetches and Thing One and Two and the Lorax.

They were creepy in the dark.

"Elin?" I whispered. I held my breath, straining to hear any reply.

Nothing.

FDR walked slowly to the door, his hands out in front of him to avoid smacking into furniture. "I don't think she's in this room," he whispered. "Where do you think she'd be?"

"The arbor area," I whispered immediately. "It's her favorite."

We made our way through stacks and shelves. FDR pulled out his phone and we advanced to the glow of his flashlight app. There was barely enough light to see four feet in front of us.

Out in the hall, every footstep echoed like a drum.

I shrugged off FDR's suit jacket—it was drowning me anyway. "Thanks," I whispered.

He accepted it in silence, holding his phone between his teeth while he put it back on.

We crept from room to room in the library, FDR holding out his phone to light our way. Shadows shifted between rows of shelves of books. I shuddered, only partly because of the cold—there was something disturbing about buildings you never saw at night.

And then I heard something.

I stopped, frozen in my tracks. "Do you hear that?" I whispered.

FDR didn't reply, but he slowed to a stop. His hand reached back toward mine, and almost unconsciously I felt myself reaching for him in return. Our fingers tangled together and I inched forward on my tiptoes, unwilling to let my heels touch the floor.

"I'm not sure," FDR began, his whisper barely audible. "I thought I did . . ."

I paused, straining my ears. I didn't know if it was my imagination, but I thought I heard . . . footsteps up ahead. My pulse quickened—Elin?

But as the footsteps grew louder, echoing in the empty hallways, I grabbed FDR's arm with my free hand and his grip on my fingers tightened.

The sounds were too loud to be a girl in heels.

The spotlight of a handheld flashlight skimmed over the wall, the footsteps growing louder from around the corner.

I stepped backward, and my heel slid out from under me, sending me tumbling to the ground. I winced at the pain that shot up my tailbone. Without missing a beat, FDR grabbed me under my arms and pulled me off my feet, wrapping his arm around my waist and preventing my heels from clicking against the tile.

The spotlight turned the corner, a barely-visible silhouette approaching.

And FDR pulled me into a broom closet.

35

Jenna Sinclair
April 18, 11:15 PM

Ket snuck me into the teachers' lounge women's room while Teddy went to find some food to sober me up. I blinked against the unflattering fluorescent light, holding up a hand to shield my vision. I groaned.

Was it only a few hours ago that I had looked as stereo-typically prommy as a girl could hope to look? Now my makeup was smeared, my skin pale and greenish. My hair was half curled and half frizzy-flat, so I retied my headband and pulled my hair into a knot at the base of my neck, hoping to gain some semblance of . . . semblance.

On the ride over, I had felt like I was going to die. Not hyperbolically, not figuratively, but *literally-in-the-literal-sense* like I was going to close my eyes and never open them again. I'd drunk too much, taken too many pain pills. I couldn't even remember if I'd taken two or three. I'd spent my whole life being fastidiously perfect and now I was a freaking cliché. What were my parents going to think? What about *Miles*? The thought sent panic coursing through my veins.

I wonder if Elin had felt like this, before. Like maybe she hadn't wanted to hurt herself, but a series of bad decisions just . . . happened?

I'd thrown up on the curb after Teddy and Ket had helped me out of the car, stomach acid coming up and burning my throat, but it had helped a little. I still looked like a sparkly nineteenth-century saloon hooker, though. At least Miles wasn't here to see me—I'd texted him to ask if he wouldn't mind going to Fisher's party and keeping Ben there until Elin could talk to him. He'd texted back that he'd head there as soon as the video game ended.

Ket leaned against the door, a guard against intruders. She was pretending to check her text messages, nonchalant, but I knew she was freaked out. "Are you sure you know what you're doing?"

"I always know what I'm doing," I said. *Equivocate: to use ambiguous language to obscure the truth or avoid committing oneself.*

"After tonight, I'm not so sure," Ket muttered.

I said nothing. She had a point. And I didn't have much fight left in me.

I'd heard on NPR once that many organizations suffer inefficiencies because of something called the "confidence gap." The least competent people were usually the most confident. The most competent people were more aware of their weaknesses, and therefore doubted themselves the most.

I'd dismissed the story. I'd never doubted myself, but I also knew—conclusively—that I was better at everything than everyone. My GPA, my extracurriculars, my teachers and coaches who adored me, my parents who trusted me, my friends who relied on me—it all proved that I had my shit together.

Except now I didn't have my shit together.

And what did it mean that I had never doubted myself before now?

Nothing good, that's what.

I had texted Hannah while Ket and I waited for Teddy to pick us up. I knew better than to just come right out and ask for what I wanted. With Hannah, you always had to dangle the carrot.

Want to double your budget for prom next year?

No other choice, I kept telling myself, there's no other choice. Not if we want Hannah to unlatch from Ben long enough to convince him to call Elin.

It only took five minutes for her to reply.

> **HANNAH:** *Are you serious?*
> *Of course I do.*
> *What's the catch?*

Done and done.

I tried not to think about how everyone would hate me when I scaled back the senior party to practically nothing after the gym prom debacle. Last year, prom had been in a hotel that got trashed, and Holly *still* managed to rent house boats for the senior party, liability waivers and all.

Once I gave Hannah half my budget for her to use on next year's prom, I'd be lucky if we could have barbeque in a park. *Quagmire: noun, one big fucking disaster.*

The trouble was, the only thing that Hannah Larson wanted more than Ben Holiday was the senior prom to end all proms. So. *Art of War* and all that.

I ran my fingers under the tap and wiped at my straying eye makeup. I already felt infinitely more like myself, but Ket was still staring at my reflection doubtfully. "I got drunk," I said finally, keeping my tone even. "But that doesn't mean that this isn't a good plan."

I might have felt like I was walking a tightrope with no net, but if I fell apart, Ket would lose it. She'd been cool for hours, but every time she checked her phone, every time she started gnawing at her fingernails, I could tell she was starting to panic no matter how chill she was trying to act. Some switch inside her would flip and she'd call her moms, call Elin's parents, call the cops, call the National Guard. And then when we found Elin at Coffee Hut or something, completely fine, she'd never talk to us again.

So yeah, maybe I wasn't completely confident that this was the best course of action anymore. But it was still the best idea we had—and that meant I had to act like I was 100% sure.

Fuck the confidence gap.

Ket stared at me, her expression disbelieving. Not for the first time I wondered which of us—if any—would stay friends after graduation. "Seriously, Jen? I think you have kind of lost it tonight. And when I think someone is out-of-control, they're seriously out to sea."

I dabbed some gloss on my lips. With every touch of shine and shimmer I applied, I willed my rage—and my nausea—back down. I smoothed out the line highlighting my lower lip deliberately, feeling my control clicking back into place with every layer of makeup I applied.

When it became obvious I wasn't going to reply, Ket rolled her eyes and went back to scanning her text messages. I gritted my teeth. She had some balls calling me out for getting drunk when she was the one who had blown the entire

Elin situation to begin with. Still. Pointing that out would hardly be productive.

And that's what I needed to do. If I was going to save Elin—again—I was going to need to be at my Jenna-iest.

I stepped back from the mirror, inspecting my reflection critically. It wasn't my best look, that was for sure, but a few steps up from the total mess I'd been a few minutes ago. "Could you find my breath strips?" I asked Ket. "They're in the zippered pocket."

Ket dumped the entire contents of my purse out—passive aggressive—and I tried not to wince. She sorted through my things noisily and then abruptly stopped.

"Jenna, why do you have two phones?"

"What?"

Ket held up two phones and I frowned, reaching for the one with fewer scratches. "This one is mine. That one . . . oh crap."

"This one is Elin's," Ket said, her voice rising as she swiped through the messages. "Why do you have it?"

"I didn't take it," I said, feeling stupid. "She must have put it in my purse for safekeeping." Elin hated carrying a purse of her own.

Ket read through the messages, her mouth hanging open. "What?" I demanded.

She handed over the phone and I read the message from an unknown number. *Hey J, it's Elin. Left my phone in your purse and I can't remember any numbers but my own. I'm fine, had to leave. If I don't see you at Fisher's after prom, I'll talk to you guys tomorrow.*

I pressed my lips together.

Elin, how could you be so selfish?

"Jenna, what the hell is wrong with you?"

I glanced up at her. "What?"

Ket was staring at me. "Dude. Do you know what happened with Elin? Like ... do you know more than me and Rosie?"

"No," I said quickly, sweeping my stuff back in my purse. "I've told you that."

E and I hadn't talked about what had happened. We had been friends since preschool, the sort of friends who you inherit from your parents. My brother Blake was friends with her brother Aron, my sister Holly friends with her sister Cat. I don't even have any memories of a time when Elin and I were not friends.

We talked about everything.

But this was something we didn't talk about.

Which meant that ever since that day, we didn't really talk.

36

Ket West-Beauchamp
April 18, 11:25 PM

I ground my teeth, refusing to call Jenna on her bullshit—because if anyone knew what had happened with Elin, it was definitely Jenna. But I needed Jenna to fix this mess, and fighting with her was never productive.

Jenna resolutely refused to discuss what happened to Elin. And Elin had only tossed a few breadcrumbs in my direction, hints about the final straw that pushed her into making a rash decision she'd never meant to make.

A couple weeks ago, after school, Elin and I were doing homework and Mom Kim was cooking. "What about you, Elin?" Mom Kim asked in an altogether too-casual tone. "Have you heard from any schools?"

It was one of those weird Utah March days. Two days earlier, we had laid out on the patio next to the Angstroms' pool, which was still covered in blue plastic, clumps of dirty snow, and dead leaves. The sun had been bright in a bluebird sky, and even though there was still a chill on the breeze, we put on swimsuits and sunscreen and soaked up the Vitamin D.

That afternoon, it was snowing.

Elin paused, her mug of hot chocolate halfway to her mouth. "No, actually," she said. "I think . . . I might be starting college next January instead."

I stopped typing and glanced over my computer screen at Elin. She was resolutely avoiding my gaze. Not starting college until January? That was news to me.

Mom Kim didn't stop chopping. "Oh, well, that's all right," she said mildly, scooping sliced zucchini into a mixing bowl. "Not everyone has to go at the same pace."

I raised my eyebrows and started to make a snotty reply— *Since when? It sure seems like I have to match Adlai's level of achievement*—but then suddenly it clicked.

College acceptance letters come in early spring—Elin had acted off ever since she broke up with Ben.

Did she forget to send in the applications?

Did she not get in anywhere?

I knew that Elin's grades had only been so-so junior year, which is why she quit her extracurriculars senior year. To focus, she claimed, though it seemed like it had the opposite effect. She was limping along, and only because our more studious friends—Jenna, Rosie, Teddy, and before their breakup, Ben— were propping her up. Even still, she had to at least have the minimum requirements for provisional admittance somewhere.

After Elin had gone home that afternoon, I'd texted Jenna, wondering if she knew anything.

Do you know what the deal with Elin and college is?

And the weirdest part was that Jenna had just written back, *No.*

No follow up. I checked my phone all night, waiting for the panicked, "Why are you asking?" The Jenna Sinclair

Special: *"She applied to the U, Westminster, and San Diego State. This is when those schools will be mailing their admittance letters and I've prepared a spreadsheet of acceptance rates, if you want to see it."*

If anyone would know where Elin had been planning to go to college, it was Jenna, who had been shooting for Princeton since seventh grade. Jenna, who had helped me write every essay and harassed me to make sure I'd filled out every application for a scholarship—not that my grades could justify one, but Jenna could be weirdly optimistic about these things.

The fact that Jenna didn't know and DIDN'T CARE where Elin was going to college was, in my opinion, the weirdest thing about this whole damn semester.

I sighed, pulling out my phone to update Rosie that Elin was fine.

Jenna was frowning. "That bitch," she muttered.

"Who, Elin?"

"No, Hannah."

I raised both eyebrows. "What?"

Jenna looked up from her phone, incredulity written all over her expression. "She wants *more* than my budget to leave Ben alone at the afterparty," she said.

I shrugged. "Give it to her."

Jenna threw her hands in the air. "The senior party!" she exploded, gesturing wildly with her phone. "That was the best I had to offer, and she wants *more*? And who even knows if it will matter—Elin doesn't have her phone so Ben *can't* call her. We're bribing her for, what, the hope that Elin comes to Fisher's afterparty, and that Miles can keep Ben there after Hannah has ditched him? Seriously?"

"What does she want?" I asked, frowning, and reaching for her phone.

Jenna jerked her phone away. "Forget it. I'm telling her no."

I snatched her phone away from her and read Hannah's text message.

I want you to change my grades.

37

Rosie Winchester
April 18, 11:20 PM

My plan to stay away from FDR, to avoid that little shiver running up my spine whenever he came too close, didn't include being crushed against him in a broom closet.

I squeezed my eyes shut. Cheeks burning from mortification. The door had barely shut behind us, clicking quietly into place. My hands were pressed against his chest, my feet barely touching the floor. FDR had one arm wrapped around my waist and one hand holding the doorknob shut, in case it hadn't latched and the door was about to burst open. I was plastered against him, knees to collarbone, and with my butt pressed against the door, there wasn't even enough room to back away.

At least it was pitch-black, because my face was probably crimson.

"Are you okay?" I whispered.

"Yes," FDR whispered, but he sounded strained. I wasn't sure how big this broom closet was, but if I was pressed against the door, I could only imagine he was backed into the handles of brooms and mops.

"Really?" I asked.

A pause. "Not really," he whispered. "Can we . . . rearrange a little?"

I nodded, not trusting myself to speak in the throes of existential humiliation.

Gingerly, FDR released the doorknob. I held my breath, but the door stayed shut, even with my backside pressed against it. I eased back onto my heels so my weight wasn't completely on FDR.

He leaned back, ever so infinitesimally, and pulled my hands out from between us. "Could you, uh . . . well, either put your arms around my waist or my neck?" he whispered, his voice so low it was almost hoarse. In that moment I knew FDR's face was burning as badly as mine.

"Sure," I whispered, and then for a second froze in indecision. Waist or neck? I wrapped my arms around his waist, underneath his suit jacket, trying—and failing—to suppress a shiver as my forearms rested against his hips.

Oh damnit, Ro, get over yourself.

I turned my head and rested my cheek against his chest. "Does that help?" I whispered, trying to keep my voice steady and professional.

(As professional as a girl plastered on a hot college guy in a closet can be.)

"It does," FDR whispered. To my relief—and a twinge of disappointment—his voice already sounded calmer. "Do you have any more room?"

Weirdly, I did, even though I was closer to him than I'd been before. Without standing on my tiptoes and my hands trapped between us, I could breathe again. "Yeah, I'm much better," I mumbled. "Are you?"

"Definitely," FDR murmured, his chin brushing the top of my hair.

And then FDR put his other arm around my waist, his thumb brushing the skin of my bare back, and I felt my heart give an extra thud in my chest—something he probably felt, since I could hear his.

I didn't want to notice anything about FDR, I really didn't. But I couldn't help the running commentary in my brain, checklisting all the boy-differences between him and me.

His chest is so hard.

His waist is thinner than I would have guessed.

He smells kind of spicy.

I'd never hugged a boy before, not even Teddy. My dad sometimes gave me one-armed buddy hugs, and Will had put his arms around me earlier tonight, but it hadn't been anything like this. This full-body, prolonged *touching*.

Despite my almost total-lack of experience, I'd read enough that I got, intellectually, the whole boy-girl-sex-thing. (And the girl-girl, boy-boy thing.) I read *Outlander* back in middle school, after all.

So I don't know what I expected, but not something this . . . foreign.

We stood in silence, the sharp lemony smell of cleaning supplies mingling with the sour mildew scent of used mop heads. I chewed my lip. "How long until we can get out of here, do you think?" I whispered.

I felt FDR's shrug. "It just seemed like one guard, right?"

"Right," I agreed.

"It takes one guard, what, thirty minutes to do a sweep of the entire library?" FDR said softly. "So, probably thirty minutes."

I frowned. "You don't sound so sure."

"Well, I'm wondering if it's not just a standard sweep," FDR admitted softly. "Like if we set off some sort of alarm."

I squeezed my eyes shut. This night could not get any worse. "Which means that he's looking for us, and he's not going to leave until he finds us or is convinced it was a false alarm."

"Right," agreed FDR.

"So . . . we just wait thirty minutes and hope for the first option?"

"I don't see that we have any other choices, unless we're willing to get arrested for trespassing," FDR whispered.

I mulled that over. "Well, at least if Elin is here, she'll probably get caught, too," I said, trying to think of a bright side to being trapped in a janitor's closet.

FDR cleared his throat softly. "Rosie?"

"Yeah?"

"Um . . . I know it's awkward to be in here with me," FDR said, his voice raspy. "I know I've been hitting on you all night, but I didn't pick the broom closet on purpose. I was hoping for something bigger. I'm going to be a total gentleman while we're in here. And . . . after we get out, as well. Always, in fact."

"Oh, totally," I agreed quickly, ignoring the burning of my cheeks. "Me too. Well, not gentlemanly. But . . ."

"Totally," FDR agreed.

The seconds ticked by. I tried to not notice the thump of FDR's heart in his chest, or that it seemed a little faster than normal.

"So how come you don't like me?" FDR asked, his voice slightly cheerier.

I frowned. "Why do you sound happy to discuss that?"

"Because I'm curious," FDR whispered. "And because understanding how you think will always be more appealing than pondering the idea of getting arrested."

"I thought you weren't going to flirt while we were in here?"

"I believe that my exact words were 'total gentleman,' which doesn't preclude a little flirting."

"Well, maybe I don't want to flirt with someone who walked into the barber's and asked for the boy-bander-special," I retorted.

FDR snorted, arms tense as he tried to laugh without making a sound. I squeezed my eyes shut, resisting the urge to bury my face in his chest. What was it about him that made me blurt out whatever was on my mind?

"I'll have you know, my cousin cuts my hair, and she told me this would look good," he said, his voice softer than a whisper.

"Sorry," I said. (It does look good.) I swallowed, and forced myself to say what I really thought. "It's working for you, if that helps."

He leaned down ever so slightly, his lips next to my ear. "I thought you didn't want to flirt?" he whispered, his breath warm on my skin.

I bit my lip, unsure of what to say. FDR brushed one hand over my hair and I tensed. His hand froze. "Sorry," he said. "Is that . . . not okay?"

I bit my lip. "It's not that I don't like you . . . I just don't know you."

There was a pause. "But you also didn't want to *get* to know me," FDR pointed out.

I sighed. "The thing is . . . I don't really do well in . . . social situations. Trust me, you don't want to find out."

"Try me."

Unbidden, my mind flashed back to the night of Teddy's birthday, two months ago. Every year, Teddy's grandparents took him out for a steak and brought him back home before 8 p.m. Teddy and I had begun the tradition of secondary-birthday when he turned thirteen. He would come over to my house and we would watch movies all night. Sometimes Teddy went home, sometimes he didn't. His grandparents were good about things like helping him with homework, but they didn't have the energy to police him.

Teddy was like the sibling I'd never had. He had open-door privileges at our house, coming and going as he pleased. My mom never objected to Teddy sleeping over. Maybe it was just that we'd been friends since we were in third grade. Most likely she assumed, like most of the boys at school, that black eyeliner meant Teddy was gay.

I don't know why it never occurred to me to wonder if Teddy was gay. I figured he probably wasn't since he'd had to cover his jeans with a throw pillow when we'd watched *Blue Crush* in seventh grade, and I'd pretended I didn't know why. But if he'd never expressed any interest in boys, he'd also never told me about girls he was crushing on—and he'd told me everything.

The night Teddy turned eighteen, there was a snowstorm, and Teddy and his grandparents came home from steaks even earlier than normal. I was waiting with an assortment of his favorite treats—popcorn, Mountain Dew, and jalapeño Cheetos. Will and my mom were spending the weekend at the St. Regis. I think my mom finally would have objected to secondary-birthday, knowing she and Will were going to be gone all weekend, but she didn't remember Teddy's birthday at all. Will did, of course, and when he'd side-hugged me goodbye he'd whispered in my ear, "I left a six pack of Coronas in the fridge. Tell him happy birthday for me."

Teddy came in without waiting for an invitation. He kicked off his snowy shoes as I was carrying my array of treats to the living room. "Hey!" I called over my shoulder. "How was dinner? Did your grandpa yell at the waiter again because his Old Fashioned was too weak?"

Teddy laughed, his voice raw from getting over a cold. "A Lawrence family tradition," he said, padding into the living room in stockinged feet. "Did you get it?"

"Duh," I said, holding up a copy of *The Good, The Bad, and the Ugly.*

Teddy, Ket, and I had decided last year that we would watch every movie on the American Film Institute's list of five hundred most important films. As of Teddy's birthday, we hadn't really made a dent, partly because we'd done a lot of rewatching. Teddy had become obsessed with spaghetti westerns, a fact that delighted Grandpa Lawrence.

Teddy and I settled into the couch, snacks between us. Teddy's legs were stretched out on the ottoman, mine were curled up underneath a blanket. It started out just like the last thousand times we'd hung out.

But something was wrong. Teddy usually commented during movies, cracking jokes, grabbing snacks, fidgeting restlessly. That night, he was still as a stone. I could hear the sound of his breathing as much as I could hear the dialogue of the movie.

Finally I looked over at him at him. "You okay?" I asked.

Teddy turned to me, his profile flickering blue and yellow in the light from the television. I could see his Adam's apple as he swallowed. "I love you," he said.

And I froze.

"Rosie?" FDR said.

I squeezed my eyes shut, remembering the look on Teddy's face right before he stood up and walked out of my living room.

"Are you okay?" FDR asked.

I felt a surge of annoyance. "Why are you so persistent?" I hissed. "Why did you even keep talking to me at that party? And don't tell me that it's because I'm 'so cute,' or whatever, since I have been rude to you all night and you just don't give up."

An awkward silence filled the broom closet, wrapping around us like a thick fog. "Do you really want to know?" FDR asked finally, a slight edge to his voice.

"Yes!"

"Fisher asked me to."

I flinched and FDR's arms tightened around me. If I could have jerked away from him completely, I would have. "What?" I asked, my mouth dry.

FDR let out a long, slow breath—I hadn't realized he'd been holding it. "Fisher noticed you weren't having a good time and your friends had ditched you. She asked me if I would try to get you to loosen up."

I nodded slowly, biting my lip.

Damnit damnit damnit. Here I was, thinking this unattainably attractive guy was *annoying* because he liked me so much—and it turned out he only did it because his girlfriend thought I was decreasing the overall level of cool at her party?

I was the personification of "humiliation."

Strands of my hair caught in FDR's stubble as he moved back slightly, like he was trying to look down at me in this pitch-black closet. "Um. Rosie? That sort of came out wrong," he said, his voice hesitant. "Let me explain."

"Yeah, I think I'd rather get arrested," I said, opening the closet door.

38

Ket West-Beauchamp
April 18, 11:40 PM

Jenna knew how to change someone's school record—which blew me away. I mean, if Jenna could fix tardies and grades all this time, *why* was I stressing over detentions and extra credit assignments?

"We could probably use Mr. Hansen's room," I said as the four of us conferred in the hall. "He leaves it unlocked."

Hannah raised an eyebrow in my direction. "How would you know?" she asked, her tone a mixture of disbelief and disgust.

I smirked. Mr. Hansen was in his thirties and the hottest teacher in our school. "I just know," I sing-songed. From the corner of my eye, I saw Teddy glance in the other direction, and I winced. *Seriously, Ket, why does everything have to be a joke?*

In reality, I knew Mr. Hansen left his classroom unlocked because I'd made out with his TA, Dave Applegate, in it a couple times. I would never make out with Mr. Hansen, but the part of me that enjoyed my Supah Scandalous reputation couldn't help but insinuate otherwise.

We snuck up to the fourth floor where Mr. Hansen's classrom was, in fact, unlocked. Hannah gave me another disgusted look, but with Teddy steadfastly avoiding my gaze, I couldn't work up the energy to act superior.

The truth was Mr. Hansen gave me serious skeevy vibes. It wasn't that he ever hit on me—it was more that he expected *me* to hit on *him*. Whenever we met about one of my papers, he made a big show of leaving the door open, but I'd catch him checking me out. If it wasn't so painfully obvious that he was doing it because he expected me to try to jump his thirty-something bones—*Oooh, tell me more about your Ragnar, Mr. Hansen*—I would have rolled my eyes.

When older guys expected you to hit on them, it was usually because they thought they were hot enough to merit it. They'd act noble for about five minutes, and then they'd reciprocate.

I flirted with Rosie's stepdad because it was funny and she hated it, but most importantly, because I could tell Will was never-ever-ever going to flirt back.

The four of us filed into Mr. Hansen's room. Hannah flipped on the lights and I whirled to smack them off. "Don't be an idiot," I hissed in the dark. "We'll just use the lamp on his desk."

I crept my way forward, holding my hands in front of me so I wouldn't crash into desks. "Wonder how you learned your way around this classroom in the dark," muttered Hannah. I gritted my teeth.

"For someone blackmailing two girls into changing her record on the school server, you're pretty judgy," Teddy snapped. I smiled in the dark. It was nice to have a defender, for once—even if that defender was under the impression I'd hooked up with a middle-aged dude.

I bumped into Mr. Hansen's desk, nearly toppling over in my heels as the pain from a stubbed toe shot through my foot. I hissed in a breath and Teddy whispered, "Are you okay?"

"Fine," I replied, blinking back the tears springing to my eyes. I patted along the edge of Mr. Hansen's desk until I found his lamp and switched it on. The single bulb, barely bright enough to illuminate the entire desk, flared to life. "Okay, Jen, work your magic."

This whole evening had been one long nightmare. Elin's disappearance, Vaughn, Rosie running off on Main Street, hacking Mr. Hansen's computer. Was Jodi Picoult right? Was someone going to need a kidney transplant next?

Jenna sat down behind the computer and logged on, setting the bottled water and bag of Fritos Teddy had bought her on top of a pile of Mr. Hansen's ungraded papers. I glanced back at the doorway, wondering what would happen to us if someone walked by, and sat down at a desk in the front row.

Months ago, Teddy, Elin, and I had been painting sets for the winter play after school. Teddy was doing it for fun, I was doing it because it was part of my final project for Art III, and Elin because she needed extra credit. Rosie, who had no interest in art but who wanted a good excuse to delay her mid-week drive down to her dad's, had gone to get us cheeseburgers while we worked late.

Elin had been sitting on the stage. She was doing makeup projects—all year long she had been a few weeks behind on homework, only doing as much as necessary to keep teachers and her parents off her back. Most were taking pity on her, offering huge amounts of credit for tiny bits of effort. Not Mr. Hansen. He wanted a fifteen-page paper on the social, economic, and political forces behind the French Revolution. Everyone who had turned it in on time had only had to do ten pages. Elin had written a whopping paragraph.

"I don't know why you're complaining; I'm sure Rosie and Jenna will help you finish it in time," Teddy had said, brushing dark brown paint to create shadows on the tree trunks.

"Mr. Hansen is a pervert," Elin had said bitterly.

"No joke," I had replied cheerily, flinging a paint splatter in Teddy's direction.

I couldn't remember what any of us said after that. Why didn't I pay attention? What did it mean that she said, *Mr. Hansen is a pervert* instead of *Mr. Hansen is a hardass*?

Why had I never insisted on her explaining what put her in the hospital?

Why had I spent so much energy being a fun friend instead of a good friend?

Teddy, who had been hovering near Jen, pulled out the chair next to mine and sat in it, his leg just a few inches from mine, his arm brushing mine. I bit the insides of my cheeks, resisting the absurd urge to rest my cheek against his shoulder. This was one area in which I could continue to be a Good Friend.

"Is this seriously happening right now?" he muttered under his breath.

"Apparently," I whispered back, refusing to lean an inch closer to him than a Platonic Bestie would.

He turned toward me, ever so slightly, and suddenly his mouth was a breath away from mine. I inhaled sharply. His lips parted slightly, like he was about to say something. I felt my breath catch in my throat. He blinked, like he had briefly forgotten what he was going to say.

He's going to ask about Elin.

He's going to say we should be grabbing Jenna and bailing.

He's going to say he was totally lying this afternoon when he said he was over Rosie.

He will never be over Rosie.

"How are you going to avoid getting caught?" Hannah asked suddenly, and Teddy and I both jumped at the sound. For the first time, she sounded doubtful about Jenna's plan. "If someone notices that my records were changed, won't they be able to figure out that they were changed on prom night? On Mr. Hansen's computer?"

Jenna paused her frantic typing. "It's not the CIA," she said, and even though we needed Hannah's help, she couldn't manage to keep the scorn out of her voice. "Even if someone notices, which I doubt, no one is going to search the meta-data and figure out when it changed."

"But what if they *do*?" Hannah insisted.

Jenna sighed. "If they do, it's going to lead back to Josh Bowman. I used his universal log-in, not mine."

"Where did you get Josh's log-in?" I asked, relieved to have an excuse not to worry about my heart pounding out of my chest.

"He leaves it on a Post It so he doesn't have to remember his password," Jenna said. "Which means it could be literally *anyone* Josh has ever let behind the front desk in the office, so every cheerleader and half the girls' soccer team."

"Why do either of you have a universal log-in?" Teddy asked.

"Because we're office assistants," Jenna said, as if that explained everything.

"So what?" Teddy asked. "Do you need to be able to access student records to utilize the stamp pass? Which, might I add, you have never shared with me."

Jenna paused again, staring at Teddy and looking seriously offended. "The stamp pass is *sacred*, Teddy."

Teddy threw his hands in the air. "You're changing a permanent record, but you can't share a few 'get out of class free' slips?"

"Shh," I said, glancing back at the door.

Jenna sighed, turning to Hannah. "Just trust me, okay? After tonight, your unexcused absences and tardies are things of the past. I've changed your transcripts, but the teacher database is going to stay the same, so if anyone notices, play dumb. They'll assume there was a clerical error when the grades were entered into the final record. No one is going to figure it out."

"So long as you guys don't say anything," Hannah muttered.

"Why would *we* say anything?" Jenna hissed.

Hannah shrugged and I felt a burst of annoyance toward her. No wonder Jenna had been complaining about her for weeks—girl was dumb as a rock.

Jenna pointed at Hannah, her face stern. "Now, I need you to remember something, Hannah. You start feeling guilty or scared about any of this? Or you don't follow through with leaving Ben alone at Fisher's? You can forget about getting my senior party money."

"*And* we'll tell everyone about the tugger you gave Josh," I added, standing and stretching.

Hannah's mouth dropped open. "You told her about that?" she asked.

Jenna smirked. "I tell my friends everything. So yeah, don't forget about the handjob, either."

"I didn't give Josh a handjob," Hannah snapped. "I made out with him, but that's it."

Jenna shrugged. "Not the way he tells it."

"Well, he's lying!" Hannah hissed.

I smirked. "Sucks to have everyone assume you're doing stuff you aren't, right?"

Teddy glanced at me, his expression unreadable in the golden light from the desklamp.

Hannah rolled her eyes. "What, are saying that your reputation is undeserved?"

I crossed my arms over my chest. "I don't have to be ashamed of anything because I don't think sex is shameful," I said loftily.

"Oh yeah, I'm sure that what you and Mr. Hansen have is just *beautiful*," Hannah said, rolling her eyes and tossing her hair. "Later, bitches."

I pursed my lips. "Seriously, what a hypocrite," I muttered, sitting on the edge of Mr. Hansen's desk and avoiding Teddy's gaze.

"Ket," Teddy said, and for one minute, I hated him for the pity in his voice. "Do . . . do people assume stuff . . . that isn't true?"

I snorted. "Nah," I said. "But I've never felt bad about any of it, so I don't know where she gets off, trying to guilt me."

Jenna turned off Mr. Hansen's monitor with a soft click. "Shut the fuck up, Ket."

My jaw dropped. "Excuse me?"

Jenna stood up, her lips pursed. "You heard me. I am so sick of your 'I'm a slut and I love it' bullshit, because you clearly do not love it."

"Jen," Teddy said warningly.

Jenna held up her hand. "No. She thinks her track record of asshats is inevitable, but when she's got a shot with a nice guy, she ruins it."

I slid off the desk and turned to face her fully. "Oh yeah, Jenna? What do you know about it?"

"I know Dave Applegate liked you!" Jenna said, standing up and putting her hands on her hips. "But you kept telling him, *oh, we're just hooking up* so finally he asked Lucy-Jean out."

"So?"

"So?! Trace *wanted* to date you, dummy, but you blew him off so he found a girl who knew how to put out emotionally! And *that's why*, Keturah West-Beauchamp, you can kiss irony's ass!"

I stared at her. "Are you done?" I asked through gritted teeth.

Jenna slumped back into the desk chair, shutting her eyes. "I don't feel so great," she said, her voice returning to normal.

"Yeah, because you're drunk and you've lost your damn mind," Teddy muttered.

Jenna opened her bloodshot eyes. "Don't act like I'm crazy when you know it's true," she said, her voice low and raspy. "Seriously, Teddy, are you going to pretend you don't know the only reason Ket has never made a move is because she's sure that a nice guy like you wouldn't want her?"

I froze. Next to me, Teddy's eyes widened and his jaw dropped open.

For one second, none of us made a sound. If Outer Ket could have said anything, she would have whispered, *"Awk-ward."*

But even she was at a loss for words.

A look of horror crossed over Jenna's face, about three seconds too late. "Oh shit," she whispered.

I couldn't look at Teddy. Couldn't look anywhere except Jenna's face, which was rapidly filling with regret.

I yanked open the door to Mr. Hansen's room and ran out into the hall.

39

Rosie Winchester
April 18, 11:40 PM

Luckily, there was no one in the hall when I stepped out of the closet. FDR muttered a sharp curse under his breath, but I barely heard him. "I think the coast is clear," I said, bending down to take off my shoes just in case. "We better get out of here before he comes back."

"Rosie . . ." FDR whispered.

"We have to find Elin," I said, trying to pretend that the pit in my stomach was from worry over my friend and not mortification that I'd been so full of myself. (Bad friend, Rosie Winchester. Bad, bad friend.)

"Rosie, could you let me explain?" FDR hissed, grabbing my arm. "Don't just run off."

"We have to get out of here before we get caught, and I don't think Elin is here," I whispered. "This idea was stupid."

I've never gone on a date. I've never been kissed, although I told my friends I had. I've never even *wanted* to go on a date or be kissed.

But for one second in that closet, I thought about . . .

I don't even want to think about what I thought about.

My phone buzzed in my purse, and I fished it out, hoping FDR didn't notice.

KET: *We've heard from Elin.*
Don't know where she is, but she says
she's okay.
We're hoping she comes to Fisher's
after-party.

Of course she was fine.

Of course I had humiliated myself for absolutely no reason.

I should have stayed home.

(I should go home now.)

FDR grabbed my elbow. "Hey, don't just run off," he whispered.

I shook him off, trying to find my way back to the window where we'd come in. "Ket heard from Elin, she's fine," I hissed. "We broke into a library for nothing."

"Well, that's a good thing, right?"

I stopped suddenly and FDR stumbled into me in the dark. We both cursed, clutching at each other as we fought to stay upright. I reached in the darkness and found a small table—we were back in the children's reading room already. I let go of him and stumbled my way back to the window.

"Could you listen to me for just a second?"

"Why? Fisher isn't here to make you."

FDR groaned behind me. "I wish I hadn't said that."

"I'm glad you did. I prefer the truth," I muttered, wrenching up the window we'd snuck into. I tossed my shoes out onto the grass.

FDR grabbed my arm before I dove out the window. "Don't hurt yourself," he whispered.

"Don't patronize me," I snapped.

"Just let me help you," he said, a hard edge to his voice.

I clenched my fists, fingernails digging into my palms. "Fine," I said, holding out my hand.

FDR lowered me out of the window. As soon as my feet hit the ground, I let go of his hands, slipped into my shoes, and turned to walk across the lawn, struggling to stay upright as my heels sank into the ground.

I heard a thump behind me as FDR jumped out of the window. I didn't turn, but his footsteps quickly caught up to mine. "Will you please let me explain?" he said, voice louder now that we were outdoors.

"What is there to explain?" I said, my voice even.

"Fisher wanted me to talk to you, but I wanted to *keep talking to you*," FDR said, his voice a rush. "You're pretty and funny, and I asked you to dance because I *like* that you're kinda mean, not because my cousin asked me to."

I stopped and FDR bumped into me for the second time. "Your cousin?" I repeated, turning to face him.

FDR stared at me, his eyes wide and his mouth snapped shut. "Yeah," he said finally. "My cousin. I keep telling you, I'm not really on a date with her."

Fisher Reese had to ask her cousin to prom? I scrambled for something else to say. "So does this make you FDR Reese?" I joked weakly.

FDR smiled, his face only half illuminated in the moonlight. "At this point, you're going to have to ask before I tell you my name."

I paused, the words on the tip of my tongue, but FDR started toward the car and I followed him. "I can't really explain," he said, pulling his keys out to beep open the car. He opened the door for me and I climbed inside, my thoughts about two steps behind what he was saying. "You won't tell anyone, right?"

"Of course not," I said dumbly. He shut the door gently.

I buckled myself in as he climbed in his side and started the car. "So, I know the cousin thing kind of comes out of nowhere, but are you not going to react at all to the other stuff I said?" he asked, his voice overly light.

"What other things?" I asked dumbly.

He laughed. "Um, the part where I said I think you're pretty and funny and mean, and I like you?"

I glanced out the window, my amusement melting away. "Don't make fun of me."

"Make fun of you?" he repeated. "Why would you think that?"

I pursed my lips. "Could you just take me to my house, please?"

"Yeah, of course," he said slowly. "But I need you to understand something—I am not making fun of you when I say that I like you."

I turned to him, injecting as much scorn into my expression as I could. "Oh really? The attractive college guy isn't making fun of me when he says he likes me?"

"To be fair, you also basically said you hate my hair, so I can't be that attractive," FDR countered, a half grin making a dimple appear in one cheek.

(Damn him.)

I glanced away again.

"Oh, so we aren't joking?" FDR said, keeping up the conversation as if I had replied. "Okay, then I will be serious. I like you, and I think you like me too. And it's fine if you never want to talk to me again after I drop you off, but I want you to know that I think you're gorgeous and I like that you make jokes about Spencer Tracy, and I would like to get to know you better. I am *not* making fun of you. What kind of assholes do you spend time with, by the way?"

I turned to him. "What?"

"What kind of *assholes* do you spend time with?" he repeated, his voice tinged with anger. "Why would you hear a compliment and jump to '*He must be making fun of me?*'"

I blinked. "I don't spend time with assholes," I said, irritated.

"Really? Your parents aren't assholes? Because that cell phone story was pretty ridiculous."

I paused. "Oh. I wasn't thinking about them."

FDR snorted. "So you agree, they're assholes?"

I crossed my legs, wishing I knew how to not respond to him. "Kind of. I guess."

FDR shook his head ruefully but didn't reply. I drummed my fingers on the armrest, my stomach clenched. I flicked my gaze over to him, but he was resolutely staring at the street. I frowned. "Why aren't you saying anything?" I blurted.

He raised one thick eyebrow and glanced at me out of the corner of his eye. "You want me to talk now?"

I blinked. "Well . . . yeah. You've been talking all night."

"You have been telling me that you dislike me all night," FDR retorted.

(Direct hit.)

"I . . . have not," I stuttered, my cheeks burning.

FDR shrugged, but said nothing. Outside, lampposts turned into glowing white streaks outside my window. Sweat broke out over my skin. The temperature inside the car was blistering—I flipped my heat vent away. Without taking his eyes off the road, FDR reached over and turned the heat down on the dash.

Something prickled behind my nose. I turned to the window, blinking rapidly to keep the tears that sprang to my eyes from falling.

It had been a long night and I was upset about Elin.

(I was upset about FDR.)

(Upset about whatever it was that was wrong with me.)

"I'm sorry," I said, swallowing hard to keep a tremor out of my voice. "I don't dislike you. It's just that ... you make me uncomfortable."

"I don't want to make you uncomfortable," FDR said softly. No hint of a smile on his face. No laughter in his voice.

I glanced down at my lap. "It's not you. It's me. I'm a disaster."

FDR said nothing in reply, but I felt the car begin to slow. We pulled over, the engine still running, and FDR put the car in park. I turned to face him, like a magnet. Like a tide to the shore.

The blue and orange lights of his dashboard reflected off his skin. He looked like a hero in a Frank Miller comic book cell—black hair falling over his forehead, faintly reflecting blue, the right side of his face hidden in shadow, the left glowing softly orange, all sharp cheekbones and thick eyebrows.

I swallowed, and for one second wondered what I looked like in his eyes.

FDR unclicked his seatbelt, turning in his seat to face me. "You keep saying you're a disaster, but I don't see it."

I laughed, but it came out all wrong—bitter and harsh. "You want to know why I am so mean? Because I think I like you too, all right? And that's why—"

His mouth met mine before I could finish my sentence.

40

Jenna Sinclair
April 18, 11:50 PM

After Ket ran out of Mr. Hansen's room, Teddy and I avoided looking at each other. "Should I . . ." Teddy trailed off.

"Go after her? Um. I don't think so. Should I?"

"Definitely not," Teddy muttered.

Bereft: sorrowful through loss or deprivation.

We turned off Mr. Hansen's lamp and crept out of his room. We wandered out to the stairwell, where I slumped down to sit on the top step, my skirt floofing out around me like a sad parachute. Even though I didn't ask him to, Teddy sat down beside me.

"What time is it?" I asked.

Teddy checked his phone. "11:52."

I nodded. I had done everything I could do, but I didn't feel triumphant. I felt hollow. "So Fisher's after-party has started. We just have to hope that Elin goes and that Miles can keep Ben there until she does."

"Are you going to tell me what is going on with Elin?" Teddy asked softly.

I stared at my dress, the millions of tiny pink circles that made up the netting of my skirt. "I read somewhere that if you're friends with someone for seven years, you'll be friends with them for life," I said. "And I thought, *That is so comforting.* I don't always get along with Ket, and Elin drives me insane, and sometimes I worry that Rosie will just disappear on all of us. But you hear that number—seven years of friendship—and think, *everything will be fine.*"

Teddy said nothing and I felt my eyes filling with tears. "And then I finished the article and realized the findings were only for people who become friends after high school."

The two of us sat in silence for a moment.

Teddy cleared his throat. "Jen?"

"Yeah?"

"I can't promise you that we will be friends forever," he said.

I nodded, my chin quivering.

"But I promise you that I will stay your friend for at least seven years after graduation."

I burst out laughing, my tears spilling over. "Thanks, Teddy," I sniffled.

Teddy slung one arm around my shoulders and I leaned into his side. "No problem," he said gently.

I leaned my head against his shoulder and shut my eyes.

April 19, 12:40 AM

I jerked awake, wiping my mouth with a clumsy hand. I blinked, trying to orient myself. "Did I drool on you?"

"Nope," Teddy said. "But you did snore."

"I did not," I said indignantly.

"Did so."

"How long was I out?" I asked, rubbing my cheek. The pattern of Teddy's houndstooth coat was imprinted on my skin.

He shrugged and held up his phone. "Long enough for me to watch two episodes of *Golden Girls.*"

I groaned. "You too?"

Teddy cracked a smile. "It's funny. You'd like it."

I rubbed my neck, wincing as my sore muscles resisted moving. "Do you think you could take me home in a little bit?" I asked. "I don't want Miles to see me like this."

"Of course. Bros before hos."

I smiled. "Are we bros or hos?"

"We're bros. Miles is a ho."

"Can I ask you a question, bro?"

"Shoot."

If it doesn't go well, I'll blame it on being drunk.

"Do you really love Rosie?" I asked. "Or do you love the idea of Rosie?"

Teddy froze beside me and I waited. "I think . . . I did," Teddy said finally. "One of those two. I don't know."

I nodded. It wasn't much of an answer, but I knew he was telling the truth. Sometimes the truth just didn't make sense. I inhaled, held the breath, and then slowly let it out. "Elin tried to kill herself," I whispered.

Teddy squeezed me tighter. "I . . . I thought that might have been it," he said, voice soft. "Hoped it wasn't, but thought it was."

"Why didn't you ask?"

"I didn't want to know."

I stared at my feet. "I'm sorry I told you what I did. About Ket. Please don't let it make things weird. I should have kept my mouth shut."

Teddy opened his mouth, shut it again. "The thing about that . . ."

My phone rang and we both jumped. I stared at the unknown number on my screen. Teddy nodded toward it. "You should answer. What if it's Elin?"

I nodded, swiping to answer. "This is Jenna," I said.

"Jenna?" asked an unfamiliar voice. "You need to get over to my place STAT. Ket is about to make a huge mistake."

41

Ket West-Beauchamp
April 18, 11:50 PM

I ran, trying to ignore the rising nausea in my throat.

I didn't know if Jenna and Teddy were going to follow me, but I suspected not. Not after that shitshow.

And even if they did, I had no intention of going back. I had one thought running through my brain, and one thought only:

Find Vaughn.

Fulfill my end of the bargain, then go the hell home.

I wanted this night over with.

I scanned the crowd of kids streaming out of the gym doors until I saw someone who could help me. "Sam!" I called, waving him over. "Are you going to Fisher's afterparty?"

"Yep," he said, grinning with his arm around his date's waist. She wore the same stinkeye expression she'd had on at the pre-party.

"Mind if I snag a ride?" I asked, falling into step with them.

April 19, 12:20 AM

At Fisher's condo, I had waited until Fisher was busy talking to Lauren Mendoza to hurriedly tell her that I needed to have access to one of her guest rooms for a half hour. She had glanced between me and Lauren, clearly not wanting to talk about anything in front of another one of Park City's richest teenage bitches, and nodded distractedly.

Anything to get the stench of Poor away from you, I guess.

I'd grabbed a cup of jungle juice in the kitchen—the Official Fuel of Bad Decisions—and ran up the stairs, knowing that if I stopped moving, I would lose my nerve.

I hadn't realized that I'd have to sit in Fisher's guest room, sipping an overly sweet cocktail of Potential Blindness, choking down my nausea, while I waited for Vaughn, who said it would take him twenty damn minutes to get there.

I stared down at the phone in my hand, the blinking text message alert. From Teddy: *Will you call me?* My throat closed with unshed tears.

The trouble was, even if I *had* been smart enough to pick Trace over Vaughn, I would have avoided the disaster I'd found myself in, but I still wouldn't be the girl with a wrist corsage. Because as cute as Dave Applegate had been, he was no Teddy Lawrence. And for that reason alone, I would have had to dump him before prom.

A nice guy like you wouldn't want her. I flinched just remembering it.

Even if Teddy hadn't been hopelessly in love with Rosie for as long as I'd known him, he was never going to go for me. And it wasn't that I was damaged goods or anything gross like that. I knew, in my brain, that I had every bit as much human worth as anyone. But the fact remained: guys like Teddy Lawrence—smart, funny, loyal, dorky, *tough* guys— do not end up with girls with so-so grades, big mouths, and deservedly bad reputations.

The look of horror that crossed his face when Jenna blabbed about my own Unrequited Love sealed the deal.

What really sucked was how pathetically wounded I felt.

As if, deep down, despite all my best efforts . . .

I had HOPED.

As if I hadn't known that this story inevitably ended with mine and Vaughn's photogenic debauchery.

I deleted the text from Teddy and put my phone in the bedstand drawer, slamming it shut.

I swallowed the last dregs of the punch. *At least my hair looks awesome*, I thought, and snickered to myself. I set the cup on the ground and flopped back on the bed, my head spinning. The bed was as firm as a hotel's and just as beige. Fisher's parents had no imagination.

This room is going to do nothing for my skintone on film, I thought. I barked out a laugh and clapped a hand over my mouth.

Not the time to crack up, Ket.

There was a knock at the door and my stomach clenched. I propped myself up on my elbows. "Come in," I called, trying to keep my voice steady.

Fisher peeked into the room and the tension in my stomach disappeared. "Can you explain to me why you need uninterrupted access to this room?" she said.

"Because it's all part of the Finding Elin Plan," I said, wishing she'd just go away.

"The part of the plan that you can't explain to me," Fisher said flatly, crossing her arms over her chest. "Even though this is my house."

We stared each other down. Her standing in the doorway, staring down her nose at me, freaking Lady Beyoncé Astoria of Highgarden. Me, sitting up and tucking my legs under myself, all too aware that my dress was a little too tight, a little too short, and a little too low cut.

But seriously.

What else does Keturah West-Beauchamp, the Park City High Bike, wear to prom?

"Why do you dislike me so much?" I asked suddenly.

"I don't dislike you, Ket," Fisher said, but she had a liar's tone in her voice.

I threw my hands in the air. "Seriously? Come on, man. Tonight I had to tell one of my best friends that I blabbed her biggest secret to the absolute *wrong* douchebag, and then that friend ran off, nary to be *freaking* found, and now I have to engage in some seriously disgusting diplomatic relations to make sure that secret never gets out, so can I just have some fuckin' honesty already?"

Fisher glanced behind her in the hall and then stepped into the room, shutting the door with a soft click. "What the *hell* are you talking about?" she whispered.

"We have hated each other forever," I said, my voice rising and not even caring. "You have never invited me to one of your parties before. What is the deal? Just because you're suddenly bud-dy-buddy with Elin, who you've never been friends until now?"

"The deal is none of your business," Fisher said coldly.

"You're an ice princess, you know," I snapped. "You think you're better than the rest of us."

Fisher narrowed her eyes. "You want to know why I don't like you? It's because of that. You've never even had a conversation with me that lasted more than five minutes, but you think you've figured me out. And frankly, it's bullshit that *Rosie Winchester's* best friend is calling anyone an ice princess."

I jumped off the bed, landing on my bare feet. My head swam for a second, but I glared steadily at Fisher. "Don't talk about Rosie. You don't know anything about her."

"You don't know anything about *me*," Fisher snapped, taking one step forward. "You've been calling me a stuck-up, frigid snob since eighth grade."

"If the shoe fits," I said, crossing my arms across my chest.

Fisher rolled her eyes. "Well, if the shoe fits, I guess you're just a skank who sold out a friend to impress an asshole. So I guess I'll take ice princess."

I snapped my mouth shut.

Point.

Set.

Match.

I swallowed, biting back any angry, snotty reply that might have been bubbling up. "You're right," I said finally.

Fisher raised one perfectly groomed eyebrow. "Wow. Didn't know you had that in you. For a second I thought we were going to throw down."

I rolled my eyes and sat back down on the bed. "There's only so far you can push me, okay? This is not the day to rub things in."

Fisher pursed her lips. "Fine. Now, are you going to update me on the Elin situation already?"

I picked up one of the decorative pillows on the bed, hugging it to my chest. "She texted to say she was fine, and that she'd find us later, but Rosie and FDR are still out looking for her."

Fisher furrowed her brow. "Who's FDR?"

"Your date," I said, waving my hand impatiently.

"Oh," Fisher said. Weirdly, she didn't even ask why. She sat beside me, not saying a word.

"You know she won't try to hurt herself again, don't you?" Fisher said suddenly.

Obviously Elin had more secrets than I'd ever guessed.

"How would you even know?" I replied miserably.

Fisher shrugged. "I know a thing or two about a thing or two."

I nodded. I had no idea what she was talking about, but I suspected Fisher was right about that much, at least.

"So what's the deal with the 'disgusting diplomatic relations'?" Fisher asked, making quote fingers. "Real talk."

I sighed. "Vaughn." I flopped onto my back. No more clarification required.

"Let me guess, he wants to raw-dog it or something?" Fisher said, her lip curled in disgust.

I raised my eyebrows at the beige ceiling. "Did the prim Fisher Reese just say 'raw-dog it'?" I joked, turning my head to face her.

Fisher didn't crack a smile. "What does he want?"

I scrunched up my face. If it were anyone but Fisher, I would try to make a joke. But somehow, it being someone I didn't even like made it easier to admit. "He wants to tape us having sex."

"Ket." Fisher sounded horrified. "You can't do that. Vaughn might not keep the secret about Elin, but he definitely won't keep that tape a secret."

"What choice do I have?" I said miserably.

"If you do this, who knows what he will make you do next," Fisher said, her eyes flashing. "He'll have *the tape*."

I sucked in a breath—I hadn't thought of that. "He's not that conniving," I protested weakly.

"He's making you film a *sex tape*," Fisher retorted.

"Maybe I want to make a sex tape," I said, sitting up, trying to get Confident Sexy Ket to take control of this conversation. "It could put me on the path to fame and fortune."

"Yeah, you really look stoked," Fisher said flatly.

I ran my fingers through my hair, trying not to notice that they were shaking. Breathe, Ket. "This may be weird to say, but you seriously remind me of Jenna right now," I said.

Fisher cracked a smile. "Really?"

I laughed, irrationally giddy. "Yes, really. I'm glad you're taking it so well."

"It's a compliment," Fisher said.

"Well, *I* think it's a compliment," I said. "Not too many people seem to get that about Jen, though."

Fisher nodded. "I could see that. I think Jenna is seriously impressive, though."

"She is," I agreed.

We sat in silence for a moment. "I really am sorry about the ice princess thing," I said finally. "I don't know why I even say some things. Well, I know. It's because your life is so effortless and perfect, and mine is such a mess. That's not an excuse, I know. I just . . . my filter is worthless."

She stared at me, her expression unreadable. "I'm sorry I said what I did about Rosie," she said finally. "You're right, I don't know her."

"She's fun," I said. A pause. "But you have to get to know her," I added.

42

Rosie Winchester
April 19, 12:00 AM

I'd read so many books that described kissing as all "soft lips" that I must have forgotten that they covered teeth and came attached to faces.

FDR's mouth was harder, gentler, *better* than I would have expected.

For one second, I froze, and then he cupped the back of my neck with his hand, and suddenly I was kissing him back.

I leaned toward FDR, and my seatbelt snapped me back. I broke off the kiss, opening my eyes. FDR blinked, looking worried with two little crinkles appearing between his eyebrows, but then I unclicked the seatbelt and he smiled, tangling his fingers up through my hair. I pushed off the seatbelt and wrapped my arms around him.

Whenever I had thought about kissing, I'd always assumed I would be bad at it. I flinched when people tried to hug me. But when FDR tilted his head one way, I instinctively moved the opposite direction. When his lips parted against mine, I copied his movement.

It wasn't something I could be bad at.

In books, they always describe how people *taste*, like mint or chocolate or strawberries. If FDR had a flavor, my brain wasn't processing it.

I was already on sensory overload.

His fingers in my hair, sending waves of tingles running over my skin.

His warm mouth on mine.

The stubble on his face softly scratching my chin.

He sucked my lower lip between his teeth and I made a whimpery sound I hadn't even known I was capable of making. I would have been embarrassed if it didn't feel so good. FDR smiled against my mouth and did it again.

It was like instinct. A conversation.

(Do you like this?)

(Yes, I do.)

(Good to know.)

I just had to pay attention.

FDR kissed his way along my jaw and I closed my eyes, running my fingers through his hair. It was softer than I would have thought, even the buzzed sides. He guided my head to one side, his lips pressing against my neck, right where my pulse beat beneath my skin.

"Is this okay?" he whispered, lips still brushing my throat, his breath warm against my skin.

I opened my eyes and leaned away from him. He stared at me, his clear gray eyes locked onto mine, a half smile on his face. I put one finger under his chin, tilting his head to one side. "Totally," I said, pressing my lips against his throat, mirroring where he had just kissed me. He sucked in a sharp breath and I smiled.

The longer the car sat idle, the colder the air in the car became, but I felt flushed. For long endless moments, he was all soft-lips and sweetness. And then suddenly he would tighten his grip in my hair, wrapping his other arm around my waist to pull me closer, his tongue sliding between my lips. Frantic, urgent. Like he couldn't get enough.

And then he'd go back to sweet and soft.

It made my head spin.

"I don't have daddy issues, you know," I said at one point when we came up for air. "Don't think that my tragic family circumstances mean I'm putting out."

(Where did that come from?)

(Channeling Ket, I guess.)

"Daddy issues are overrated," FDR said, looking slightly dazed. He pulled me closer, pressing his lips against mine.

I broke off the kiss. "Shouldn't I know more about you?"

"*Now* you want to get to know me?" FDR asked, grinning and pulling the bobby pins out of my hair so he could run his fingers through it.

"Number of brothers and sisters, favorite food, favorite sport, go," I commanded.

"One older brother named Bronson, steak enchiladas, football," FDR said. "You?"

"No siblings, yellow curry, I can't stand sports," I replied, grabbing his tie and pulling him back for another kiss.

A few moments later I paused, leaning away from him. "Bronson?" I asked. "Are your parents big *Death Wish* fans?"

FDR frowned. "He was named after a transcendentalist."

I shook my head. "The point is, your family must be really confident in the caliber of genes they're passing along. Can you imagine living life as an acne-prone, chubby girl named *Fisher*?"

FDR grinned, and I couldn't look away from his perfect, swollen lips. "Are you trying to get me to tell you my name without you having to ask for it?"

"Of course not." (Lie.)

"I can tell you're curious," FDR said, running one finger-tip along the edge of my ear.

I squirmed, trying not to reveal how much I liked him tickling my ear. "I am not," I said. (Biggest lie.)

FDR smiled, the dimple in his cheek appearing. "Just say the word and it's yours," he whispered, resting his forehead against mine.

43

Ket West-Beauchamp
April 19, 1:00 AM

After we realized we had nothing left to say, Fisher left to attend to her guests, promising that she would tell me if Elin arrived at the party. She didn't ask me to promise not to give in to Vaughn's demands—I guess she knew that nothing she said was going to help make up my mind.

I paced the room, trying to decide what I was going to do. To Sex Tape or Not To Sex Tape? I seriously couldn't believe that was the question.

I scrolled through my phone, hoping for a distraction. And a solution. Or maybe instructions on how to build a time portal. Prom picture after prom picture scrolled through my feed. Ugh, the happiness.

I paused on a selfie Vaughn had taken just thirty minutes ago. He was standing in the locker room at school, making his Patented Sexy Face in the mirror. I rolled my eyes. *He fixed his stupid pompadour.*

In that one second, with that one stupid thought, everything became clear.

It wasn't about embarrassing my moms or Adlai.

It wasn't whether Teddy Lawrence was ever going to look at me like a girl instead of his oversexed buddy.

It was about me.

And the fact that I would rather walk on nails than let VAUGHN HOLLIS touch me one more time.

"I'm not gonna do it," I whispered out loud, if only so I could hear myself say it.

I stared at the selfie, my heart thumping in my chest. Now what? I wasn't going through with it, but I couldn't let him take Elin down, either.

Think, Bizarro Jenna said—only now she sounded like real Jenna.

What Would Real Jenna Do?

"The party's ending," read his caption. *"Adios high school. #prom #senior #natski"*

Natski.

National Ski Team.

I sat back on the edge of the bed, staring at my phone as the idea unfurled in my brain. Holy shit. Was this what being a genius felt like?

I was gonna have to ask Jenna. As soon as she was sober. And I wasn't pissed at her.

1:15 AM

When Vaughn walked through the door, I was sitting on the edge of the bed, leaning back slightly, my legs crossed at the perfect angle so they'd look a mile long, a wicked smile on my face.

I wanted him to get one long, last look before I dropped the hammer.

"Hiya buddy," I said.

Vaughn smirked at me, shutting the door behind him. "Glad this is finally happening."

I widened my smile. "Oh, Vaughn. This isn't happening."

Vaughn hesitated, a brief look of confusion crossing his face. "What?"

I picked up my phone. "*Membership on the National Ski Team is a privilege, not a right,*" I read. "*All athletes agree to conduct themselves according to the values of the team, including integrity and respect, both during competitions and in their personal lives.*"

"What is this?" Vaughn said, his voice rising.

"It's the code of conduct you signed," I said brightly. "It's right on the National Ski Team website, did you realize that? It includes stuff like not drinking underage, which we both know you did tonight, and it even says you can't use profane or abusive language. Do you think Sex Blackmail is covered there?"

"Beauchamp," he said warningly, a dark look on his face. "You are blowing this way out of proportion."

"I'm really not," I said, tucking my phone into my bra. "You can tell whoever you want about Elin, but I will literally destroy you if you do. And holy shit dude, code of conduct aside, can you even *imagine* what sponsors would do if this all came out because you were bullying a suicidal girl? That's such a bad look."

Vaughn stared at me, his jaw hanging open stupidly. He swallowed visibly and plastered on a weak smile. "Hey, Beauchamp. You know I've just been kidding around, right?"

I rolled my eyes. "Sure."

"Seriously," Vaughn insisted, and somehow his voice was back to normal, like he hadn't had an I Just Shit My Pants look on his face three seconds before. "No hard feelings, right?"

Outer Ket wanted to chuckle and agree, just to avoid the conflict. But Inner Ket was running this show. "I have *all* the hard feelings," I said, standing. "Don't look at me ever again. Don't look at Elin ever again. Maybe do some charity work, I don't know. But don't stop looking over your shoulder, because seriously, screen shots are forever."

A muscle in Vaughn's jaw tensed. "You wouldn't."

I shrugged, waltzing past him and out the door. "That's the thing about girls like me, Vaughn. You just never know what we will or won't do."

1:25 AM

I came down the stairs in a daze. *You did that*, Outer Ket whispered, amazed.

Sure as shit did, Inner Ket said with a smirk.

The party was even bigger than it had been before prom, the living room packed with kids. Fisher caught my gaze from where she was standing in the kitchen and raised her eyebrows. *What happened?* she mouthed.

I shook my head, and Fisher excused herself, making her way over to me by the stairs. "I didn't do it," I whispered, glancing around. "I, like, *crushed* him."

Fisher's lips curled infinitesimally upward—which I guess was her version of a grin. "Good," she said.

"Did Elin ever show?" I asked.

Fisher's smile faded. "No. Ben's still here, but . . ."

I swallowed. "Rosie made us promise that we would tell Elin's parents if we couldn't find her at midnight," I admitted. "She's probably already told them."

Fisher's shoulders slumped. "I'm still sure she's fine," she said, the first bit of doubt creeping into her voice. "But I really thought she'd show back up, even just for the chance of seeing Ben."

"Me too," I said, feeling defeated. Elin had said that she'd see us at the party or sometime tomorrow—Awesomely Helpful there, Elin—which meant she was probably fine.

Except, if it was fine, why couldn't any of us find her?

We stood in silence for a moment. Fisher cleared her throat. "You should know, Jenna is asleep upstairs. Teddy helped her into a guest room."

I blinked, my mouth suddenly dry. "Teddy?" I asked, trying to sound cool.

For what may have been the first time in her life, Fisher actually looked abashed. "Yeah, sorry. I was really worried about you, so I called Jenna to talk you out of it. But she got here and basically passed right out before she could even make it upstairs. I don't think she handled the drive all that well."

"Oh," I said, my head swimming. "Um. Did you see where Teddy went?"

"I think he left," Fisher said, glancing around.

I nodded, a mixture of relief and disappointment twisting my gut. "Well. I'm going to step outside and have a smoke," I said finally.

"I'll join you in a minute," Fisher said.

I raised my eyebrows. "What about your poor Grandma?"

Fisher lifted one shoulder, the most glamorous shrug I'd ever seen. "They're both alive. Sometimes I just can't help being a bitch."

I laughed, heading toward the door. "You and me both."

1:30 AM

I stepped out onto the porch, letting the door slam behind me, and glanced up at the stars, heaving a sigh.

"So how was the sex taping?"

I froze and slowly turned. Teddy was sitting on the porch bench, elbows on his knees. Face in shadow.

Fisher Effing Reese. I take back all the nice things I thought about her.

I plastered on a wobbly grin. "Oh yeah. Thanks for the rescue effort, but I really did have it handled."

"Did you," Teddy said flatly.

I swallowed. On scale of Mad to Mount Vesuvius, Teddy Lawrence speaking in that inflectionless tone of voice fell somewhere around one step away from Total Meltdown.

I took a step backward, miscalculating the distance of the stairs and stumbling in my high heels. I swallowed, sitting down on the step in one motion. This Is What I Meant To Do All Along. "Yes, it was handled," I said, staring out at the road and trying to ignore the cold seeping into my under-clothed butt. "You know I'm saving my Sex Tape Virginity for the first available member of the band formerly known as One Direction."

"Could you stop?"

I snapped my mouth shut, refusing to look at him. In all the years I'd known Teddy, he'd never used that tone of voice—low and soft, like every word was coming from some cavern deep inside his chest. "You know Jenna is *so drunk*, right?" I blurted. "All that stuff she said in Mr. Hansen's room—I mean, whoa, right?"

Silence.

"So, if I told you I liked you, you'd say you didn't feel the same way?" Teddy said finally.

I blinked and turned toward him. "Are you serious?" I said finally.

"Of course I'm fucking serious," Teddy snapped. "Why does every girl I say that to respond with, 'Are you serious?'"

I flinched. "Don't," I said, my voice shaking. "Don't compare me to Rosie when you're telling me you like me." I stopped, unable to say anything else as my throat choked closed.

Teddy stood and walked over to me. I refused to look up at him, biting the inside of my cheeks.

He sat beside me. Not touching me.

"I like you," he whispered—whether it was to me, or to himself, I didn't know. "It's not because of Rosie. It's because *I like you.*"

Slowly, like he would bolt if I moved too quickly, I turned to look at him. I forced myself to say it. "What about Rosie?"

Teddy swallowed, his Adam's apple moving in his throat. "Rosie always felt . . . expected. Like she was my missing piece."

I stared at my shoes and Teddy shook his head beside me. "No, that's not right. It's like . . . it's like all four of you are my missing pieces. Jenna has always been with Miles, Elin's with

Ben, and you were out of my league. I just assumed it was going to be me and Rosie. I never thought about another girl until she said no. And when she did . . . tonight, when Jenna said what she said, I thought you ran off because you were embarrassed for me."

I stared out at the street, the old-fashioned lampposts casting long, skinny shadows on this long, skinny street. "You think I'm out of your league?" I whispered.

Teddy bumped his shoulder against mine—friend move. "Ket. Duh. You're gorgeous and funny and three inches taller than me. Of course you're out of my league." He put his hand on the edge of the step, fingers brushing mine.

Not a Friend Move.

"Were you really going to have sex with Vaughn tonight?" Teddy asked suddenly.

I wrapped my arms around myself, trying to keep away the chill. "I don't know. I didn't want to, but I couldn't think of what else to do."

Teddy said nothing, just stared up at the moon. I hadn't realized until just now—the clouds had finally dissipated.

"There's one thing I should say," I said finally. "What Jenna said tonight about my 'act.' It's only partly true. I'm not embarrassed that I like sex. I'm not embarrassed people know that about me. I'm just embarrassed that I've had sex with guys like Vaughn. Because that was seriously, *seriously* the worst call on my part."

Teddy bumped his shoulder against mine again, but then stayed within an inch of my side. Friend-Not Friend.

I chewed the inside of my cheek, impatient for his reply. "So?"

"So what?" Teddy whispered.

"Soo, do you really want to date a super slut like me?" I asked, my voice deliberately light.

Teddy froze next to me. "Ket. Don't say stuff like that about yourself. I would like you no matter what. You should like you, too."

I sucked in a breath. "I like you," I whispered.

Holy.

Shit.

I just told Teddy Lawrence I liked him.

Teddy Lawrence.

I turned toward him. Teddy leaned in. His face was inches from mine.

I jerked back. "Wait. I have to clarify one thing."

Teddy stared back at me. "Okay."

"So you forgive Rosie?"

I expected him to roll his eyes at me, but he never broke his gaze. "There's nothing to forgive," he said simply. "She didn't like me. And anyway, she was right. We would have been awful."

I bit my lip, trying to hide a smile. "So you guys are friends?"

Teddy cracked a rueful smile. "If she wants to be friends after I was such a little bitch."

I pressed my forehead against his, our fingers tangled together. "She wants to be friends," I whispered. "I've got her friendship power of attorney."

His face tilted toward mine.

The front door crashed open and we jerked apart.

Jenna stood in the doorway, her skirt glowing a flaming pink around the edges. Nonsensically, my brain scrambled for an excuse—*we weren't doing anything, I swear!* But Jenna stared right through us, like she didn't even register.

She stumbled down the stairs to sit beside us, not bothering to shut the door. "I want to go home," she said, her voice raw. "Can one of you drive me?"

I patted her on the back awkwardly, glancing over at Teddy. Half his face was illuminated by the golden glow in the hallway, the other half in shadow, the moonlight unable to compete. He wore an unreadable expression. "Yeah, of course," I said to her, looking at him. I bit my lip, one eyebrow raised.

To Be Continued?

Teddy nodded, almost imperceptibly, and I grinned. He may have told me that he liked me five minutes ago, but I still couldn't quite believe it wasn't a total hallucination on my part.

Teddy and I helped Jenna to her feet as I felt the vibration of a text message coming in from my phone. I struggled to pull it out of my bra and swipe it open as the three of us made our way down the walk.

And then I came to a halt, Jenna stumbling slightly beside me. "What?" asked Teddy.

"You guys are not going to believe this," I said.

44

Rosie Winchester
April 19, 1:30 AM

I was turned in my seat, shoes kicked off and my knees tucked up. I had placed my cheek against my headrest. FDR sat across from me, his posture mirroring mine. Between us sat two bags of fast food trash, smelling of sugar and salt and fried fat.

We were a few feet apart, but it felt like we were even closer than we'd been in the closet. There was something weirdly intimate about sitting across from him, him not breaking eye contact with me.

I supposed that's sort of normal after you make out with someone for an hour.

We had finally stopped kissing when FDR heard my stomach growl. "Are you hungry?" he'd asked, pulling on his seatbelt and turning the car back on.

"I'm not," I'd lied, just as my stomach released an enormous gurgle. He'd raised an eyebrow at my stomach, and I'd wrapped my arms around it defensively.

"I'm buying you dinner," he'd said. "Would you put your seatbelt on, please? I've kind of got a thing for safety."

I'd paused, intending to argue with his claim that he'd buy me dinner, but distracted by the seatbelt thing. (Safety first.) But when we pulled up to the Wendy's drive-thru, I'd tried to stop him from paying. FDR responded by grabbing my purse and tossing it in the backseat. "Is it just physically impossible for you to let people be kind to you?" he'd asked.

I'd smiled despite myself. "Sometimes," I admitted.

"That's going to be a problem," he'd said as he handed me my food, his eyes literally twinkling as he studied my face. "Because I really like taking care of the people I like."

And for some reason, I smiled instead of shutting down. "Me too," I admitted.

"Well, here's to that then," he'd said, raising his frosty cup. I clinked mine against his. And then he took the longest possible route to Elin's house.

The night that Teddy told me how he felt about me, I felt ... panic. Like this was the worst thing that could have possibly happened. And even though my life had been darker even since Teddy had removed his friendship from it, I knew that I had made the right choice. Teddy and I were not going to work. *I* was not going to work like that.

Ket and Jenna and Elin had not understood. Like Teddy, they seemed to think that all my grim messed-upped-ness was the perfect match for Teddy's. I didn't even know how to try to explain that every instinct I had said otherwise. Just ... no. How did anyone suddenly see a friend, practically a brother, as someone you wanted to ... date? It felt weird to even think about.

Sitting across from FDR, I finally recognized the feeling that had plagued me every time I met FDR's eyes.

It was the exact opposite of the feeling that told me Teddy was wrong for me.

"So what are you waiting for?" FDR asked, nodding toward Elin's parents' house.

I fiddled with my seatbelt. "To get brave, I guess."

FDR smiled faintly and said nothing.

I'd been so wrapped up in kissing FDR that I hadn't even noticed that Ket had texted me, telling me that Elin hadn't showed up for Fisher's afterparty. That my chosen deadline of midnight had come and gone, and we still had no idea where our friend was.

"What's your real name?" I said finally, still staring up at the house.

FDR grinned. "You won't believe me if I tell you," he said.

I'd always thought those moments they talk about in books and movies—the moments that last an infinity within mere seconds—were exaggerating.

But that moment before I turned around to look at FDR? It lasted a delicious infinity.

"It's Lincoln," he said, his eyes never leaving mine. "Lincoln Baer. But you can keep calling me FDR if you want."

I clapped my hand over my mouth, trying not to laugh. "Seriously?"

He laughed. It was wild—I had never been so worried in my life, over Elin, over Jenna and Ket, and yet as Lincoln smiled at me and I grinned back, I felt a weight I hadn't even realized was there fall off my shoulders.

"I'm going to wait here for you," he promised.

I took a deep breath, my smile fading a little, but I straightened my shoulders. "Thanks," I said. I opened the door, putting one foot on the sidewalk. The combination of the heat of the car and the cold April air made me light-headed. Shivers ran over my skin, and I looked up at the Angstroms' house. I'd give anything to delay this moment.

I turned to FDR—Lincoln—one more time. "I'm glad I got to know you, Lincoln Baer," I said.

A slow smile spread across his face. "Give me your phone number, Rosie Winchester."

I refused to allow myself to smile. "What are you going to do with that?"

He lifted one shoulder, a luxurious shrug. "I'm going to ask you on a date," he said. Like it was no big thing.

Which I guess . . . it wasn't.

I didn't know whether I should smile or laugh, so I just nodded. "Give me your phone," I said, and I saved my number in it myself.

Lincoln stared at me, a half-smile on his face. I couldn't believe I hadn't noticed it before. He and Fisher had the same resting expression—like they were always looking for the bright side of things, no matter how dark it was. "It's going to be okay," he said.

And even though I knew there was no way he could guarantee that, I believed him.

I pulled Lincoln's jacket tighter and took off my shoes to walk up the Angstroms' path on bare feet. It was cold, but I couldn't stand the pinching any longer. I swallowed, wondering what I was going to say to Elin's parents.

(Sorry we lost your daughter?)

(Sorry we let her steal a car?)

(Sorry she doesn't know how to return a text?)

I tried to imagine how my parents would react to finding out I had helped my suicidal friend sneak out of the house for prom, and then lost her. I tried, and failed. The only one I could visualize was Will, and I didn't like to think about Will being disappointed in me.

That's when I saw it. A faint, flickering light coming from the backyard.

Coming from Elin's treehouse.

"Holy crap," I whispered.

And I pulled out my phone to text Jenna and Ket about everything.

45

Elin Angstrom
April 18, 8:07 PM

"Hey, Elin!"

Elin turned. Miles was walking toward her, waving cheerfully, a wide grin on his face. Dress slacks and a dress shirt, no tie or coat. "Have you seen Jenna?" he called. "I've been looking for her everywhere."

She forced a smile, trying to shake thoughts of Ben out of her head. "I'm sure she's off saving the day somewhere," she said. "I'm looking for Ket. I think Rosie and I might split, get some dinner, pick up J when she's done with all this."

Miles hesitated. "E . . . can I ask you something? It's about Jenna. You don't have to tell me if you don't want to."

Elin glanced behind her. A few girls were waiting in line for the ladies' room—a few guys milled around, waiting for their dates. None of them were paying attention. "Sure," she said, leaning against the wall, matching Miles's stance.

Miles's eyebrows knitted together, forming two wrinkle lines on his forehead. "I don't know what happened . . . at the beginning of March," Miles said softly. "But . . . did it involve Jenna?"

Elin felt the color wash out of her face, like she was a faded chalk drawing on the sidewalk and someone had taken a hose to her. "What?"

"Jenna has been acting so weird," Miles said, rubbing the back of his neck with one hand, a worried look on his face. "I mean, she's always intense, but she calms back down, you know, once her project is finished or whatever. Now it's like she's been getting more and more wound up for weeks, and there's no . . . release."

"I don't . . . are you sure?" Elin said. "Jenna is always . . ." She trailed off, unsure of how to end that sentence.

Nuts?

Crazy?

Psycho?

Suddenly the descriptors they'd always used to describe that special brand of Jenna-ness seemed so *off*.

Miles nodded. "I'm sure. I've been waiting for her to tell me what's wrong, but I don't think she's going to. I've wanted to ask you for a while now—"

"Why me?" Elin interrupted. Too loud. Too defensive. Miles glanced over her shoulder and she turned around. A few of the kids had been looking in their direction, but they stopped once they were caught.

Elin turned back to Miles. He looked uncomfortable, but he soldiered on. "It's fine with me if you want to keep . . . whatever it is . . . a secret," Miles said softly, and Elin nodded. "But if it involves Jenna, you're the only person who would tell me. Rosie and Ket won't, you know that."

A faint, bitter smile skittered across Elin's lips. Wouldn't they? Even though he and Rosie were fighting, it sure seemed like Teddy knew, every time he looked at her with his perma-sad eyes. As for Ket, how was Elin supposed to know she hadn't told more people than Vaughn?

Jenna's parents told Elin's teachers, Ket's parents, and Rosie's mom and stepdad. And now Elin's parents, who had been friends with Jenna's parents since before she was born, weren't even speaking to them.

But . . . Miles didn't know.

Which means that Jenna didn't tell him. Jenna, who told Miles everything.

Which means that of all the people who knew, only Jenna had managed to keep Elin's biggest secret to herself.

And if Miles was right, and Jenna had been spinning out of control, ever since March . . .

It was Elin's fault.

And if Elin told him, Miles would know that.

Elin plastered a smile on her face. "I'm sure it's just planning prom and track and stress about AP tests coming up," she lied. "I bet you anything she's better tomorrow, with all this off her plate."

Miles smiled in relief, because Miles always believed the best of others, even liars like Elin. He said something, and Elin said something in reply, but her mind was light-years away. He needed to get back to his game, and he waved as he turned down the hall.

Elin turned, blinking. Trying not to burst out laughing, which was the last thing she wanted to do. But sometimes, it seemed like she didn't have control over her laughter any more than she could control her anger or her tears.

Ben and I are not getting back together, she thought, all thoughts of sushi and the dance erased from her mind.

Ket had told Vaughn, who would tell everyone.

Nothing was going back to the way it used to be.
But worse than all of that.
Jenna was not okay.

46

Jenna Sinclair
April 19, 1:15 AM

Teddy helped me up to one of the guest rooms in Fisher's condo. I felt boneless, weightless. He tucked a throw blanket around me, over my giant stupid dress, saying nothing before he walked softly out of the room, shutting the door gently behind him.

The last thing I wanted to do was dream. I knew what was coming.

But I was just so damn tired.

Capitulate: surrender under agreed upon conditions.

BEFORE
March 6, 8:50 PM

I pulled up to Elin's house and put my car in park, stifling a yawn. For a second, I thought about calling Elin, asking if she could just run my copy of *Frankenstein* out to me, but she'd stayed home from school today with cramps. I turned the ignition off and climbed out of my car—no sense in bothering her when I'd been letting myself in and out of the Angstroms' house since I was eight.

I punched the code to the Angstroms' garage—2232 for Aron, Cat, and Elin Angstrom—and yawned again as I waited for the door to rise enough for me to duck underneath. I was so tired, I couldn't believe I agreed to an evening prom committee meeting on the same day I'd had an early morning officers' meeting and track practice.

The foyer was dark, so I flipped on the lights in the kitchen as I made my way to Elin's room. I didn't hear anything, not even the TV, and hoped that she hadn't already gone to bed. I expected her to be up watching *America's Next Top Model* or something. I was bursting with stories about Hannah Larson—and because Hannah had not-so-subtly been after Ben all year, Elin disliked her even more than I did.

I knocked softly on Elin's door. I couldn't tell if there was any light coming through the cracks. I frowned. Should I just come back the next night? But I was scheduled to babysit the Monroe twins the following day, and I wanted to finish reading during their nap so I would be ready for the quiz on Monday.

I turned the knob and stepped inside. "E?" I said softly, flipping on the light. And blinked in surprise.

For the first time in months, Elin's room was clean, her bed perfectly made. I glanced around, as though she might be hiding somewhere. Did she go to the lodge with her parents?

I spotted my copy of *Frankenstein* on her nightstand, right beside the lamp where I'd left it, and heaved a sigh of relief. I did not want to go buy a new copy. I crossed the room, picking it up and thumbing absently through the pages.

Then I saw a folded piece of paper on Elin's pillow, labelled *Aron, Cat, Mom, and Dad.*

A chill washed over me, and without knowing why, even though it was none of my business, I reached over and unfolded the paper.

I'm sorry. I love you so much. Please don't ask why.

"Oh my God." I turned in a circle, panicked. Where was Elin?

The sound of running water came from Elin's bathroom.

I dropped the paper and my book.

The door opened. I opened the door.

Elin was in the bathtub.

Elin's mouth and nose were under the water.

I ran to her side, slipping on the bathmat, which was soaked through, and banged my knee against the side of the tub. One of the candles on the edge of the tub toppled into the water, and for a second, I thought, *Fire!* but the water put it out.

I reached into the water, turning my white sweater pink, and slid my arms under Elin's armpits. She was heavier than I expected, slippery as a fish, and she hit the tile floor with a wet slap as I fell backward and cracked my head against the knob on the cupboard under the sink. My scalp stung.

Her arm was oozing blood.

I reach for my waist, but I hadn't worn a belt that day, so I turned to the drawers and yanked the first one open so hard it came off its hinges, scattering bobbypins and nail polish bottles everywhere. Elin's flatiron. I pulled it out and wrapped the cord around Elin's arm as tight as I could and pressed one hand against her bleeding wrist as I fumbled for my phone in my back pocket.

"911, what is your emergency?"

"My friend, she tried to kill herself. Hurry, you need to come." My voice was not mine.

"What is your address?"

My mind went blank. The Angstroms have lived one street over and two blocks up from my family my entire life—had I ever known their address? "I've got to call you back," I blurted, hanging up.

I called my dad. "Jen, you better be home in twenty minutes," he said when he picked up, sounding annoyed.

"Dad, where do the Angstroms live?" I gasped, and now my voice sounded like mine.

"What?"

I started to cry. I couldn't believe I wasn't already crying. "Where do the Angstroms live?" I sobbed, pressing my hands against Elin's wrist. "The 911 lady needs to know their address."

I heard nothing for one second. "Are you at the Angstroms'?" my dad asked, his voice flat and calm.

"Yes!"

"Your mother will call 911 and tell them the address. What's wrong?"

I told him and I heard the *ding-ding-ding* of him climbing in his car, the growl of the revving engine. He told me to stay calm and he would be right there. His voice in my ear was even, telling me to check for Elin's pulse, telling me he was a block away, telling me not to worry because Mom had called, asking if Elin had a pulse and telling me it was good that I could find it, asking if I could remember anything from my CPR class, it's okay that I couldn't, just stay calm, he was outside and coming through the door, and then I heard him running and shouting my name over the phone, his voice echoing through the house.

"I'm here!" I screamed, and my dad came through the door.

My dad hit his knees next to Elin, next to me. "Move, Jenny," he said, and he hadn't called me Jenny in years. "Other side." There wasn't enough room for him to kneel down between Elin and the cupboards.

I scrambled to the other side as my dad checked for Elin's pulse. Her face was white, her hair plastered to her cheeks. He tilted her head back and checked her airway. How did I forget that step? So stupid.

My dad reached over, gripping my shoulder. "You're going to do the compressions," he said, his eyes staring into mine, and for some reason him telling me to do them instead of asking me helped me remember how it was supposed to work.

"Her arm," I said weakly, knitting my fingers together over Elin's chest, pressing my palms over her chest. Doctor or not, she would be so embarrassed if she knew my dad was seeing her naked.

"It will be fine," he says. "We've got this, okay? You and me."

I leaned over Elin, my arms straight, counting out loud. I heard a crack and my dad leaned over, his hand under Elin's neck, blowing into her mouth on my count. Her chest rose. I repeated those actions for I didn't know how long, and then my arms got weak and my elbows started to bend and I knew I wasn't doing it right anymore and my dad said *It's fine, Jen, they will be here soon* and then my dad was doing the compressions himself and leaning over to blow into Elin's mouth and I wasn't helping at all.

I leaned back and stared at my dad. I felt so fucking stupid. Captain Von Trapp. Ket calls my dad Captain Von Trapp because his posture is so straight and his hair is always perfect, but he didn't look like Captain Von Trapp anymore. He was starting to panic, and wasn't it a bad sign when a surgeon starts to panic?

I heard footsteps in the hall. "Paramedics!" someone shouted, and my dad and I yelled, "In here!" at the same time.

My jeans were clinging to my skin. I looked down. The faucet was still running, the tub overflowing. I was sitting in a puddle of Elin's watery blood. I should change. Elin would have let me borrow a pair of her pants, she would understand that I didn't want to leave the house in bloody jeans.

My dad pulled me to my feet and me out of the bathroom, giving the paramedics room to work, pulled me down the hall to where my mother was waiting, her face tight and white, and she wrapped her arms around me so tight it hurt, not a hug, a vice.

"What were you doing here, what were you doing here?" she kept whispering into my hair, and my dad wrapped his arms around both of us and I heard him start to sob.

I blinked, staring over my mom's shoulder through the open front door at the ambulance parked at the curb, red and blue lights flashing. "Prom committee went late," I said.

47

Elin Angstrom
April 19, 2:00 AM

Dr. S told Elin to talk about herself in the third person whenever she found talking about her feelings too difficult. If talking was too hard, she should write it.

Once upon a time, a girl with no feelings but sad tried to escape her life. She was rescued at the last moment and sent to a white castle. When she returned to her old life, she found that she no longer wanted to leave—but she still wasn't happy, either.

She didn't know if she'd ever be happy again.

Cheesy, right?

The third person idea was bullshit.

"Hey!"

I sat up, setting my book down. I pushed off my blanket and crawled over to the window, peeking down into the yard.

Rosie, Ket, and Jenna stared up at me, all wearing identical expressions of annoyance.

"Do you know how long we looked for you?" Rosie hissed.

"*Young lady,*" added Ket, hands on her hips. Even with a scowl on her face, she couldn't resist making a joke.

"I texted you," I said, puzzled. "Jenna should have gotten it."

"Seriously?" Jenna snapped, grabbing onto the rungs of the ladder. "That text told us *nothing*, Elin." She began climbing, stumbling a bit as she stepped on the hem of her skirt. I reached out to help her into the treehouse.

One by one, Jenna, Ket, and Rosie crammed into the tree house. All four of us sitting on the wooden, slatted floor, Jenna knee-to-knee with me and Rosie, Ket tucking her legs neatly underneath herself by the entrance. I shared my blankets around and we spread them over ourselves as much as we could, Jenna's skirt doing its poofy part to keep everyone warm. I moved the camping lantern to the center of our circle.

"So," I said, a grin spreading over my face. "How was the rest of the dance?"

"Too soon," Ket said, scowling.

"Sorry," I said, widening my grin. "I know it's not funny."

"It really, really isn't," Jenna muttered.

Rosie was looking around the treehouse. "How long has it been since we were in here?" she said softly, almost reverently.

Ket put her hand on the window sill, looking around. "Jeez. Years, for sure."

"I remember it being bigger," Rosie said.

"We were smaller," Ket countered.

My parents had the treehouse built for me when I was eight. Jenna and I would spend hours up here after school and all summer long; we had filled it with old throw pillows so the floor wasn't so hard. I'd save my allowance and buy things to make it nicer. A shelf to house our model horses. An antique birdcage. A sachet of potpourri that I hung from the ceiling with a ribbon, thinking it made the place homey. After we became friends with Rosie, Ket, and Teddy, the treehouse became filled with books and comics. Jenna brought over an old Igloo cooler and we'd fill it with ice and glass bottles of soda—because glass bottles just seemed more special.

The five of us would hang out for hours, laying on our backs, our feet propped up on the window sills. We'd talk about the adventures we'd have after high school. Jenna knew she wanted to go to Princeton, like her dad, and work for an international philanthropy. She wanted to get married and have two kids and a pool in the backyard. Rosie was going to move to some cool city and live in a lofted apartment over a Chinese restaurant, writing books, and only the four of us and Will would be allowed to visit, and she would only go see her parents when she wanted to. Teddy wanted to become a musician and tour the world and fly his grandparents out to see him. Ket changed her dream weekly—fashion designer, makeup artist for movie stars, a person who created floats for parades. She and Jenna had fought over whether that last one was even a real job.

I never dreamed as big as they did. "Oh, I want to go to college, but I want to move back to Park City after. Get my own cat from a rescue. Live near my parents." But none of them, not even Jenna, ever made fun of how simple my dream was.

Eventually Ket and Teddy decided they wanted to paint the treehouse. My parents wanted it to stay white with blue trim on the outside, but gave us free reign to do what we wanted on the inside. We painted a midnight sky on the ceiling, mountains on the north and east sides, a lake on the south, a forest on the west, all under Ket's directions. It stank like chemicals for weeks, but we thought it looked so cool. And then we all sort of lost interest, the way kids do after a big project.

It still does look kind of cool.

But Rosie was right.

It did used to seem bigger.

I stared at Rosie, suddenly realizing what was wrong with the picture. "Whose jacket are you wearing?" I asked, pointing at the overly large suit jacket she had on over her dress.

Rosie glanced down, and I could have sworn she blushed in the shadows. "Umm . . ."

Ket's jaw dropped. "You dirty whore! Did you steal Fisher's date?"

"No!" Rosie said.

"Then whose jacket is that?" Ket demanded.

"Well . . . yeah, it's Lincoln's. I mean, FDR's."

"You're on a first-name basis with FDR?" squealed Ket.

"Who is FDR?" Jenna and I said simultaneously.

"Fisher's date," Rosie said at the same time Ket said, "Rosie's new boyfriend."

I leaned against the wall of the treehouse, grinning. "Jeez. I ditch one dance and Rosie gets a boyfriend?"

"He's not—" Rosie began.

"Ket and Teddy were holding hands on the ride here," Jenna blurted.

Rosie and I turned to her, eyes wide. Ket smacked Jenna, who smirked unrepentantly.

"Umm. So I guess there's something I need to tell you guys," Ket began, in her signature *everything is super fun* voice. "I sooorta have a big crush on Teddy."

"No kidding," Jenna said at the same time Rosie said, "Seriously? Teddy?"

"What?" Ket said defensively to Rosie. "Just because you didn't like him like that doesn't mean that no one would."

"I know that," Rosie said, leaning back in surprise. "I just . . . you never said anything. You tell me everything."

Ket shrugged, glancing down. "I figured you would come around to him. And then it would be weird that I liked him."

"It's not weird," Rosie assured her. "And I was never going to come around. He's like my brother."

Jenna pursed her lips primly. "So. To recap the evening. Rosie broke into the city library and has evidently hooked up with Fisher's date—"

"Not a hook-up," Rosie interrupted.

"Ket, who was apparently *this-close* to making a sex tape with *Vaughn Hollis*, confessed her crush to Teddy, who, judging from the aforementioned hand-holding, received the information favorably."

"Yeah, he did," Ket said, waggling her eyebrows suggestively.

"Also, who did you go clubbing with?" Rosie interrupted, turning to me. "We found a bunch of creepy older dudes who said they saw you with some girl?"

"What? Oh." I shook my head. "Alex Kingston, from physics. I used her phone to text my phone. Why didn't you just call her? I ran into her outside of school, her date was off puking and she was pissed. She said her sister could get us into this club, so I figured why not? I didn't want to go back to the dance and I figured I'd meet up with you guys later."

"And you guys stole FDR's car?" Ket asked, her eyebrows raised.

"I didn't think he'd care," I said. "It's not like I had to break into it. I had his keys and just beeped them until I found it. Was he mad?"

Rosie threw her hands in the air. "I mean, not really, but is that actually the point?"

"I mean, kinda," I said, shrugging. "If he wasn't mad, then it wasn't really stealing."

"Dude, that is not how that works," Ket said, smirking. "But at least you weren't the only one breaking the law tonight." She nudged Jenna, who sighed.

"Right," Jenna said, shaking her head ruefully. "Me. I committed many infractions, misdemeanors, and possibly a felony, the worst of which was promising Hannah Larson my senior party budget. I hereby swear I am never drinking again."

"Hallelujah," said Ket.

"Amen," said Rosie.

"And Elin, who was elected prom queen—you're welcome, by the way—was in her clubhouse all along."

"I'm prom queen?" I said.

"Congratulations," Jenna said dryly. "Have I missed anything?"

"How is Miles?" I asked.

"Gorgeous, as always." Jenna met my gaze for the first time in weeks and grinned.

"I like how no one is congratulating me about the fact that I *didn't* make a sex tape, but that I was willing to," Ket complained.

Rosie put her arm around Ket's shoulders. "That really was the friend moment of the night."

"Why would Vaughn even want to make a sex tape?" I asked, puzzled. "I thought you said his ween was crooked." I held up a pinkie finger to illustrate.

"Don't ask me to explain that boy's thought processes," Ket said, leaning her head on Rosie's shoulder. "Maybe he was planning to work his angles."

"Also, why didn't you just tell us that Vaughn was bullying you?" Rosie asked, playing with Ket's hair. "We would have helped."

Ket shrugged. "It just seemed like something I had to solve on my own."

"That was dumb," Rosie said.

Jenna leaned her head against the wall. "I am so tired," she said. "I did not get enough sleep at Fisher's."

"Oh! I think we're friends with Fisher now," Ket said suddenly. "Well. Maybe not Rosie, since she stole FDR."

"His name is Lincoln," corrected Rosie.

Ket shrugged. "I'm sticking with FDR."

"I'd like to note for the record that you didn't deny stealing him," Jenna remarked, eyes still closed.

"Oh my gosh, I did not steal him," Rosie said, crossing her arms over her chest.

"Then why do you have his coat?" Ket asked, elbowing her in the ribs.

"Because he's a gentleman," Rosie said defensively.

We all stared at her—even Jenna sat up, and for a second there she had looked like she was about to fall asleep. "Did you really just have something positive to say about a guy who isn't Teddy?" Ket said.

Rosie huffed. "If I admit we made out a little, will you guys get off my back?"

The three of us gasped simultaneously. "He's so gorgeous," I whispered. "Is he a good kisser?"

"Are you guys going to start dating?" asked Jenna.

"Rosie's first kiss!" Ket squealed.

Rosie frowned. "No, my first kiss was at Bear Lake in eighth grade."

"None of us believed that," I assured her.

"Not for a second," Jenna added.

Ket stretched her arms out in front of herself and then folded them behind her head. "Oh Rosie, I knew one day my whorish influence would rub off on you."

"Could all of you just shut up about it?" Rosie asked, glancing down. "Gosh, you're making me feel defective."

"No," I said. "I'm the one who is defective."

The light-hearted feeling in the treehouse evaporated. My friends glanced at each other—they'd been doing a lot of that lately—and then down.

Looking anywhere but at me.

I cleared my throat. "You know Will tried to talk to my parents about it. After," I said finally.

Rosie looked up. "Really?"

"Yeah. Do you remember when we did Comparative Government homework at your house, a few days before?"

"Of course," Rosie said. "I couldn't stop thinking about it. After."

I swallowed. "Well, you left for a minute to go grab some-thing, and I asked Will to take better care of you. He didn't get what I meant. I told him it was about Teddy and college and stuff. But later, obviously, he put it together."

I glanced over at my friends. The three of them were staring at me, their eyes locked on my face. "So he called my parents after. To apologize, I think, for not saying something earlier. That's why I'm not allowed to go to your house unless your mom is there."

"What? Why?" Rosie asked, her eyebrows knit together in puzzlement.

I shrugged, my cheeks flushed in the cold air. "My mom and dad keep saying the best thing will be to just move on, think positively, but what they mean is to pretend it didn't happen. When Will called, they unleashed all their anger about everything on him. I heard my dad on the phone. 'What kind of grown man is so interested in teenage girls.'"

Rosie's eyes widened and Ket sucked in a breath. "Will never said anything," Rosie said softly.

"They don't talk to my parents, either," Jenna said suddenly, her arms wrapped around her knees, eyes wide. "But my parents aren't being any better about it. They're so pissed."

"At my parents?" I asked, my eyebrows raised.

"Yeah," Jenna said. "I mean, at first I think they wanted to help, but when your parents got mad, they got mad back. They think . . . you know, that your parents should have known that you were upset. Why you were upset."

I shook my head. "It's not their fault," I whispered.

The four of us sat in silence for a long moment. "What happened?" Ket asked finally.

"You don't have to talk about it if you don't want to," Rosie said quickly.

"No." Jenna stared at me, her jaw set. Ket and Rosie looked at her, but she stared at me. "You really do have to talk about it, E," she said.

I glanced down. "It's kind of a long story," I said finally.

"We've got all night," said Ket softly.

48

Elin Angstrom
April 19, 2:20 AM

When I woke up in the hospital, after, my mother was holding my hand. She was gripping it so tightly that, for a long moment, I didn't even notice I was strapped to my bed.

My dad was behind her, asleep on the stiff, small couch, his feet wedged into a corner, his bent knees hanging off the edge, his head laying on an armrest at an awkward angle. I wondered how he could be sleeping. I didn't even feel bad for him; I was just puzzled because it looked so terrible.

I found out later it was because the nurse had given him a tranquilizer.

My mother studied my face. Usually when my mother looked at me—when anyone looked right at me, really—I glanced away. I don't know what I thought they would see written in my expression, lurking in the depths of my eyes, but this time I held still. My mother's eyes, red-rimmed and shining, darted from my eyebrow to my chin to my nose to my ear. Memorizing me.

I didn't know what else to say, so she was the first person I told the truth. My voice felt thick and raw from disuse, but I got the words out. "I wake up sad."

My mom burst into silent tears, her hand clapping over her mouth, her shoulders shaking as the sobs ripped through her body. I stared at her, knowing I should feel sad or guilty, but feeling nothing.

I didn't know if she believed me, or understood what I meant, but in that moment, I felt like she had heard me and would try to understand.

I lie to myself a lot.

I lie to my friends more.

Around me, their faces lit by the cold blue-white light of the lantern, the three of them stared at me. Waiting. Their perfect hairstyles undone, their dresses looking wilted, like they'd spent their night surviving a natural disaster and not a dance.

But still beautiful. My beautiful friends.

I cleared my throat, swallowing against the dryness in my mouth. My doctor says that you have to admit the truth to move forward. So . . .

"I have depression. I have . . . for a long time, I guess."

Since elementary school.

It got bad this year.

"I didn't realize it. The thing about depression is that it creeps in so slowly, you don't even realize that all you ever are is . . . sad."

Sad is the wrong word, but I don't have another. I was sad, then sadder, and then something deeper than sad, so dark and thick the word *sad* doesn't begin to cover it. Anxious, tired, lonely, hopeless—none of them are quite right. I was so sad that I couldn't feel anything else—and then, eventually, I didn't even feel that anymore.

I felt nothing.

And one day, I realized I thought more about dying than I thought about my future.

"But . . . you didn't seem depressed," Ket said.

She, Rosie, and Jenna were staring at me, all wearing similar expressions.

Puzzled.

Disbelieving.

They were just like my family. Their memories of me—joking around, cheerful, happy, always *so damn happy*—did not match with what I was telling them was the reality.

I shrugged helplessly, wishing there was an easier way to explain this.

That there was someone else who could explain it for me.

"I put on a good front," I said finally. "I'd gotten so good at pretending everything was fine, it was second nature. To act happy, even when I wasn't. Usually, even when I was at my worst, I didn't even have to think about the fact that I was faking."

I stared down at the folds of white fabric. The silver beading sparkled dimly, the stars on a misty night. I couldn't look up at my friends, watch their expressions slowly change as they realized I was telling the truth. As they mentally catalogued every giggle, every inside joke, every conversation, sleepover, study session, and party.

Trying to figure out what was real.

What was fake.

Not that I could even begin to figure it out myself.

I couldn't imagine they would want to be friends with me after this, but they deserved to know what had been going on.

I cleared my throat, anything to break the silence. "My therapist says it's called 'smiling depression.' People with it seem fine. But one of the big symptoms is, like, anxiety about other people finding out, so they—I mean, I guess, *I*—work really hard to cover it up. And then the anxiety about people knowing can feed the depression, and . . . things can . . . spiral. Things were fine junior year, but I guess that was just the calm before the storm. This year . . . it just got harder and harder. I wanted to sleep all the time, but I couldn't sleep. I'd stay up all night watching TV. I didn't ever want to have sex, but I couldn't tell Ben that."

I heard a choked gasp and glanced up involuntarily. Rosie was staring at me, her eyes wide, and I knew that Rosie had reached the conclusion that I dreaded her reaching.

Be honest.

That I wanted her to reach.

Because it made it easier on me.

My stomach churned, but I knew I couldn't stop now. "That's another thing my therapist told me. Depression . . . it messes with your sex drive. I just thought I was crazy, liking tons of sex and then suddenly hating it for no reason. But I never told Ben how I was feeling, because I didn't want him to think something was wrong with me."

I glanced away from Rosie's frozen expression. I forced a smile, a self-deprecating giggle, twirling a piece of hair around my finger.

Old habits die hard.

Like me, I guess.

Ha.

"It's so weird, when you think about it," I said, making my voice lighter. Familiar. Less real, but more comfortable. "I thought I was crazy because I didn't like having sex with my boyfriend . . . but I *didn't* realize I was crazy when I couldn't ever get out of bed. It was like I lived in a fog. I thought the fog was normal, so when it got thicker I didn't . . . I didn't even realize what was happening. All I knew was that it was getting harder and harder to act happy when all I felt was this overwhelming, crushing sadness."

I trailed off.

The last piece was always the hardest to explain.

I guess that's why it's last.

I stared at my nails. Shell-pink, a perfect gel manicure. My mother took me two days ago, an appointment my dad set up for us last week. He calls me every day at lunchtime now, texts me constantly. He never asks me how I feel, but it's obvious he's checking to make sure I haven't run into oncoming traffic or something. So I tell him about my classes and he tells me about work, and we make plans to go see movies . . . in a few days.

I don't have the heart to tell my dad that if I wanted to try to kill myself again, it wouldn't be the idea of seeing a romantic comedy with him next weekend or a spa day with my mom that would keep me from doing it.

He is comforted, knowing that he is doing his best to keep me safe.

It would be wrong to tell him that his best is . . . not pointless, exactly.

Beside the point.

There is nothing my parents or friends or boyfriend could have done.

Because there is no reason.

It's worse, somehow, when you have to admit that you tried to kill yourself because you were sad. There was no triggering event—no big trauma.

Embarrassing.

I didn't have a pregnancy scare or a sketchy abortion, my boyfriend didn't hit me, no one date-raped me, nobody died. My grades were terrible, but I didn't care. Whenever I tried to sit down and complete an assignment, I just got so anxious that I had to give up. I quit track, thinking that with more free time I would feel better, but the hopelessness just got worse.

[Some people can point to something and say, *"Look, that's where it was. The moment that sent my life off the rails. If that hadn't happened, I definitely wouldn't have done what I did."*]

But all I can say is that my brain chemistry makes me this way. I'd been in the fog before, but it always lifted after a while. But this year, it just felt like it would never lift. I couldn't pretend it wasn't there. I couldn't smile my way out of it. And I . . . I couldn't stand it anymore.

"I'm sorry I let you guys think there was a reason," I choked out finally. "There . . . there isn't a reason."

But if I had told Rosie that it wasn't Ben's fault, if I had told Ket that it wasn't a whim, that I planned it for weeks and held on to my plan like it was a dream, the dream I traded college and Ben and prom and everything for . . . I'd have had to admit that there was no reason.

Just my brain. Being legit crazy.

And to say anything to Jenna . . .

There is nothing I can say to Jenna.

I stopped. Jenna's lip was trembling.

Rosie and Ket stared at her. "What's going on?" Rosie said, glancing back and forth between the two of us.

Jenna stared at me. For one moment, it's like I remember every version of her I have ever known.

Five-year-old Jenna at swim lessons, telling the instructor that she didn't need the float board.

Struggling not to cry after she fell roller skating and split her lip at my ninth birthday party, my mom holding a carton of melting ice cream to her face.

First-day-of-middle-school Jenna standing next to me in the cafeteria, clutching her tray and pretending she wasn't scared. Spying a pretty Indian girl with thick bangs, a short boy with curly dark hair, and a girl with glasses too large for her face and saying, "Let's sit over there."

Eighth-grade Jenna, the only one of us who stepped forward to hug a screaming, raging Teddy after his mother checked herself out of rehab early without saying goodbye.

Sixteen-year-old Jenna, coming over to my house to tell me everything about her first date with Miles. Swooning as she fell backward onto my bed.

Beginning of senior year Jenna, giggling helplessly as she struggled and failed to shut her locker door with her backpack, gym bag, and tennis racket inside.

End of senior year Jenna, avoiding looking me in the eye.

I pretended that I didn't know why Jenna doesn't come over to my house anymore, but that was just me lying to myself again. I knew why, but I was too big of a coward to say, *I am so, so sorry you were the one who found me. I am so sorry you were the one who had to save me.*

Except that sounds wrong, too, since if Jenna hadn't saved me, no one would have. And I guess I am glad that someone did. Really, I'm just sorry I was such a bitch afterward.

"Why didn't you tell them?" I ask her finally.

Jenna shrugs. "I don't know. I didn't want to think about it. They just . . . assumed."

"What?" Ket demanded, her voice rising.

"Jenna saved me." I smiled faintly. A real one.

2:40 AM

I explained everything that happened that night.

For a moment, none of them said anything. Jenna fiddled with a torn piece of tulle on her skirt and Rosie's mouth hung open, her forehead wrinkled with concern. Ket's arms wrapped around herself, like she didn't want to hear any more, as she glanced back and forth between me and Jenna.

I glanced down at the bracelet encircling my wrist. "I never . . . thanked you, Jen," I said finally.

"I don't want to be thanked," Jenna whispered, her voice rough. "You're my best friend."

"Best friends can save each other and be grateful, too," Rosie pointed out. "You're like Han Solo and Chewie."

Jenna sniffled, wiping tears off her cheeks. "That's actually just kind of a racist trope."

Ket smiled, that half smile of hers that managed to dazzle brighter than most people's full smiles. "That's our Jenna."

Jenna cracked a smile of her own. "Damn straight."

I couldn't help it—I laughed.

That was real, too.

And just then, I remembered something Dr. S had told me. Something I hadn't really understood at the time.

I lie to myself a lot.

But there's a funny fact about lies.

Last week, as I waited at the curb for my mother, Dr. S took a seat on the bench next to me. Eloise-Katherine-Whatever Her Name Was That Week had already left, and he sat right in the spot she usually occupied. I tensed involuntarily, wondering what he was doing.

This isn't working for you.

He's going to send you back to the hospital.

"Do you know why she picks a different name every session?" Dr. S asked suddenly.

We were both staring straight ahead, people walking by on the sidewalk, but there was no doubt that he was talking to me. Not asking me why—asking me if I knew why.

Which meant he knew.

And I desperately wanted to know.

But I couldn't open my mouth.

"It's a reminder," he went on, as if I had answered. "Something she started doing after I told her what I am about to tell you. I think it's working for her. Either that, or she really likes jerking the other girls around."

I smiled faintly.

"I know it can be hard to admit the truth about yourself sometimes," Dr. S continued softly. "But Elin, no matter how hard things get, I need you to remember one thing."

The pause stretched out for an eternity, and I knew this time he wouldn't say any more unless I spoke. I swallowed. "What?"

Dr. S exhaled softly, and I realized he'd been holding his breath. "That no one, not even you, will ever lie about you like your depression will."

Neither of us said anything after that, and my mother pulled up a few moments later. She nodded curtly at Dr. S, and he smiled as if she'd been friendly, and I opened the passenger door and got in.

And as she pulled away from the curb, I thought, *That's it?*

That's the big secret?

That my depression lies to me?

But suddenly, like a clap of thunder in a silent night, I got it. Got it down to my bones.

My friends looked for me all night. They ditched dates and broke into buildings, made deals with douchebags, missed the last dance of high school, and realized it was all for a crazy girl who was camping out in her treehouse.

And they're still here.

I can tell my friends anything.

They will love me anyway.

"The first week on anti-depressants, I didn't notice anything particularly different, but my therapist said I needed to give it time," I said, my voice steady and soft. "My parents checked me out of the hospital. About a week after I came home, the pills started to do the trick. My emotions came back, bit by bit, though some of them were mixed up. Amused and lonely and hungry and disappointed, all put in a blender and coming out at the wrong moments. My doctor promised me they would stabilize soon. And then . . . I came back to school."

I went to bed at night, and I could sleep. Strange, vivid dreams like I'd never had before. Supposedly that was normal. I could focus in class. I could sleep at night.

The fog was gone. Gone so completely I was almost scared that I'd imagined it before.

"The hard thing is, now that my emotions are mostly back to normal, I am sort of . . . confused."

Why had I wanted to do what I'd done? I remembered the feeling—all I had to do was think about it and I remembered, muted but there, rushing back over me like a wave. The crushing blackness, the overwhelming anxiety. The numbness. The need to escape.

But on the pills, I couldn't understand *the reason*.

I was just sad?

That was all?

That made no sense.

And if I couldn't understand why I did what I did, how could I expect anyone else to?

"You can't tell anyone this next part," I said suddenly.

Rosie took my hand. I blinked, surprised it was Rosie, not Ket, who voluntarily reached out to squeeze my fingers between her own. "We won't," she promised. I squeezed her hand back.

"I've only made one friend in therapy. Fisher. She's the only one who gets it. The not-getting-it part. But I wouldn't even be friends with her if it weren't for group therapy, and we just don't talk about that stuff outside of the group. We kind of just . . . pretend we were always friends."

Fisher got it, but Fisher's problem was still different than mine. Fisher's brain kept reliving a bad episode of her life, no matter how hard she tried to focus on other things. She was on medicine for an anxiety disorder, and she was supposed to work on her therapy goals every week, but I understood enough of Dr. S's psychiatry talk to understand that Fisher would one day move past what had happened to her.

"Some people . . . they try to kill themselves, and they get help, and then they're better. And then some people get help, and then . . . they just manage things. And I'm in that group. I still have no idea what I am supposed to say about it. I feel so much better, but it's not like I can ever stop taking the pills. They won't cure me."

I had known there was no cure, but that hadn't stopped me from hoping for one anyway. I had spent the last weeks thinking about how great it would be when I got back together with Ben—the last person who mattered who didn't know what happened. When I had someone who loved me again, when I could prove to my parents that I was back to my old self, that I was normal and stable and capable of heading off to college. Then I would be better.

And on some level, I knew it was wrong to try to break him up with Hannah, even if they weren't serious. Maybe he did deserve better than Hannah, but he probably deserved better than a girlfriend who lied to him and dumped him, too.

Except another level, a darker part of me, just felt like I *deserved* him. Because I was there first, and for longer, and I *needed* him. He was the last ingredient I needed to return to the person I'd been last year, before things had gotten so massively screwed up. Not the sort of thing you could admit and still be a good person, but it had felt like the truth.

Except that it was a lie, too. Because with or without Ben, I couldn't keep pretending that everything was fine.

I rested my cheek against my knee. "Some people will graduate from therapy."

Fisher will graduate from therapy.

"And I will not."

And this is how it's going to be forever.

49

Rosie Winchester
April 19, 2:50 AM

"That's bullshit," I said finally.

"Ro," said Ket disapprovingly.

"No, she's right. It's bullshit," said Jenna, her mouth set in a thin line.

Elin glanced between me and Jenna, looking like a smaller version of herself, wavy blonde hair falling around her like a waterfall. "What?"

"First, it's not 'just depression,'" Jenna snapped, making air quotes with her fingers. "It's *fucking depression*. It's a nightmare, that's what it is, and don't ever think it's something to be embarrassed about."

Elin rolled her eyes at Jenna, and weirdly, I felt encouraged.

Because I'd rather have her show us how she really felt than just pretend to be happy.

And if that meant I had to talk about some feelings, well then dammit, I was going to talk about some feelings.

I stared at Elin until she looked back at me, resisting the urge to retreat and let Jenna handle this alone. "She's right," I said, hoping Elin knew that I meant it with everything I had. "You may have it forever, but it's not going to be like *this* forever. *This* is going to get better."

Ket took my hand, and I convinced myself not to pull it away. I gave it a squeeze and saw her smile in the darkness.

"Everyone is messed up, in one way or another," I said. "Some of us more than others."

(Teddy and Jenna, struggling to control their tempers.)

(Ket, pretending she was carefree and confident, even when she wasn't.)

(Me ignoring all of it, trying to avoid any emotional situation that was messy or unpleasant.)

(And apparently the beautiful, perfect Fisher Reese, hiding some problem I never would have or could have guessed about.)

(And Elin, staring at me with an expression that looked a lot like doubt on her face.)

I squeezed Ket's hand extra hard, hoping to borrow a little of her courage. "But the solution isn't to think we're broken. I think it's to admit that we're all the same. And *not* pretend that everything is fine when it isn't."

"That was wise, dude," Ket said approvingly.

I raised my eyebrows at her. "Speaking of things that aren't fine? Making a sex tape with someone you hate."

"I didn't!" Ket burst out.

"You almost did," I said, and Jenna nodded, looking stern.

"But she didn't," Elin said defensively.

"You gotta work on that self-esteem, Ket," Jenna said. "It is seriously so awful."

Ket raised both eyebrows, her dark eyes shining in the dim lantern light. "Tell me more, Little Miss PTSD."

Jenna rested her cheek on her knee, but she was smiling. "Yeah, yeah."

Ket yawned, stretching her arms above her head. "Well, the *really* important thing is that I found a way to shut Vaughn up for good. So yeah, I definitely suck for blabbing in the first place, but overall, go me. Am I right?"

"Definitely," Elin said, fighting a smirk.

We all leaned back against the four walls of the tree house, like we were one connected organism relaxing at once.

And then I heard a snap.

"What was that?" I said, eyes wide. All around the circle, my friends stared back at me, mouths open slightly, eyes shadowed by the lantern, heads tilted, straining to listen.

A creak—and suddenly Jenna was tumbling backward, a board in the wall behind her tumbling to the yard below. "Holy shit," she gasped as Ket and I lurched over to grasp her hands and pull her back up.

"Get out, get out!" Elin yelled as wood snapped and cracked. Ket squealed, scrambling to her feet and jumping out onto the lawn, not bothering with the ladder. Jenna's dress snagged on a splinter and ripped as she followed, cursing as she landed. I grabbed my skirt and held it up by my knees, pulling my shoes off and tossing them into the darkness as I crouched in the doorway.

I turned, but Elin was already reaching for me. We jumped together.

It wasn't like jumping when we were kids—we spent summers in the treehouse, leaping out into the air and landing on soft, well-watered green grass.

I winced as I hit the ground, pain shooting up my shins, and threw my hands out to catch myself as I fell over, dry twigs cutting into my palms. Elin hissed beside me, stumbling in the other direction.

Ket helped us to our feet as Jenna looked for my shoes in the dark. "Didn't that seem easier when we were twelve?" Elin said, shaking her head. "Are we old already?"

"Apparently," Jenna said, grimacing as she handed me my shoes. "Old and heavy."

We turned and stared up at the treehouse, the moon silvery and bright behind the bare branches that surrounded it. From the outside, it looked like it was still stable, if you ignored the sagging west side. But I knew if any of us tried to climb back inside, the whole structure would come crashing to the ground.

"I'm just gonna say it," Ket said finally. "If that was the universe sending us a message about the end of childhood, the metaphor was a little heavy-handed."

3:00 AM

The four of us ended up walking the half-mile to Ket's house, arms wrapped around each others' waists and shoulders. Jenna's car was still downtown—and Jenna probably still couldn't have passed a breathalyzer, even if it were there. Teddy had said that we could call him for a ride, but even though Ket swore things were going to go back to normal with Teddy, I was sort of glad when Jenna said, "Let's call him to meet us for breakfast tomorrow. Let's have it just be us right now."

Just us sounded perfect.

"Did anyone figure out what happened with Ben?" Elin asked.

We stopped. *Ben.*

I groaned. "Oh man, I've really got to apologize to him." (Ugh, I hate apologizing.) (But I am going to try harder.)

"Yeah, you do," Ket said.

"It's not her fault," Elin said. "I should have just explained from the beginning."

"I think the fact that we got Hannah to ditch him for the rest of the night is apology enough," said Jenna. "Honestly, he should be thanking us."

"You got Hannah to ditch him? Why?" asked Elin.

Jenna waved a hand. "Too tired. I'll explain it tomorrow."

"Speaking of boyfriends, yours is worried about you," Elin said, bumping Jenna with her shoulder.

"Miles? Why?"

Elin shrugged. "He can tell something is wrong. You can tell him what happened, I know he wouldn't repeat it."

Jenna stared at Elin. "Back up. Why is he worried?"

Elin shrugged again. "Because he said you've been acting so crazy. Crazier than normal, anyway. I saw him at the dance, before I left."

Jenna stopped in her tracks. "I don't understand what you're talking about. I spend a ton of energy making sure Miles doesn't know how intense I am. He thinks that I'm, like, chill."

The three of us laughed. "The ship has sailed there, kid," Ket said, throwing her arms around Jenna in a bear hug.

"Miles knows you're not chill," I said, shaking my head in amusement.

Jenna huffed. "Whatever. You guys don't know what you're talking about. I am the coolest girlfriend ever. He thinks I am *so* laidback."

Ket laughed and Elin smacked her. "You are a *good* girl-friend," Elin clarified. "You are way more thoughtful that I ever was with Ben. But, you know that he's seen the spread-sheets, right?"

"And he's heard you complain about Josh Bowman?" I added.

"And he's got eyeballs and ears." Ket grinned. "But why do you even care? He adores you. And have you not noticed that Miles isn't exactly cool?"

Jenna gasped. "Miles is *so* cool."

Ket, Elin, and I glanced at each other.

(Are we talking about the same Miles Brooke?)

"He's really not," Ket said flatly. "And you should be glad. *Vaughn* is cool. Miles is Grade-A nerd, but people don't notice because of his jump shot. Clearly nerd is the way to go."

"Just accept it," Elin said. "You two were made for each other. And he's worried about you. So you should probably text him. I'm serious."

Jenna glanced down, a smile fighting to emerge. "Okay," she said simply.

The sky was an inky midnight blue, the moon hanging low in the sky, a huge silvery disc. The clouds had cleared, but I couldn't see many stars—the lampposts were too bright. Considering it had snowed a few hours before, the temperature was practically balmy.

That's Utah for you.

"So I have an announcement," I said suddenly.

"You're pregnant with FDR's baby?" suggested Ket eagerly.

I rolled my eyes. "No. I'm going to stay for college in the fall."

Ket and Elin squealed.

"I'm the only one who is going out-of-state now?" Jenna complained.

"No," I said, turning to walk backward. "I'm going to transfer out-of-state for my sophomore year. I still want to get away, just . . . not yet."

"Is this because FDR goes to the U?" Ket said, a wicked smirk on her face.

I shook my head. For once, I was telling the whole truth and nothing but the truth. "Don't be ridiculous. It's because *you* are going to the U. And Elin's going to be there or Westminster by spring semester, right?"

"Right," Elin promised.

"And Teddy, who will hopefully finally forgive me," I pointed out. "Besides, who doesn't want to knock out their generals with half tuition?"

"Your dad is going to be so gloaty," Jenna warned.

I shrugged. "Gloaty is actually one of his more endurable character traits."

Ket skipped over to the curbside, balancing along with her arms spread wide, shoes held in one hand. "Admit it though," she said, pointing one long leg like a gymnast on the beam. "FDR being there will be a nice bonus."

(Well, now that you mention it . . .)

"Ket! We made out once," I scolded.

"Yeah, but for you, that's practically accepting a marriage proposal," Ket pointed out.

"He's probably going to get to know me and then hate me," I said.

Elin laughed. "Eeyore, everyone who gets to know you loves you."

50

Ket West-Beauchamp
April 19, 3:20 AM

I unlocked the front door and crept in quietly. Jenna, Rosie, and Elin followed, tiptoeing behind me.

"Ket?" called Mama Leanne from the living room. "Could you come in here, please?"

I winced. The gig was Officially Up. "Crap. You guys just go up to my room, okay?" I flipped on the hallway light since there was no point in the subterfugery anymore.

I expected at least a sympathetic backward glance, but Jen, Elin, and Rosie were too tired even for that. They filed up the stairs, yawning and carrying their high heels in their hands.

I opened the French doors to the living room. Mama Leanne and Mom Kim were curled up under a blanket on the couch, Mom Kim's feet propped up on the Ottoman of Shame. The TV screen was blue—whatever movie they'd been watching had shut itself off long ago.

Well, there was one piece of good news. They looked too tired to move, which meant my lecture was delayed.

"How was the dance?" Mom Kim asked, stifling a yawn.

"Good," I said slowly. Was it possible that they didn't know I'd missed my curfew by two and a half hours?

If so, I definitely wasn't going to point it out. Another Prom Night Miracle!

"Did the other girls have fun?" Mama Leanne asked.

"Yup," I said.

They exchanged a knowing glance as they both sat up, stretching and wincing. It was like a silent communication that you'd probably have to be an adult to read.

I paused before I shut the doors. "I'm going on a date this weekend," I said. "With Teddy."

My moms stared at me. They normally had to pry boy information out of me with surgical tools.

"He's a very nice boy," Mama Leanne said.

I beamed. "Right?"

"And you deserve a nice boy," said Mom Kim hesitantly—not like she doubted it.

Like she was worried I would argue with her.

I paused. "Right," I agreed, the stupid grin still plastered to my face.

I turned to go upstairs and then paused one more time. "Love you guys," I said.

"Love you too, hon," said Mama Leanne, sounding vaguely stunned.

Up in my room, Jenna and Rosie were changing into their pajamas, their dresses tossed over my reading chair, a mass of pink and a slash of emerald. "Elin is brushing her teeth," Jenna yawned, pulling on a tank top.

Rosie climbed into my bed, curling up, as Elin came back from the bathroom. "You think you get the bed? I'm all post-suicidal-ly," complained Elin.

"You don't get to play that card," Rosie mumbled, snuggling her face down into my pillow. "You let me be a total c-word to Ben for a month."

I unzipped my dress and kicked it aside, opening my chest of drawers to find sleep shorts and a tee-shirt. "I'd like to point out that, one, it's my bed, and two, Rosie, you still broke your promise to me about leaving Ben alone."

"I broke it out of love," Rosie mumbled as Elin curled up next to her, wrapping herself in my old baby blanket. "Besides. Now I'm obligated to help Elin make up with Ben, too, so it sort of worked out for the best."

Elin raised her head from her pillow, a sleepy smile spreading over her face. "Really?"

"Of course," Rosie said, patting Elin's arm absently.

"Between the four of us, that boy doesn't stand a chance," Jenna said, yawning and unzipping her sleeping bag.

I eyed Rosie and Elin, who were making no move to get off my bed. "So Jenna and I have to take the floor?" I said incredulously as I pulled on my PJs.

"Speak for yourself," Jenna said, stretching out at the foot of the bed and pulling her unzipped sleeping bag over herself. "Would you grab the light?"

"This is my bed, you bitches!" I said, but I couldn't help but laugh.

Elin raised her head, eyes barely open. "Climb on in," she said. "There's always room."

Acknowledgments

After what feels like a lifetime of trying to achieve this dream, the words "thank you" feel insufficient. But I am going to do my best.

Thank you to Rachel Stark, who acquired this book for Sky Pony, and for Nicole Frail, who edited it. I feel infinitely lucky to have worked with two fantastic editors who both saw something special in my book. Thanks to the entire Sky Pony team for their support.

Thank you to Maria Vicente, my amazing agent. You're like my personal Good Witch of the Great White North and I wouldn't have made it here without you.

Thank you to Emily Martin, Brenda Drake, the entire Pitch Wars team, and the Table of Trust. You guys were the first thing in 2014 to change my life permanently and for the better. Because of Pitch Wars, I became a better writer, I found an agent, but more importantly I made amazing friends.

Thank you to my critique partners, beta readers, and everyone who offered their time and feedback—Sarah Clift, Melanie Stanford, Chris Wharton, Hailey Archer, Lindsey Nikola, Kristin Button Wright, Gina Denney, Rosalyn Eves, Melinda

Nevarez, Alyssa Witting, and Prerna Pickett. You have all made this book a little bit better and I will always be grateful that you took the time to read these words and offer your thoughts. Thanks to all the friends who encouraged my writing through the years, there are too many of you to name—which just goes to show how very lucky I have been.

Thank you to the Novel Nineteens and the Class of 2k19—you guys have made debuting an absolute joy, and I can't wait to see what else all of us are going to do in the future.

Thank you to my parents, who encouraged a love of reading in me from a young age. To my mom, for taking me to the library multiple times a week. To my Dad, who encouraged my writing but also told me to get a job that could pay my bills. Good call there, Dad. Thank you to my grandparents—it is one of the biggest blessings of my life that I got to grow up next door to two of the all-time greats. I'm sorry for all the swears in this book.

Thank you to Kris and Doyle, who raised one of the best men I've ever met.

Thank you to all the teachers at Samuel Morgan Elementary, Fairfield Junior High, and Davis High and the professors at the University of Utah who helped make me into the writer, thinker, and person that I am today.

Thank you to my girlfriends, who inspired the friendship between Jenna, Rosie, Ket, and Elin. They're kickass girls because you all are kickass women.

Apologies to Park City, Utah—I played pretty fast and loose with your geography, landmarks, and buildings . . . but you are a city and you probably don't mind.

Finally, thank you especially to Nick, who makes my life immeasurably better every single day. You, Rooster, Spencer, and Scout are all I could ever ask for.

And I love you more, so there.